THE
DAEMON
PARALLEL

THE
DAEMON
PARALLEL

ROY GILL

 Kelpies

For RDP

*Thanks to Ann Cook and Isobel Nesbit – who I hope would
see the funny side*

Mum and Dad – for tea and cake, and labradors on loan

Lindsey – who saw I was stuck, and managed to unstick me

 This book is also available
as an eBook.

Kelpies is an imprint of Floris Books
First published in 2012 by Floris Books

The publisher acknowledges subsidy from
Creative Scotland towards the publication
of this volume.

British Library CIP data available
ISBN 978-086315-869-8
Printed in Great Britain
by CPI Group (UK) Ltd, Croydon

1. An Offer Over Coffee

It was over coffee and biscuits that Grandma Ives offered to return Cameron's father from the dead.

"It won't be easy, of course. A resurrection spell is old magic, and quite unwieldy. You would have to be both strong and brave, and I'd have to speak to Mrs Ferguson, which is never pleasant. But I can do it. If you want me to."

Cameron stared at her. The old lady had made her proposal just as casually as she now pushed a plate of biscuits towards him.

"What do you mean, 'a resurrection spell'?"

"Revitalise. Bring back. Make as if he'd never died. I'd have thought the meaning was quite obvious." Her eyes narrowed. "Do you think I'm bluffing?"

You've got to be. Cameron's heart quickened in his chest. He looked away, choosing to examine Grandma Ives' living room rather than reply. The winter sun was poking over Blackford Hill and light flooded in the balcony window, picking out the gold spines on the books, and showing up dust swirls on the bulgy grey screen of the old television. In the corner alcove, a jazz LP spun on the ancient record player and a warm fuzzy voice sang of *love gone bad,* and *a man who done me wrong...*

He'd been living with the old lady for nearly a week now. She'd done nothing in that time to suggest she was mad, or likely to make up wild stories.

But she can't really mean it. She can't really be offering to bring Dad back to life.

"Well, young man?"

Cameron took a biscuit, put it in his mouth, and crunched it.

"It's good." It wasn't really. Nothing was, these days. The biscuit tasted of dry paper and the sort of marzipan he always picked off Christmas cakes.

This can't be happening...

"You do *miss* him, I suppose?" Grandma Ives spoke the word as if a hair had got stuck on her tongue. "Not that I know why I should bring him back; he was trouble enough the first time. Never listened to a word of my good advice—"

"Of course I miss him!" Cameron shouted, unable to help himself. "Can't you tell? Isn't it obvious?" The thing was, deep down, he worried all the time that he should've begun to miss his dad a little bit sooner...

It was now just over two weeks ago, that first night Dad hadn't come home. Cameron had come in from school, and slung his bag in the corner. He'd booted up his dad's PC and logged on. The computer was nearly as old as he was, and it'd crash if you put a game anywhere near it, but it did alright for checking message boards and downloading music. When it got to 7.30, and he'd still not heard the rumble of his dad's van in the driveway, Cameron went to the kitchen and got on with making his dinner. There was a stack of ready meals in the fridge.

"When I win the lottery I'll cook," his dad would say. "I'll be like Number One Super Chef! Even Jamie Oliver won't touch me."

Cameron chose tuna and tomato bake. The label promised it was "delicious" and made to the "best ever recipe", but somehow he doubted it. As he ate the stringy pasta he watched *The Simpsons* and then a bit of a talent show. Some of the contestants could sing, but they couldn't dance or didn't have the right look. Others had great hair or clothes, but screeched and wailed like angry cats.

He picked up his bowl, pausing on his way to the kitchen as he caught a glimpse of himself in the mirror over the fire. His best friend Amy said he wasn't bad looking, if he'd only have a bit of confidence. Cameron didn't see it. He was tall for his age, sure, but he was thin too, and not exactly broad about the shoulders. He ran his hand through his hair, which fell down in a dark thatch over his eyes. Maybe he should get it cut to look like one of the guys off the telly? Amy would love that. She'd go on about it for a week. Then again, interesting hair got you noticed, and he didn't want to do anything to make himself stand out more at school...

He channel hopped for a while, then reluctantly went up to his bedroom to get on with his homework. He put his stereo on loud; perhaps the noise would help drive some particularly dull maths problems into his skull. The driveway was still empty when he went to bed at 11.30, falling asleep to the sound of his headphones whispering in his ears.

The truth was, his dad was so often home late, Cameron had stopped finding it unusual. He ran Duffy's Quick Clearances, and spent his days emptying houses after their owners died, or moved away, or went bankrupt. He would sort out the things worth selling, and take the lumpy old furniture nobody wanted to the dump. When Cameron was small, his dad sometimes took him along. He would run wild round strange, slowly-emptying spaces. Sad-eyed relatives of the departed would look at him fondly, and slip him fifty pence. Other times he'd get shouted at for being a nuisance and making too much noise.

Now his dad hardly ever wanted to take him, even if the jobs were at a weekend.

"You've got to study. Find out what you want and how to get there," he'd say. "Don't just fall into something like I did."

Cameron would ask what he meant, but his dad would always push the question away.

Sometimes emptying a house meant working late into the night. People would leave it to the last minute to call the clearers. Malcolm Duffy and his lads would have to put in long hours to get the job done. If a client's house was far away, Cameron's dad would sometimes even bunk down in his van. When he came home the next day, he'd shake his head sadly and say, "You wouldn't believe how much stuff people collect."

Cameron would nod, thinking how his dad kept loads of odds and ends, all packed into the spare room; stuff he hadn't been able to shift but insisted might be useful. The garage was crammed too, and the van usually had to sit outside. On cold mornings, the engine would cough over and over before it shuddered back to life...

On the second day his dad did not come home, Cameron had gone round to Amy's. Annoyingly, all Amy wanted to do was talk about some boy in the sixth year she'd got a crush on. Cameron hadn't been sure what to say. He concentrated on checking out which new tunes Amy had added to her laptop, and waited for her to change the subject.

"Stay for dinner, Cam," said Amy when her mum got in from her shift at the hospital. Her mum's eyes were red around the corners, and Cameron didn't think he should push his luck. He caught the bus home instead.

Fireworks popped and crackled above his head as he walked along Scott Street. People were getting ready for bonfire night early this year. As he turned the corner, he saw that the van was still not back in the drive. In the kitchen, his dirty plates lay untouched in the sink. If Dad had been in during the day, he'd have expected to find a clutter of mugs there too.

Cameron wasn't sure what to do. The odd evening on his own was kind of fun; after a day in school, with its overheated cabbagey corridors, he enjoyed the space.

If Dad wasn't going to make it home tonight either, Cameron told himself he wasn't bothered. He would make the most of it. He'd raid the fridge, have a fry-up, and pig out in front of the telly. He'd put on that music channel that played nothing but rock and indie, the one that always made his dad glare and plug his ears...

He grinned. It was an excellent plan! But when he sat down on the sofa, with his skilfully cooked plate of food – bacon brown and crispy, eggs running into the beans – it didn't seem to taste right.

He tried his dad's mobile. He hadn't bothered before, when it had just been another late night. Two days without a message or text was definitely odd, though. When an answering *Brrrupp!* came from the old donkey jacket hanging up on a peg by the door, Cameron thumped his hand off his head in frustration. His dad was always leaving his phone in the wrong coat.

He looked up the tatty address book by the hall phone. There was no one permanently on the payroll of Duffy's Quick Clearances, but there were a couple of guys his dad used regularly. Big Joe had the biggest beer belly you've ever seen. Scribbled in the phone book was "Try Black Bull" next to Joe's name, so Cameron called the pub.

Big Joe hadn't heard a thing. "Dinna concern yersel', lad. It'll all come oot fine in the wash." He was keen to get back to his drinking.

Cameron called Eric next. Eric was trying to make it as a singer, when he wasn't shifting furniture. Dad said Eric was sensitive, which Cameron took to mean his songs tended to go on a bit.

Eric was on the way home from band practice. "I haven't been out on a job in weeks, Cam, and I'm noticing it. Listen, are you alright there, mate? Do you want me to head over?"

"Nah. It's cool. I'm ok."

Cameron went back to the living room to worry. Not long later, the doorbell rang.

"I'm fine, Eric, really—"

It wasn't Eric on the doorstep. The two policemen invited themselves in, asked a load of questions, and made several cups of tea Cameron didn't want. They spoke on their radios, looked at each other gravely, and offered to make more tea.

About an hour later, another police officer arrived. She was young and pretty, with dark hair pulled back into a ponytail. When she opened her mouth to speak, Cameron noticed an odd little gap between her bottom teeth. As she told him about the way they'd found the van by the caves on the beach at Weymss, the body on the sand, he found himself focussing on that gap, as if concentrating hard enough could keep him from crying.

The next week and a half passed in a painful sort of blur. Amy's mum put him up at first. Amy hadn't known what to say. She kept apologising, saying she was there for him, and asking if he wanted to talk. Cameron just wished she'd shut up and leave him alone.

Moving in with Grandma Ives hadn't been Cameron's idea. He barely knew the old lady. He had only vague memories of a woman with steel-grey hair, who'd turned up once on his seventh birthday. She'd given him a wooden music box, then sat in the corner, watching him intently. Cameron's dad had been angry for some reason, and had taken the box away.

"He's not going to be like you. You and your daft old ways! You keep your hands off!" he'd said, before showing her the door.

Cameron's dad never made any secret of the fact he didn't get on with his mother. There were cards that came through the post at Christmas, but no more visits. So Cameron had been amazed when his dad's will said Mrs Isobel Euphemia Ives-Duffy of 24 Observatory Road, Edinburgh was to be his guardian.

Cameron had tried to explain to Carole the social worker that he didn't know the old woman at all. She hadn't listened.

"Crises like these, they have a wonderful way of bringing family together. You're only thirteen. There's no way you can live on your own."

Cameron's house turned out to be owned by his mum and dad together, but no one knew where Elaine Duffy was these days, Cameron included. There were only a few precious things he remembered about her, she left so long ago.

"There are all sorts of complicated legal things to be sorted before the will can be settled," Carole said. "You're best off with your gran. And your school has agreed to send work home for now."

She helped the boy pack some of his possessions, and drove him in her battered Volvo to Grandma Ives' house in the south of Edinburgh. Even though it was only fifty minutes away from his home in Cauldlockheart, Cameron had never been to her house before. As they sat in Grandma Ives' living room, Carole promised she'd drop in soon. Grandma Ives insisted that would not be necessary. Her tone suggested she was used to getting what she wanted.

"I can see you'll both get on famously!" Carole said, as she packed up her notes in her leatherette briefcase.

Cameron had exchanged a wary glance with his newly acquired Gran. "Grandma Ives" – that's what he was supposed to call her. She looked smart in an old-fashioned sort of way, and thin, and more than a bit stern.

Not like a proper granny at all...

A proper granny would never offer to bring her only son – his dad – back from the dead.

"I can tell by your face you don't care for the biscotti. That's alright. You don't have to eat them."

He looked down at the plate she'd pushed towards him. Dad wouldn't have put out biscuits like that, with their posh paper wrappers and icky-acid almond taste. You'd get a torn-open packet of Hobnobs, or maybe some Jaffa Cakes. The coffee wouldn't come in a glass pot with a plunger either...

Cameron's hands went to his stomach. Everything normal, everything he had grown up with, had been taken away. The pain of losing Dad felt like someone had cut a vital muscle from his guts, and it wasn't getting any better. He still went about, day by day, walking and talking and eating as if he were normal and healthy, but all the time he was trying to hold himself together, to stop the gap from spreading. He blamed himself for all sorts of things: for not noticing something was up with his dad; for not calling the police sooner; for not starting to worry when something still could've been done. And now the old woman was offering to put that missing part back, to give him the chance to find out what really happened, to magically make it all better...

"Did you mean what you said, about bringing him back?" Cameron hardly dared to believe it.

"I always mean what I say." Behind Grandma Ives' wire-framed glasses, her eyes were calm and steady, without a hint of doubt or playfulness.

"Yes," he said quietly. "Please. Bring him back."

"What was that?" The old lady leaned closer.

"Bring him back. Just tell me what I have to do."

Grandma Ives smiled. "Good boy," she said.

2. Night-time Stories

Cameron's trainers scrunched along the beach. The night sky above him was dark blue, and the waves that hit the shore sounded oddly muffled. Where was he? How had he got here? The answer seemed just out of reach, like when you try to name a song half heard on the radio, and the lyrics nag you all day long.

He turned his questions into a rhythm, beaten out by his trainers on the pebbles. Where – am – I? I'm – on – a – beach. Which – beach – where? I – don't – have – a – scooby. No. No, that wasn't helping. He stopped and looked all round him. He could see water, sand and pebbles, and a scrubby sort of headland with a yellowish glow breaking through the grass. The air smelled of salt and of something slightly rotten. Perhaps a dead bird or animal was lying on a rock somewhere, just out of sight. He decided to head towards the light. As he scrambled up the shallow cliff that separated the beach from the land, the glow resolved itself into the headlamps of a familiar white Ford Transit. Cameron broke into a run.

"Dad? Where are you? Dad?" His voice seemed to vanish into the night, the words coming out dull and flat. The driver's seat was empty, the inside of the cab its usual mess of newspapers, roadmaps and old cassette tapes. He tugged at the door handle but it refused to click. He had more luck round the back: one of the rear doors was unlocked. Cameron yanked it open and ducked into the darkened interior, taking in the familiar scent of mothballs, oil, and old fish-supper wrappers.

The back of the van, usually crammed to the roof with furniture, was almost empty. A crumpled shape slung in the corner turned out to be his dad's duffel bag. Kneeling, Cameron unknotted the bag's drawstrings and examined the contents: a pair of his dad's jeans, some T-shirts, a jumper... Tucked in-between was a scattering of photographs he recognised from the walls at home. Here he was as a wee boy, building spaceships from Lego. Then a shot of him and Dad on the dodgems. Next, him and Mum at a picnic, back before she left. She was holding out a plate of sandwiches, her face pretty but sad. What were the photos doing in the bag? Where was Dad going that he needed to take them?

A movement in the corner of his eye caught Cameron's attention. Something had passed the windscreen, breaking the light from the headlamps. It might have been an animal, but the shape felt all wrong for that. He peered through the gap between the front seats and out of the windscreen. This time he saw it: a figure in a long dark cloak – its hood pulled down to hide the wearer's face – hurrying towards him across the sand.

Suddenly terrified, Cameron scrambled to the rear of the van. He grabbed the door and pulled it closed as quietly and quickly as he could. There was no way to lock the rear doors from inside, but he figured if he hunkered down by the duffel bag then maybe he wouldn't be seen in the shadowy interior.

There was no sound from outside. On the beach Cameron's every footstep had been reported by the pebbles, but up here on the grass there was nothing to let him know if someone was coming. He shifted slightly in his crouch and his kneecap cracked. Cameron swore under his breath. It sounded like a gunshot to him – would anyone have heard outside?

There was still no indication of movement. What was he to do? He could pull himself over the seats into the front of the van, but he didn't know whether the key was still in the ignition. The front door had been locked, so it didn't seem likely... He had to chance it. If the key was there, he'd start the van, and try to drive it. If not, he could open the driver's door and make a run for it into the night. He tensed himself for action.

A creak from the rear door gave him his cue. It eased its way open, and Cameron just saw a set of long white fingers creep their way around the edge before he flung himself at the gap between the front seats and the roof. The leg of his jeans caught on the gear stick as he vaulted over. He tugged it free. Something grabbed at his other foot. Hoarse breath rasped in his ear. He struggled and yanked, but the bony grip was tight upon his ankle...

Cameron woke, drenched in sweat. All at once he knew where he'd been: the beach at Weymss where they'd found his dad. He tried to sit up, and found the bedsheets had wound themselves into a knot around his legs. His feet fizzed with pins and needles. He shook them free, drew his knees up to his chest, and hugged himself.

Cameron had dreamt a lot about his dad since he'd died. Those dreams were usually vague and sad, but this one seemed so real. He could still half smell the sour and salty air in his nostrils...

Don't think about it. He forced himself to lie back down. From his pillow, he could see 01.24 in blue glowing numbers on his mobile. There was still an awful lot of night to go. He reached for his headphones, but of course they weren't there. His mini-system was stranded on a table by the window, near the only free socket. When he'd moved in, Grandma Ives had given him this huge upstairs room to himself. Unlike the ordered neatness of the rest of her house, it was clear she'd been using it for storage. There were boxes and books piled on every surface. He'd even found a stuffed mongoose – its furry limbs raised up, ready to pounce – lurking in the clutter on top of the bed.

"That's Monty," Grandma Ives had explained. "Came from India. He's been in the house for years and I can't bring myself to throw him away. You don't mind sharing?"

Cameron had examined the dead animal's glassy eyes and yellow teeth. "I'll cope. As long as he doesn't bite."

"You're quite safe, unless you're a snake." She put the mongoose on top of a bureau, and Cameron later chucked a T-shirt over it. It snagged on the creature's claws, but at least he didn't have to look at it.

"It'll take us a while to sort things out," Grandma Ives had said, "but I hope we'll find a way for you to be happy here."

Over the course of the first week, they'd set to and cleared the room. Bit by bit Grandma Ives' junk went out, and Cameron's things moved in. Bags and boxes of CDs, books and clothes arrived, and his posters were stuck up over the old flowery wallpaper. His dad's PC sat in the corner, gathering dust. It was doubly useless now, as Grandma Ives didn't show any signs of getting broadband. There were still tons of things back at the old house, his dad's stuff mainly. But Grandma Ives said that was a problem for another day.

Cameron turned over in bed. His mouth was dry, and every time he closed his eyes he had the feeling he was going to end up dreaming about the beach again. He decided to get up and get a glass of water. He swung himself from the bed, and grabbed a sweatshirt off the back of a chair.

Downstairs the kitchen light was on. Grandma Ives was up too. The old woman was wrapped in a green velvet dressing gown, her hair hanging loose about her shoulders in long silver strands. She was shaking flour into a large mixing bowl on the table.

Cameron didn't know where to look. This was nothing like him and his dad in their T-shirts on a weekend morning, grunting at each other over their teacups and cereal bowls. He turned to go, but she'd already seen him.

"Good evening, Cameron. Or should I say good morning? What brings you down here?"

"I need a glass of water."

"Well, help yourself. There's cocoa on the shelf if you prefer. I find it calming after bad dreams."

"Who said I had bad dreams?" A flush of anger ran through him. If anyone was to blame for his nightmare it was her, with her mad outrageous promise of bringing Dad back. She'd clammed up after he'd agreed to her plan, but the idea had been festering away at the back of his mind. It wasn't the sort of thing you could easily forget.

"I just want a drink, that's all. I'll get it and go."

"Bad dreams wouldn't be unusual, given what you've gone through." She held out her hands in a calming gesture. "That was all I meant."

There was an uncomfortable pause. Cameron sipped his water and watched as she began to stir the mixture in the basin.

"What are you doing?" he said eventually.

"I'm making dough for bread. I suffer from sleepless nights too. A little activity helps me relax." She held out the wooden spoon to him and smiled. "You could stir this for me, if you like."

"I guess." Cameron took the spoon. It wasn't like he was in a hurry to go back upstairs anyway.

"I don't usually have a helper for my nocturnal bakery." Grandma Ives collected a wooden board from the cupboard and began to cover it with flour. "Would you like a story, to help time pass?"

"If you want to," he said guardedly. "Don't you think I'm a bit old for bedtime stories?"

"Oh, this story won't send you to sleep, far from it. It has a little to do with our earlier conversation. Shall I begin?"

Cameron shrugged.

"I'll take that as a yes." Grandma Ives tipped the dough onto the board, and as she told her story, she began to knead. "The last trial for witchcraft was in 1727, did you know that?"

He shook his head, a little surprised at her choice of subject. Did she really think talk about witches was going to cure his insomnia?

"It's more recent than people think," the old lady continued. "Not long after, all of Europe began to look to Scotland and to Edinburgh for inspiration. There were new ideas about science, about philosophy, about engines for movement, about how the Earth came into being. They said it was a period of enlightenment, and superstition and the old belief in magic began to recede. Why do you think that might be?"

"I thought this was a story, not a history lesson," Cameron grumbled.

"It's always good to ask questions, Cameron. That's how you find out how stories work."

Cameron rubbed his eyes and reluctantly engaged his brain. "Ok. When you're a kid, you believe in things like the tooth fairy and Santa and monsters under the bed. But when you get older, you stop. You realise they're made up. Maybe that's what happened? People just sort of grew up."

"Good thinking. Completely wrong, of course, but nicely reasoned. How about this... Perhaps it wasn't the people that changed. Perhaps it was the world?" She gave Cameron a very direct look.

"Go on." He folded his arms across his chest. "You're not boring me."

"I'm so pleased." Grandma Ives attacked the dough with renewed vigour. "There was once a great and powerful man called Alexander Mitchell. You won't find him in the official history books. His family had for years held great power in their hands, both in this world and in the daemon world beyond—"

"The *daemon* world?"

"*Where dwell those creatures that are not man, no nor angel either,*" she recited. "Where do you think the monsters people used to believe in came from?"

"Ri-ight." Cameron had the distinct impression this conversation was running away from him. "And this daemon world would be where exactly?"

Grandma Ives took her hands from the dough, rinsed them, and plucked some fruit from a tray on the counter. She set an orange on the table in front of Cameron.

"Imagine the Earth as a spinning sphere." She added an apple, right next to the orange. "Imagine the daemon world as another sphere, occupying a fractionally different space." She walked her fingertips from the top of the orange across to the apple. "The two were so close, at times you could step from one to the other."

"But the world's not really like that," said Cameron dubiously.

"Oh? And how do you know that?"

"There've been spaceships up there. Satellites take pictures all the time. We'd know if there was another world nearby."

Grandma Ives sighed. "Lower your head, so your chin touches the table."

"Why?"

"Indulge me."

Feeling a little daft, Cameron did as he was asked.

"How many fruits can you see?"

"Two." The orange looked large and juicy, right before his nose. She lifted the apple, and put it directly behind the orange.

"And now how many?"

"Just one."

"Which is what your rocket-ships and sputniks would see: the Earth alone in outer space."

"But I *know* the apple's still there!" he said stubbornly. "You've just hidden it."

"Just as I *know* the daemon world exists alongside ours." She stuck a finger under his chin and lifted it up. "You simply need the right perspective to see it."

Cameron glowered, and rubbed flour from his neck. "That's not fair."

"Life rarely is." She returned to kneading her dough. "Alexander Mitchell – of whom I was about to speak – didn't care for the idea of dual human and daemon worlds at all. Far from being part of the natural order, he believed the daemon world was exerting a corrupting influence on its partner. He reasoned that if there was some way to free us from it permanently, we could evolve along a uniquely human path of science and rationality, and leave the dark days of magic well behind.

"Over in the daemon world, a mage called Astredo had been plotting along similar lines. He believed daemonkind would flourish best in a world of magic alone, untainted by man's ideas. Together, Mitchell and Astredo contrived a plan to separate the worlds."

"But if they'd always been so close," said Cameron, toying with the orange, "wouldn't that be really dangerous?"

"Insanely, stupidly so," agreed Grandma Ives.

"So how were they going to do it, this mad plan of theirs?"

"They used their dark skills to find a fissure point, a magical fault line where the connection between the worlds was weak. By exerting enough force, they hoped to separate the worlds entirely. Mitchell's fissure point was right here in Edinburgh, above Salisbury Crags on Arthur's Seat."

Cameron knew those hills. "Arthur's Seat used to be a volcano, didn't it? Millions of years ago."

Grandma Ives nodded. "Whatever subterranean clash threw it from the Earth also uncovered the fault line the conspirators would exploit. With Astredo and his coven ready to channel their power from the daemon world, Mitchell called together his followers. It was a dreadful night, the sky black and moonless, and the wind howling around the cliffs. The men clutched their hats to their heads, and the women wrapped their shawls tightly. The air was so cold it chilled you to the bone."

Cameron shot the old lady a quizzical glance. "You sound like you remember it..."

"Cameron Duffy, I may be a little past my prime, but really! Now, where was I?"

"On the crags," he prompted. Grandma Ives was giving a great performance, her eyes flicking round the room, and her floury fingers gesturing as she brought the story to life.

"Now, as the two covens focussed their magic, the tortured worlds screamed out their protest. The covens pushed and pushed, but no matter how much power they threw in, the worlds resisted. Rather than the clean separation they hoped for, they merely forced open a rift: a howling void neither of one place nor the other.

"When Mitchell's coven saw the terrible void they'd created, their confidence left them. One by one, their nerves broke, and they fled screaming into the night. Mitchell tried to hold on, but he didn't have the strength. He was sucked into the rift, and it swirled closed behind him. We can only assume a similar fate befell Astredo, for neither of them have been seen alive since."

Cameron realised he'd been holding his breath, and slowly let it out. He could almost *feel* the chill of the storm-swept hillside, and see Mitchell's terrified followers running away, leaving him alone to be drawn helplessly into the void. "So what happened next?"

"Well, for a start, movement between the worlds became a lot rarer. The daemon world's influence on ours began to decline, if not as completely as Mitchell might have hoped..."

"And that's when all those new ideas about science and engines and so on started to happen." Cameron began to understand. "From then on, there were no more goblins, witches and ghosts for us."

"Fewer, certainly." Grandma Ives nodded with approval. "Most of the old magic left the human world that night, leaving behind only the occasional pale glimmer that leaks across the gap. In time, people found other things to be scared of."

Cameron thought about the TV news. It was full of terrorists and pollution, bank crashes and job losses. Nobody had time to care about *proper* monsters any more.

"The story's not over though, is it? What about the void? Is it still there?"

"Do you know the expression, 'nature abhors a vacuum'?"

"Yeah, I think." Cameron racked his brains. "We did something about it in school. It means empty spaces aren't normal, doesn't it? Amy kidded on she thought it was something to do with Hoovers."

"Amy sounds like an amusing girl. Remind me to ask her to dinner," said Grandma Ives, her eyebrow raised. "Yes, that's what it means. The gap that opened up couldn't remain empty forever. It had to be filled."

"What with?"

"Whatever it could draw into itself. It snatched echoes, and stole distorted reflections from the worlds it bordered. It fed on memories of leftover places that were knocked down or forgotten. All the old creatures and things otherwise lost to time found a new home there. Slowly the in-between place became a mixture of human Edinburgh and daemon Edinburgh, all churned up into one. It is the route by which those who still can pass between the worlds. It's a wonderful place in its own right."

"*Those who still can.* But who are they, exactly? Who do you mean?" Cameron gripped the table.

Grandma Ives gave him a half-smile. "Are you sure you don't know?"

"Tell me."

"The people who were in Mitchell's coven that night – some went mad, some became mystics, some never spoke of it again – but they all shared one thing. That little glimpse they had of the void *changed* them. From that moment on, they always knew how to find their way back, to pass into the in-between place, and to use it. Their children had the gift too, and their children's children, and so on, right down to the present day. People like you and me, Cameron. People like your father, although he never wanted to admit it."

Cameron stared at her. "But I'm normal. I've never seen anything mad like that. I've never been anywhere but here."

"Perhaps. But that might not always be the case."

Grandma Ives lifted the dough, and smoothed it out into a tin she took from the cupboard. "This can rest for a while, and in the morning I'll bake the bread." She stretched her fingers. "I'm quite tired after that little workout. I think I shall sleep well."

"You can't go to bed now! You need to tell me more!" Cameron protested.

Grandma Ives leant forward and kissed him gently on the forehead. "There'll be time enough tomorrow, Cameron."

"But..."

"Turn the light out when you go up."

She swept out, leaving him in the cold kitchen with his long-forgotten glass of water, very much awake.

3. A Shop in Two Places

Cameron woke up full of questions, but when he went downstairs to speak to the old lady, he found a note stuck to the fridge:

Cameron,

I have some business to attend to, but I'll be back by lunchtime. Could you pick up some milk for the cat? You'll find some change in the kitchen drawer and a door key on the dresser. It's about time you had your own.

Go out the door, down the hill, and turn left. Keep going until you see a sign marked "Montmorency". You can't miss it.

Grandma Ives

Cameron picked up the key. How come he'd never seen the cat? It must be hiding somewhere, still uncertain about this strange new person it was going to have to share its house with... He knew how it felt.

He grabbed a couple of buttery slices from the still-warm loaf resting on the table, slipped some money into his pocket, and ducked out the front door. Grandma

Ives' house was one of a neat stone-built row that lined the steep road up to Blackford Hill. An observatory nestled on the hilltop. Cameron set off in the opposite direction. He was in the mood for a walk anyway. It might help clear his head.

10.45 on a Thursday... If he was back in school, it'd soon be his least favourite time of the week. In fifteen short minutes, his classmates would swap the eggy warmth of the science lab for the changing rooms, and two full hours of P.E. The last Thursday he'd been there, they'd all been sent outdoors for football. He was put in defence as usual, along with the fat kids and the space cadets. Bored of watching the ball roll pointlessly about the field, he'd drifted into a daydream, thinking up a name for the great band he was going to be in, if he ever got it started... The ball went shooting past, straight into goal. He'd not been popular in the changing rooms. Wayne Sneddon had chucked a boot at him, saying he'd find that harder to miss.

Morons, thought Cameron, trudging down the hill. He'd had nothing but trouble off Sneddon and his mates since he started Cauldlockheart High. Maybe if he didn't have to see them for a couple more weeks, they'd forget he existed.

Yeah, that'd be right. He kicked at a discarded Coke can, and watched it go skittering and bouncing down the slope. Grandma Ives hadn't said anything about him going back yet. She hadn't even made him do the work he'd been set. The letter she'd written to the headmaster said he was still grieving. Was that true? It wasn't like he cried all day, or screamed until he had to be slapped, like people did in rubbish old movies. All he had left inside him was this nagging pain that reminded him something important was missing.

The morning air was cold around his fingers, and he pulled his hands into the cuffs of his sweatshirt. The old woman's offer to bring back Dad, her tales of a daemon world that existed alongside this one – they had all seemed so believable when it was just him and her. Here and now though, as he slouched down the road for a pint of milk, with his trainers rubbing against his heel because his feet had grown again overnight, it all seemed a bit, well, *mad*.

His phone rang. He dug it out of his back pocket.

"Hiya, Amy."

"Hey, Cam-boy. What's up? I'm a bit bored now my sidekick's not here."

"I thought you were *my* sidekick?"

"You *wish*," snorted Amy. Her voice sounded odd and echoey.

"Where are you?"

"Girls' loos. I told Mr Robertson it was a 'girl thing'. He went red and said, 'Very well, make it quick, Miss Giovanni.'"

Cameron laughed.

"I reckon I've got ten minutes at the most before he sends out a search party. So, tell me the latest. How's the mysterious Granny?"

"She's ok." Cameron was uncertain how much he could tell his friend. "Some of the stuff she comes out with is a bit odd, though."

"What like? No TV with dinner? Speak when you're spoken to? Or does she still think it's 1945?"

"Nothing like that." He struggled to find the right words. "It's like... she reckons there's more going on than most people realise... like there are strange things lurking beneath the surface."

"There's always more going on than *you* realise, Cam."

"Like what, exactly?"

"Oh, stuff. Things you don't notice right under your nose—"

There was a crackling sound, as if the phone had suddenly been shoved in a pocket. Cameron heard a stern woman's voice say, "Are you talking on the phone in there, young lady? That's strictly forbidden during school time, as well you know!"

"No, honest, I'm not! I'm praying. This is my religion, see? I've got to meditate three times a day—"

The phone clicked off.

Cameron grinned. Amy could talk her way out of anything. She was a good mate, but she would never believe him if he told her the truth. And Cameron wasn't sure if he was ready to say it out loud yet. He had to give Grandma Ives a chance, didn't he? He had to see if she could really do what she'd promised.

He stowed the phone back in his pocket.

The corner shop took up the ground floor of a block of tenement flats. It had obviously been there some time. Beneath posters and flags advertising *Edinburgh Evening News*, lottery scratchcards and mobile top-ups, there was an older plainly written sign marked:

MONTMORENCY'S GENERAL STORES
Newspapers & Confectionery & Fancy Goods

Cameron pushed the door open, causing the bell to dance and ring. A stocky man behind the counter looked up from a portable telly that was blaring out a daytime chat show.

"No thieving," he said by way of greeting. He tapped his finger against his glasses, and Cameron noticed one of the lenses was blanked over with sticking plaster.

"I'm gonna get some milk, that's all."

"I've got my eye on you, mind." The man returned his attention to the telly.

"Yeah, just the one eye though," muttered Cameron.

He made his way down the aisle, taking in the usual small shop smells of newsprint, flour and powdery sugar. At the back of the store there was a chiller cabinet and a paper rack. Cameron picked up a pint of Lo Fat, then turned his attention to the magazines. If he couldn't get online at Grandma Ives', he could at least *read* about the bands he should be listening to.

He flicked through *Sound Express*, which had a good free CD stuck to the front. Something clicked in his ear: a short sequence of pops that rose and fell. He shook his head. *Probably a bit of water...* It hadn't been that long since his morning shower.

He put the magazine back, and reached for *Axe God*. It came with a fingering chart with "the chords every songwriter needs to know". That'd be useful, if he could ever get his hands on a guitar...

There was the sound again. It was more like music this time, but the tune was indistinct – a sort of mixed-up sound, like you might get out of an old radio tuned halfway between stations. He glanced around to see what it might be, but there was only the shopkeeper's telly.

"There's a library on Fountainhall Road," called the man from the front of the store. "I mention this as a service, that's all."

"I'm making my mind up," said Cameron. "That doesn't cost anything, does it?"

He fished out his wallet. Great huge wads of tenners were sadly notable by their absence. Grandma Ives hadn't said anything about an allowance, and he wondered how to go about subtly mentioning it. He'd have to put *Axe God* back for now.

As he stretched out his hand to put the magazine on the shelf, the mysterious noise came again. This time it positively roared, and a cacophony of random notes filled his head.

"Turn it down!" he yelped. His hand clenched, scrumpling the magazine.

"Headphones playing up, son?" The shopkeeper's attention was still focussed on his chat show. "Take 'em out. They're bad for your ears."

The sound gibbered and howled, and Cameron's vision seemed to go fuzzy for a second. He dropped the carton of milk – *splot* – to the floor. He had to get out of here! Clutching his head, he staggered forward.

To his amazement, the shelf to his left started to rotate. The side he had seen when he came into the shop spun giddily to face the wall, and a new side swivelled out. The familiar tins of soup and beans had vanished, and in their place was a line of containers with labels he didn't recognise.

What kind of crazy shop was this? The other shelves were following suit, rotating jerkily to reveal strange new products. In the chiller, bottles of dark red liquid stood in place of pints of milk. There were still eggs on display, but they were green and rubbery looking.

If that came out of a chicken, it wasn't well...

Cameron laughed, a little hysterically. Everything was different! The light was dim and yellow, and everything seemed distorted – looking towards the shopkeeper's counter was like peering into a tunnel. On the paper rack, creamy rolls of parchment hung on pegs. "Which souls in torment make the sweetest sounds?" he read. "Our panel decides!"

"What the—"

"Last copy," hissed a voice. "I saw it first!" A hand pushed him out of the way, and Cameron stumbled...

The odd music roared again, and once more the shelves began to spin. Cameron ducked as a corner edge whipped past his face, causing him to bump into a stand of cards. A stack of *On Occasion of your Wedding* – showing a dopey-looking couple holding hands – scattered across the floor.

"Right old mess you've made." The shopkeeper looked up at last from his telly. "What's up with you? Been hanging about the bus stops, drinking stuff you shouldn't?"

"Don't blame me, it's your shop that went mental..." Cameron started to protest, but all around him, everything had returned to normal. There was only the dropped carton and strewn cards to show anything had happened.

He leant against the chiller cabinet, trying to pull himself together. He couldn't have imagined it, could he? Cold air smelling faintly of milk and cheese pumped past his nostrils. His stomach churned and his head spun as if he'd just stepped off a fairground ride.

"I think I'm gonna be sick—"

"Oh no, not in here." The man swung the counter open, and came barrelling down the aisle. "I'm going to call someone. They can come pick you up and shout at you, or take you to the hospital. I'm not fussed which. Come on, lad! What's your dad's number?"

"I haven't got one any more." Cameron groaned. "I live with my Gran."

The shopkeeper moved closer. He removed his sticking-plaster wrapped glasses, and brought his hand up to shield the eye that had previously been uncovered. His newly exposed pupil was a bright and piercing green.

"Flamin' hell, lad. You've been world-shifting, haven't you?" The shopkeeper blinked. "Who did you say your granny was?"

4. The Eyes Have It

"Peppermint tea," said Grandma Ives. "Wonderfully calming for the stomach."

Cameron took a sip. It tasted like Polo mints stewed in warm water. "I don't think I'm a fan."

They were in a room at the back of Montmorency's shop. Amongst the piles of boxes and supplies, the shopkeeper had somehow managed to squeeze in a living space. Cameron sat on a battered and crumb-ridden sofa, Grandma Ives on a hard-backed chair by the sink. She'd made a point of dusting it down with a handkerchief. The old lady had arrived remarkably quickly after the shopkeeper called. It was clear she and Montmorency knew each other.

"We share a similar family history," she explained to Cameron. "But while you and I are direct descendants of, well, the human side present at the world-split, Mr Montmorency's ancestry is a little more mixed."

"Mum was a daemon; that's what she means," said the man cheerfully. "I'm half and half." He nudged Cameron's hand. "Drink it up. I had to rip open a fresh box. Not much call for peppermint tea."

Grandma Ives glared.

"Not that it isn't always a pleasure," he added.

"Is that the shop bell?"

"It could be. I can certainly take a hint." He hefted a box of loo rolls from a nearby stack, and disappeared back to the shop.

"If he's half daemon, doesn't that make him evil or something?" Cameron said when the man was out of earshot. He checked his surroundings. "Is this an evil corner shop, then? Did you send me to an evil corner shop?" He laughed a little nervously.

"Being a daemon does not mean one is evil, no more than being human means one has to behave respectably." Grandma Ives screwed up a discarded crisp packet with an expression of distaste. "Do you think I would have sent you here unprepared if there was any great danger?"

Cameron hadn't known Grandma Ives long enough to come to any firm conclusions about what she might or might not do, but he could tell when he'd been set up.

"You didn't really need a pint of milk... You don't even have a cat."

"Not lately, no," she admitted with a thin smile. "It's been a while since I had a feline friend."

"And you knew I was going to see... *stuff* if I came here, right?"

"I thought there was a good chance. This store is a common meeting point, one of a number around this old city. The edges of the worlds are well worn from visitors crossing to and from the in-between place. After our conversation last night I wanted to check your abilities." She leant forward in her chair. "What exactly did you see?"

"I dunno... it was only a few seconds. It was like the same shop, but different. Filled with things I didn't recognise."

"Definitely a world-shift! You've got your grandmother's talent, and no mistake." She clasped her hands together tightly in front of her chest. "I'm proud of you, Cameron. You and I are going to do great things together."

"It was all true, then," he said slowly. "Everything you told me."

"Did you doubt me?"

Cameron looked away. "Just a little," he admitted. "But not any more." He could feel the excitement growing inside him. The sick feeling he'd had earlier was completely gone. "A whole new place, part way between here and the daemon world... Do you reckon I'll be able to go there properly?"

"There's every reason to suppose you'll be very good at world-shifting."

"I don't know." He pulled a face. "I felt like I was going to puke."

"Simple spatial-dislocation symptoms," she said firmly. "You'll get used to it."

"Your mate Mr Mont-what-thing wasn't keen when he thought I was going to redecorate his floor. What is it with those glasses of his anyway? I thought he had a lazy eye at first—"

"Should my ears be burning?" said the shopkeeper, coming back into the room. "I have this strange suspicion I'm being talked about, and in my own shop too."

Cameron reddened.

"My grandson was remarking upon your innovative eyewear," said Grandma Ives smoothly.

The shopkeeper gave Cameron a look. "You've got to watch out for these quiet ones. They notice things. I should know." He perched on the corner of a table. "I wasn't much older than you when my daemon side came on. It was a right nuisance at first. I'd get these blinding headaches, seeing two places all at once. That's why I came up with these..." He tapped his plaster-covered spectacles. "These are my glasses for here, and these are my ones for *there*." He dug in his jacket pocket and produced a smarter pair, with a piece of smoked glass covering the opposite lens. "Useful, eh?"

"They're genius." Cameron reached for the spectacles eagerly. "Would they work for me?"

"I shouldn't think so, lad. It's just ordinary glass. It's how you see things that's important." The shopkeeper took off his current pair of glasses, and Cameron saw for the first time that the man's eyes were of contrasting colours: one an iridescent green, the other a more subdued brown.

The shopkeeper winked. "See. Told you I was half and half, didn't I?" He put the smoked-glass spectacles on, hiding his brown pupil. "This is all I need to do to find Edinburgh Parallel." He switched back to the sticking-plaster pair. "And these are me everyday specs. Nice and ordinary. Doesn't frighten the human customers."

"Edinburgh Parallel," breathed Cameron. "Is that what they call it then? The other place?"

"It's as good a name as any for a gap wedged between two worlds," said Grandma Ives.

"But why *Edinburgh* Parallel? Doesn't the gap run everywhere? Or does it only exist right here?"

"We are in Edinburgh, and so is the parallel, and that is all we need to concern ourselves with for now," Grandma Ives sniffed.

Way not to answer a question...

Cameron turned to the shopkeeper, who shrugged. "When do I get a chance to go off on holiday and find out about other places? Having a shop here and in the parallel gives me two sets of customers, and that keeps me busy enough. And I'm not the only one into that game. Take your granny here..."

Cameron shot the old woman a curious glance.

She stood up at once. "Excuse me, Mr Montmorency, I prefer to keep my business to myself."

"Of course," said the shopkeeper hurriedly. "Wouldn't dream of stepping on anyone's toes."

"We'll say no more about it then." Grandma Ives spoke lightly, but Cameron could tell the subject was closed. It was the same no-nonsense voice she'd used on Carole the social worker.

"Old charmer, isn't she?" Montmorency whispered. "It's probably a full-time job just tending the bats in her belfry."

Cameron looked at his feet, trying to keep his face straight.

"Well, Cameron, I think we shall be going." Grandma Ives drew a twenty-pound note from her handbag. "I trust this will cover any disruption? We'll take a pack of sausages too, and my special order if it's arrived."

"No problem. It's in the fridge." The shopkeeper glanced at Cameron. "There were a couple of magazines the lad was pawing at. All crumpled they are. Couldn't possibly sell 'em."

She sighed and revised her estimate.

They followed the shopkeeper to the cash desk, where he bagged up their purchases. He handed the carrier to Cameron. "See you about, lad. Don't let her boss you around too much."

"Do you reckon I get a choice?" Cameron turned to go. "Thanks for the magazines!"

The shopkeeper wasn't listening. He was talking to someone over Cameron's shoulder. Cameron looked round, but there was nobody there.

"He's had a hard life, Jack Montmorency," Grandma Ives said as they set off back home. "It wasn't easy for him growing up in this world, not fitting in. His eye, you know. People can be cruel. Children especially."

Cameron looked at Grandma Ives. What had she been like when she was young? Was she always so confident, so in command?

"Did you always fit in, then? What were you, captain of the school hockey team?"

Her lips went tight. "My childhood was a long time ago. I don't care to remember."

She stalked up the hill in brisk strides. Not like an old woman at all, thought Cameron.

"You've had it easy the last few weeks, my boy," she said firmly, as he struggled to keep up. "I've been neglecting your education."

Cameron's heart sank. "But I don't want to go back! You can't tell me about other worlds and daemons, then send me back to Sneddon and P.E!" He was conscious of his voice going all small and whiny. *Way to go, Cameron... Now she's really going to listen.*

"There *is* more than one sort of education, Cameron. We are going to be too busy for you to return to school, or to 'Sneddon', whatever that might be."

He stared at her in disbelief. "Sneddon's an idiot, but that doesn't matter. Woo-hoo!" He leapt up and punched the air. "Do you mean it? I don't have to? Not yet? Really?"

"Calm down! You'll shoogle the groceries." The old woman fumbled in her bag for her door key, but Cameron found his more quickly, and slipped it into the lock. "It's of no concern to me if you don't go back at all. I have far more important things to teach you."

"Like what?"

"How to use your talent properly. How to shift into Edinburgh Parallel. How to trade with daemons. How to deal with Mrs Ferguson—"

"Mrs Ferguson..." He'd heard that name before, when Grandma Ives made her offer. "Is she important?"

"She certainly likes to think so." Grandma Ives took the shopping bag from Cameron, and handed him his magazines. "I've requested an audience this afternoon, which just about gives me time to instruct you on what to do. Sausage sandwiches for lunch, then we'll get started."

"Instruct me?" he repeated, shooting her a glance. He grinned. "Why, what happens if I mess up? Will she throw a strop?"

"Very possibly. So you'll have to pay attention." Grandma Ives hung her coat smartly on a peg. "For if we don't do things right, Mrs Ferguson will not give us what we need, the resurrection spell cannot be made, and your father will have to stay dead."

Suddenly, the hollow feeling in Cameron's gut was back with a vengeance – that terrible reminder Dad was gone.

"We'd better get it right then, hadn't we?" he said.

5. A Visit to Mrs Ferguson

On the bus ride to Mrs Ferguson's, Grandma Ives sat bolt upright. She'd whipped her grey hair into a high-up fancy do, and put a silver chain with a locket round her neck. Her head, framed in profile by the window, reminded Cameron of something off a postage stamp.

She's all dressed up, like she's going on a state visit. He glanced down at the dull and sensible school clothes she'd insisted he put on. *And I look like a dork on a day trip.*

He shifted in his seat. Hot air belched from a vent near his feet, and it seemed to be setting off some kind of reaction with the "special order" from Montmorency in Grandma Ives' bag. A sour and unpleasant smell was drifting into the cabin, and Cameron knew he wasn't alone in detecting it. The woman in front had already moved seat, but only after giving them both a disgusted glare.

Grandma Ives just looked past her, but Cameron was more than a little embarrassed. Grandma Ives had explained that it was very important to take "exactly the right gift" when visiting. Cameron's suggestion of a box of chocolates wouldn't do at all. He hoped Mrs Ferguson was going to appreciate the effort they were going to.

"Hey," he said, trying to gain his gran's attention. "What's this Mrs Ferguson like anyway?"

"She's no better than she should be."

"Well, *great*. That just tells me *everything*."

Grandma Ives studied him for a moment. "We can rely on her to keep to the letter of the law. That is why it's so vitally important you know the rules. Perhaps you could repeat them to me?"

Cameron frowned. Grandma Ives had talked of little else but "the rules" all the way through lunch. He'd have thought she could trust him to remember a simple list.

He counted off on his fingers. "One, I have to be polite."

"Very polite."

"Got it. Two, I can't accept anything from her, unless you say so."

"That's extremely important."

"Three, I'm not to tell her anything about myself I don't have to."

"If you are in doubt, you probably shouldn't say anything at all. Excellent! Abide by my instructions, and you'll be fine."

"Uh-huh." Cameron was getting a little sick of all the repetition.

The bus lurched on, down through the cobbled streets of Edinburgh's New Town and into Stockbridge. Grandma Ives beckoned him to get up. Out on the frosty road, she started to head towards the rows of colonies houses, and Cameron realised he'd been here once before. It had been on one of his dad's clearance jobs. The streets between the houses were pretty narrow, and

Dad had sworn himself purple trying to manoeuvre the van into a space. In the end he'd given up, and handed the wheel over to Big Joe.

"I'm gonna quit driving. It's not worth it in this city." Dad stood and fumed while the big man did his work. "I'm gonna ride a bike instead."

"Not a bad idea," Cameron said, "but it'd be pretty difficult to get all that furniture in the basket."

"Oh, is that what you reckon, Cameron Duffy?" His dad's face crumpled into a smile. "What if I learnt to balance huge bundles on my head, like those old men and women in India? What about that, eh?" He had popped his clipboard on top of his baseball cap and, arms outstretched, tottered off down the road while Big Joe watched from the van, shaking his head.

Cameron smiled at the memory. His dad could be properly daft sometimes. If he was going to get Dad back, he hoped it would be *this* dad, the one who could joke and laugh and talk about the world, not the sad and serious person he'd increasingly become.

But any dad at all would be better than none.

"If you're quite finished daydreaming?" Grandma Ives' brisk march had come to a halt outside a ground-floor flat at the end of the row. She touched her hair, checking everything was in place. With a quick glance at Cameron, she took a deep breath and pressed the bell.

A small girl of around nine or ten opened the door.

"Ms Ives and her grandson," said Grandma Ives, "here to call upon Mrs Ferguson."

The girl looked at them blankly. She showed no signs of moving, or even having heard Grandma Ives speak.

Cameron had a strong urge to poke her with his finger, just to check she hadn't frozen into a statue.

A cheerful voice sang out from the passageway. "Visitors, is it? Bring them in, Eve, don't let them catch their deaths!"

The girl stepped silently to one side, and Cameron followed Grandma Ives down the narrow hall to the living room. Although it was still light outdoors, there were thick velvet curtains drawn over the window, and the room felt cosy and snug. Every surface was covered with china ornaments, shiny glass and decorated plates, and there were many, many framed pictures of children. It reminded Cameron of the times he'd been round to Amy's nan's place. It had the same sort of homely clutter.

"Come away in, come away!" Mrs Ferguson called from her seat by the fire. She was a round-faced old woman with curly brown hair. She wore a bright floral print dress and comfy slippers.

She beamed at her visitors. "Have yourselves a seat. You'd surely like a cup of tea, and something for the lad?"

"Please don't trouble yourself." Grandma Ives sat carefully on the sofa, and gestured to Cameron to join her.

"Oh, it's no trouble, dear." Mrs Ferguson clapped her hands. "Eve, pet lamb, would you bring us some drinks?"

"You're too kind," said Grandma Ives.

A moment later, the girl who'd opened the door reappeared with a tray. She set a cup and tea-cosied pot down before Grandma Ives, and a steaming mug of hot chocolate by Cameron. There was barely a clink from the crockery as she went about her task.

The statue-girl's become a robot, thought Cameron. *She's definitely the weirdest thing here.* Even the way she dressed seemed a bit odd and old-fashioned. Her hair was tugged back into two tight pigtails, and she wore a dark blue dress with white stockings and smart black shoes. After dispensing the drinks she gave a small bow, and left the room as silently as she'd arrived.

"My little Evie," said Mrs Ferguson proudly. "She's such a help to me."

"It looks like she's making herself most useful," said Grandma Ives.

"Just one of her little games. She likes to pretend. Yesterday she was a gardener, today she's a maid. She's my wee treasure!"

"You must be delighted to have her," observed Grandma Ives.

"Oh, but they always have to go away so soon, don't they? What about yours?"

"This is Cameron, my grandson and ward. He's staying with me quite voluntarily."

"What a handsome lad! He'll be nice and big and strong once he fills out."

"Actually, it is on his account that we've come to call on you today, is it not, Cameron?"

Cameron wasn't really listening. As far as he was concerned, Grandma Ives and Mrs Ferguson had slipped into standard old-lady chat. Mrs Ferguson seemed sort of, well, *nice*; not at all what he'd expected. If she had something for a resurrection spell, he was starting to think she must've won it in a raffle, or bought it by accident in a jumble sale.

His attention shifted to the hot chocolate. The walk to Mrs Ferguson's had been cold, and lunch was a long time ago. He supposed the drink fell under Grandma Ives' bizarre rule of not accepting anything from their host, but even if he couldn't drink it, there wasn't any harm in warming his hands on the mug, was there? He picked it up.

"Go on, dear. Drink it while it's hot." Mrs Ferguson gave him a cheery smile. "It'd be a shame if it went to waste, after wee Evie put all that effort into making it."

"I guess so." There were tiny marshmallows arranged on top of the thick brown froth, and a scattering of chocolate dust. It looked and smelled great; probably the best hot chocolate he'd ever seen...

Grandma Ives opened her mouth as if to say something, and Mrs Ferguson swiftly held up a hand. Grandma Ives pursed her lips, a look of intense frustration passing across her face.

"*Such* a shame you're on a diet, Ms Ives," laughed Mrs Ferguson. "No yummy hot chocolate for you! But it's just the thing for a growing lad. Cameron, won't you take a sip?"

"I want to..." The rich chocolate smell was teasing Cameron's nostrils.

"So drink it, dear. Drink it all down."

"I can't..."

"Don't be silly, now. I'll be most offended if you don't have any."

There was something in the bright eagerness of her voice, her determination for him to drink, that jolted Cameron. He glanced at Grandma Ives. Although her mouth was closed, her eyes were darting furiously from the mug to Cameron and back.

"I can't drink it," he said quickly. "I can't take anything from you."

"Oh, really?" Mrs Ferguson's eyes sparkled with amusement. "Why ever not?"

"Those are the rules," he said, more confidently now. "I can't unless Gran says so. And she hasn't said a word." He put the mug back down.

There was a pause, then Mrs Ferguson lowered her hand. "My, she has taught you well."

"Yes, I have." Grandma Ives rubbed her jaw, and Cameron noticed her hand was trembling very slightly. "Might we now stop playing this charade?"

"What charade would that be, dear?" said Mrs Ferguson. She was smiling as benignly as ever, but now Cameron thought about it, he reckoned it was an empty sort of smile. It was like she'd pulled the corners of her mouth into all the right places, but underneath she wasn't pleased at all.

"This pretence we are but two Edinburgh ladies quietly taking tea," said Grandma Ives. "As if you could ever be something as straightforward and respectable as that."

"Oh, very well," said Mrs Ferguson. "You never were any fun, were you? Just give me a moment to change..." Her voice tailed off.

Cameron watched with a mixture of horror and fascination as Mrs Ferguson's eyes rolled back sharply in their sockets. A long, drawn-out breath hissed from between her lips, like the last bit of air being squeezed from a plastic bag. The old woman became quite still.

"She's having a heart attack! We've killed her, just cos I wouldn't drink a lousy cup of chocolate!"

Grandma Ives snorted.

Gingerly Cameron went over to Mrs Ferguson, and waved his hand in front of her face. There wasn't the slightest movement. The old lady wasn't breathing.

"Gran, I'm serious. I think she's dead."

"No, she's not. That thing wasn't properly alive. The body sitting in that armchair is simply an avatar." Grandma Ives didn't look in the least bit concerned.

"An avatar..." Cameron paused. "Do you mean like online?"

"On a line of what?"

He laughed nervously. "On the internet. Like when you post on a message board or play a game. It's the picture or character other people see. It stands in for you."

Grandma Ives raised an eyebrow. "And does this picture resemble the person sitting typing into their computer equipment?"

"Well, sometimes." He thought of his own avatar on the *Sounds Express* site: Johnny Tremor, lead singer with the Sidewalks. "Sometimes it's more who you want to look like, or really want to be."

"Then I should say an online avatar and a daemonic avatar are similar, and equally misleading."

The implication of Grandma Ives' words sank in. "So Ferguson's a daemon?" He stepped back from the armchair. "Like Montmorency?"

"No. Not at all like Montmorency."

"Oh," he said. "Thanks for the warning."

"You're welcome," said Grandma Ives, oblivious to his sarcasm.

"Are we going to, you know, world-shift?" He steeled himself for the strange sudden rush of sound. "Some kind of heads-up would be good, you know."

"There's no need," said Grandma Ives. "Mrs Ferguson can change into her daemon self any time she likes. Her true form is not very... *compatible* with the human world, but she usually finds a way to twist it to her needs."

"Oh great." He looked at her grimly. "So what do we do now then?"

"Sit down." She patted the sofa. "But be on your guard. We must wait and see how the real Mrs Ferguson chooses to manifest herself."

Cameron scanned the room, alert now to every little sound or movement. The fire in the grate hissed and cracked. In the corner, a clock with the face of a cat ticked, its eyes sliding from side to side with each wag of its pendulum tail. Grandma Ives said nothing, just sat with her hands clasped tightly on her handbag.

Cameron found himself looking again at the children in the photographs. Now he studied them, he saw they were all dressed in old-fashioned clothes, much like Eve had been. Were they just as quiet and well behaved? Or were the photos faked, like Mrs Ferguson herself? He snuck another glance at the avatar. It didn't matter what Grandma Ives had said, he couldn't shake the uncomfortable feeling he was sharing the room with a dead body. The old woman's face had taken on a distinctly grey colour, and there was a little trickle of drool running out the corner of her mouth.

Gross... He looked away, staring instead at the spots of sunlight on the closed curtains. High up by the curtain rail, they bobbed and weaved...

Except – there was no other window in the room. So where were they coming from, those red streaks of light?

He looked closer. The more he stared, the more the spots seemed like dancing eyes, and the crease in the material above, a stern, heavy brow.

One of the "eyes" blinked, and Cameron started. *There's definitely a face in the curtains.* And it was staring right back at him.

He gulped and nudged Grandma Ives. "I've found her. Look..."

A fold in the curtain shifted abruptly, and formed a crooked mouth.

"He's sharp, this one," breathed a raspy voice.

The fabric puffed out, twisting and distorting into a new shape. Soon the eyes and mouth were revealed to be the centre of a disc-shaped head-body, about the size of a dinner plate, around which the faint outlines of eight legs rose twitching from the velvet. One by one, they wriggled free until they were joined only at their very tips to the curtain from which they'd formed.

Cameron was appalled. It was as if some colossal mutated spider was pushing its way into the room, and yet he was utterly convinced there was nothing hidden behind the curtain. The fabric was being re-shaped by the power of the daemonic Mrs Ferguson alone.

"Oh, he's so adorable, so bright and so bold." The creature's red eyes ran over him. "Couldn't you just eat him up?"

6. Eve

Grandma Ives considered her response. "I would certainly say that Cameron has many admirable qualities."

"So kind of you to have brought him as a gift." A leathery tongue licked around the edges of the daemonic Mrs Ferguson's mouth.

"I'm nobody's gift..." began Cameron. He distinctly did not like the way the creature was eyeing him.

Grandma Ives shushed him quickly. "I'm afraid you misunderstand. Cameron is here as a supplicant only. We have come to beg trade for a certain item required for a resurrection spell."

"When petitioners consult me, they must bring offerings. That is the correct method of approach." The velvet material that had formed the spidery creature's body bristled, as if a million tiny hairs were standing on end. "Perhaps I no longer walk freely in the human world, but that is still NO CAUSE FOR RUDENESS!"

The room darkened, and all the china plates and knick-knacks vibrated as the voice rose to a shout. An ornamental mug with a "World's Best Auntie" logo threatened to topple from the mantelpiece, but Cameron saved it and put it back, more from instinct than anything else. He sat quickly back down by Grandma Ives, hoping he hadn't drawn any more attention to himself.

The old woman seemed quite unfazed by this outburst of daemonic temper. "I've been an adept for many years, Mrs Ferguson. I'm fully aware of the terms for dealing with entities like yourself."

Reaching into her shopping bag, she drew out the mysterious white packet that had caused Cameron such discomfort on the bus. He caught a glimpse of a printed sticker that said:

MacGregor's Family Butchers: Retail & Wholesale
Deliver to: Montmorency's General Stores
Offal – customer special order

So *that's* what she'd picked up at Montmorency's. What was she going to do with it? He glanced up at the Ferguson daemon. She couldn't really be going to feed it?

Grandma Ives broke the seal and opened the wrapping. A new wave of sour stink wafted into the little room. The packet's contents were brown and glistening, and had stained the papers a dark rich red. Up on the curtains, Mrs Ferguson's eight legs began to twitch with anticipation.

"At my command, High Priest MacGregor took the pride of his beasts and slit its throat in your honour." Grandma Ives held the open packet aloft. "From the bull's belly he tore its liver, so we might bring you vitality. From its head he plucked its brawn, so we might gift you determination. And from its breast he took its heart, so we might offer you strength. Humbly we place these tokens before you, and beg you to spare us and grant us our desires."

Her words had taken on a sing-song tone, Cameron noticed, as if she was reciting a poem, something that had been said many times before. It seemed to please the daemon, whose red eyes now focussed on the meat.

"A plain offering, Lady Ives o' the Black Hill. The delivery could be fresher, but I suppose we must move with the times. Perhaps it might be that bit more palatable if the boy presents it to me?"

Cameron looked at Grandma Ives. "She's not serious, is she? I don't have to?"

"Remember, best behaviour," Grandma Ives said quietly. "I would tell you if it wasn't safe."

Gritting his teeth, Cameron took the greasy paper. He tried not to look inside, or even breathe in. The smell was turning his stomach.

"Bear the sacrifice up to me, boy!" The daemon's head-body thrust forward. Reluctantly, he edged closer, holding the sticky paper at arm's length. The daemon's mouth stretched wide, and he caught a glimpse of yellow teeth stretching back into its maw – like a row of brass curtain hooks that had been filed into sharp points – then the lumps of meat were snatched away.

He backed off as swiftly as he dared. The appreciative chewing sounds coming from the daemon weren't exactly helping the queasy feeling in his gut.

Eventually, its jaws slowed, and it gave a contented sigh. "De-lic-ious."

"Now that messy little ritual is finished, perhaps my grandson may withdraw?" Grandma Ives' voice was cold and business-like.

"Why the hurry?" Mrs Ferguson growled. "Do you want to spoil my digestion?"

"Perish the thought. But we do have business to discuss."

The creature's gaze returned to Cameron. "A resurrection spell, is it? And who is it you wish to call back, should such a thing be possible?"

"It's Cameron's father—"

"*I'm addressing the boy!*" the daemon screeched. It paused, and its ragged voice took on a warmer tone. "Don't interrupt, dear, or I may change my mind about co-operating. A lost father, is it? How old are you, lad?"

Cameron wasn't really in the mood for a conversation, certainly not about something so private and sad. But he remembered Grandma Ives' instructions. She had told him to be polite, but also that he shouldn't share any unnecessary information.

"I'm... I'm old enough," he said carefully, "to know what I want."

The daemon laughed. "I can see that. You are quite grown up. You must like being independent, striking out on your own?"

"I suppose..."

"Of course you must! A spirit such as yours needs space to stretch out, to discover its boundaries, to explore... Am I not right?"

A vision of himself in his old house on Scott Street swam into Cameron's mind. He was lying on his bed, his headphones pressed tight in his ears. He remembered how he used to enjoy those evenings he had to himself. He could be alone with his thoughts and his music...

"So nearly a man. Almost full grown." The daemon's velvet body quivered from side to side. "A boy like you could go places, with the right creature of power to sponsor you. You could have anything you want."

"Anything?" said Cameron slowly. A claggy dreamy feeling had spread over him. "What... what do you mean?"

"Anything at all." Mrs Ferguson's eyes shut down to two pinpricks of brilliant red light. *Like a couple of rubies...* For such a strange and ugly creature, they were oddly beautiful.

"So why not give up this silly quest, and do something more fitting with your life instead?" the daemon purred. "What need have you of humans, when you could stand alone? What need have you of fathers to tell you what to do?"

"No." Cameron shook his head. "That's not right..."

Deep down, he *knew* those evenings alone were only good because they weren't every night. He missed the time he had with his dad: teasing him about his tone-deaf singing as he rustled up dinner; arguing about what movie they were going to watch together. All those daft things they used to do.

"Being alone's no fun if it's not my choice. I still want him back." Cameron glanced at Grandma Ives. Her approving look made him feel he'd somehow passed a test.

"Sentimental rot." Mrs Ferguson belched, sending a gust of sewer-like air into the room. "A newly-hatched

Weaver daemon's first meal is the corpse of her brood-parent. That seems a better arrangement to me."

Cameron's stomach gave another terrible lurch.

"As Cameron is evidently not susceptible to your charms," said Grandma Ives lightly, "might we continue to business?"

"Oh, very well." The daemon quivered. "It'd be best to remove temptation. The boy may join Eve in the kitchen."

Grandma Ives nodded her agreement.

Never taking his eyes from the curtain, Cameron backed from the room, pulling the door closed behind him. Out in the darkened hall he leant against the wall, willing the sick feeling to pass.

Something cold and damp touched his leg, and Cameron yelped. His eyes swiftly adjusted to the gloom. It was the small girl Eve, carrying a mop and bucket. She shot him a look approaching scorn, and continued down the passageway.

Cameron collected his pride. It seemed ok to be alarmed by a ranting curtain-daemon with bad breath; it was a bit less cool to be startled by a little girl with a bucket.

"Hey! You don't say much, do you?" He followed her.

The kitchen was an L-shaped room at the back of the flat with a door leading to a yard outside. The place didn't look like it'd been decorated in years.

Eve was at the back door, wringing out her mop.

"So are you just another made-up thing, like that freaky old lady?"

The girl did not reply.

"Did you hear me?"

She finished her wringing and slooshed the dirty water into the yard. Stepping smartly past Cameron, she gathered up some crockery and got ready to wash up. Her pink gloves were clearly meant for someone much older, and went way too far up her arms. She had to fetch a box to stand on, as she was too short to reach the sink.

Cameron sniggered, and the girl shot him an irritated glance. If nothing else, it kind of settled his mind that Eve was human. A proper daemon wouldn't stand on a stupid box. Wouldn't it just hover?

Eve was still in silent robot mode, so he decided to look around the room. The tail of the L-shaped section had been curtained off to form a nook. He peered suspiciously at the curtain, but it seemed completely normal – faded and well worn – so he ducked his head round it into the area beyond. There was a camp bed and wooden chair, and a neatly folded pile of clothes. This couldn't be where Eve slept?

"That's private," said a voice.

"Oh, you can speak then?"

With a barely audible sigh, Eve put down her cloth and stepped away from the sink. She crossed to the press cupboard by the fireplace, and dragged out a big box.

"You can play with these toys if you want," she said in a high, firm voice. She returned to the sink.

Great, thought Cameron, *I'm being condescended to by a little girl*. He glanced towards the kitchen door. Grandma Ives was still in conference. There didn't seem to be anything for him to do. Grumpily, he hunkered down and examined the toys. He recognised the Transformers and Action Men, but there was also a load that looked much older, like the teddy with a pointy snout, the carved Noah's Ark and the collection of tin cars. He picked up a fire engine with an extendable ladder. It had the word "Dinky" on the base.

"These toy cars are worth a bit. My dad used to clear houses. I know all about the sort of things people collect."

Eve continued her washing.

Cameron tried again. "You could sell these, and buy yourself some new clothes or something... pretty. I bet my dad's workmate Joe knows someone who'd buy 'em."

There was a distinct pause in the scrubbing sounds. "I'm not interested."

"I was just saying you could have fun for a change, not just slave away here."

"They're *boys'* toys," Eve said, with some distaste.

Ok, thought Cameron, *if that's the way you want it*. It seemed a shame to let them sit here in this old box, in danger of going rusty. He laid the cars in a line along the floor. They seemed in good nick, mostly, and there were about a dozen in all. Even if they were only worth five to ten quid each, that would still be around a hundred pounds. You could get a second-hand electric guitar for that...

He smelled a sudden odour of washing-up liquid and bleach. Eve was standing behind him. "Have them if you like. I don't care for the little engines at all."

"For real? You're sure you don't want them?"

"You may have them all."

61

According to Big Joe, the reason Cameron's dad never had any money was that he was too honest. If they ever turned up something of value in their work, Malcolm Duffy would always tell the house owners. But it wasn't like Mrs Ferguson was a grieving relative... *And Dad's not here now, is he?* Cameron would have to look out for himself. He stretched out a hand...

There was the sound of a door opening down the corridor, and he heard Grandma Ives, clearly agitated about something.

"Go on, take them, take them quickly."

Cameron twisted round, startled by the urgency in Eve's voice. The little girl's face was pale, and there was an odd darting redness to her eyes. He jumped up and backed away.

"Nearly got you that time," smiled Eve.

Grandma Ives appeared at the kitchen door, and addressed the room at large. "Mrs Ferguson, are you in here? Even setting aside the discourtesy of leaving me talking to an inanimate set of curtains, I would remind you we are under terms of parlay. I presented an offering in line with ancient rite. You are bound at least to listen to what I have to say."

Eve's eyes narrowed. "It's my right to hunt wherever and whenever I choose, particularly here in my own domain. I do, however, concede you may have a point about etiquette. Very well, I will return." She winked at Cameron. "See you later, delicious boy." The little girl hiccoughed, and sat down abruptly.

"And you," snapped Grandma Ives to Cameron, "I trust you are remembering the rules?"

"Of course, Gran." Cameron stared down at his feet, his heart thumping. He couldn't believe how close he'd come to taking the cars! He was furious at himself for letting his defences down.

"Stay alert." Grandma Ives stalked back down the corridor.

He looked at Eve. The little girl was slowly getting to her feet, and Cameron saw the dancing light in her eyes was gone. She looked more like the sullen-faced kid who'd served tea in the living room.

"Are you ok?" he said gently.

Eve nodded.

"How long was that daemon thing controlling you?"

"I'm not supposed to talk." Eve's eyes darted round the room, scanning the walls, the corners, and the folds of the faded curtain.

"It was still me until you started going on about the other children's toys." She shot Cameron a glare. "I really didn't like you looking in my bedroom!"

"I'm sorry." Cameron followed her to the sink. "I didn't know it was yours. I didn't reckon anyone would really have to sleep there..." He trailed off guiltily.

Eve got back on her little box, and returned to her dishes.

"Hey, how about a joke?"

The plates squeaked slowly.

"Doctor, Doctor, I feel like a pair of curtains – Well, pull yourself together!"

It was a lame joke, real Christmas cracker material, but Cameron found himself laughing a bit hysterically. He saw the corner of Eve's mouth twitch, but if it was a smile or a sneer, he couldn't quite tell.

She washed-up for a while, then turned on the tap to top up the basin. A torrent of water poured in, causing the bottom pane of the window behind the sink to steam up. Cameron watched her take her hand from the water, and with the tip of one finger draw a 6 on the misty surface, then quickly wipe it away. She tapped her finger to her wrist – where a watch would be worn – then pointed out the window to the corner of the street. Finally she looked round at Cameron. He nodded very slightly, to show he understood.

"Auntie Ferguson says I mustn't speak to boys like you," she said in a particularly prim voice.

"Oh, yes. Good thing too. You've no idea where I've been. Tell you what, I'll go over here, and we can both not talk together. Deal?"

For the next half hour, his mind raced. He wandered round the kitchen, itching with frustration. There was nothing to do, he couldn't speak to Eve, and after the incident with the toy cars, he didn't dare poke his nose in anywhere. Finally, after what seemed like an eternity, Grandma Ives called him back into the living room.

Grandma Ives' whipped-up hairdo had started to wilt, and she looked worn out.

Mrs Ferguson was back in her avatar form, and was as cheerful and rosy cheeked as ever. "Cameron, dearie, so nice to have met you! I do hope your granny brings you again, and next time you can stay for dinner..."

"You don't give up, do you?" began Cameron, but a look from Grandma Ives warned him to drop it.

"We'll see ourselves out," she said firmly.

Cameron was desperate to find out what had gone on.

When they were safely out on the street, he bombarded his gran with questions. "How was it? What happened?" He paused, building up to the really big one. "Did you get what we need – to bring back Dad?"

Grandma Ives held up her hand. "Later."

"But I *need* to know."

"I said later. Right now we're going home. I did my best for you, but things may be more complicated than I had hoped."

Cameron bit his lip, uncertain what to do. He'd been going to tell her about Eve, but now he could see the old lady wasn't up to investigating. He couldn't let this opportunity slip away. He needed an excuse, and quickly.

"I was thinking, we're down near town anyway, so maybe I could get the next bus back? I could go have a look in HMV or something..."

"I see you've recovered your spirit." Grandma Ives raised an eyebrow. "Well, if you must. Try not to be late for dinner. And be careful!"

Cameron walked her as far as the bus stop. She was going slower than usual, he was sure. Whatever had happened had taken a toll on her, but he couldn't allow himself to worry about it now. He was still trying to puzzle out the reason for Eve's message.

Why on earth did she want to meet him? Could she really slip out of the house without Mrs Ferguson finding out? Did she know something important, perhaps about the crucial deal Gran was trying to strike?

He shivered slightly. There was another possibility. It might just be a new trap...

7. The Unravelled Heart

It didn't take Cameron long to find the street on to which Mrs Ferguson's property backed, and spot the window where Eve had written in the steam. He held back, not wanting to get too close and give himself away. Any twitch in the curtains or sudden chink of light made him nervous. He had no way of knowing if these were caused by the little girl or if Mrs Ferguson was lurking, staring out into the night.

He checked his watch for what was probably the twentieth time that past half hour. Nearly six. He paced back down the alley, catching glimpses of people in the flats he passed. They were making their dinner, or watching soap operas on the telly, lounging around with computers and reading books. He'd once been just like them, he realised, unaware of all the strange things that went on around him. They probably thought Mrs Ferguson was a jolly old woman with a quiet, well-behaved niece. There was no way they could suspect they lived on the same street as a daemon.

Near the end of the row someone had wedged a shed into their tiny garden, hard up against the fence, and Cameron leant upon it. The slatted planks pressed ridges into his back, and he drummed his fingers on their surface.

"Come on, Eve. Where are you?"

"I'm here. In the garden."

Cameron twisted round. Under the yellow streetlight, Eve's pale features and old-fashioned clothes made her look like a ghost.

"You're really jumpy for a boy. Come on, this way." She motioned him to climb over the fence, and follow her into the shed. "The owners are away. Nobody will notice."

The inside of the shed was cramped, and Cameron found himself crushed up against a lawnmower, while Eve perched on a sack of compost.

"It is *you*, isn't it? Proper you, I mean." He studied her in the dim light.

"Of course it's me. Idiot."

The scornful tone of her voice was definitely familiar, and her eyes held none of the terrible hunger he'd seen when she'd been possessed by Mrs Ferguson.

"What did you say to me in the kitchen? Just after Ferguson de-possessed you and Grandma Ives came in."

"I said I wasn't supposed to talk, then I told you off for nosing about in my bedroom," said Eve with a frown. "Then you told a rubbish joke, then—"

"Ok, ok, I believe you! You're definitely nippy enough. How did you manage to sneak out?"

"She's listening to an opera. She always does when she's pleased. She's fed recently too, so she'll likely fall asleep. I left the window open, so I can tell when it's nearly over."

She tilted her head, and Cameron realised he could hear a mournful bass voice echoing faintly down the street. There was a pause, then an answering chorus of strings.

"I know this one," she said. "There's a while to go yet. Radames and Aida still have to be buried alive in the tomb."

"Sounds like a laugh a minute," said Cameron.

"It's very romantic," said Eve. "They die together, but at least they're not alone."

There was an awkward silence, and Cameron shifted about, trying not to stand on anything sharp.

"Anyway," said Cameron eventually, "I don't know what you're on about, saying I'm jumpy. I've a right to be. That Auntie Monster of yours tried to catch me and eat me. Twice!"

"I'm not sure she *does* eat people," said Eve. "At least not all the time. I think it's worse than that."

"Like how?" Cameron recalled the sharpness of the daemon's teeth, and the greed with which it gobbled the meat. "What's worse than being eaten?"

"Remember the toys in the cupboard? You know how some of them are really old?"

Cameron nodded.

"I found this." She held out her hand, and showed him a wooden Noah. It clearly belonged with the toy ark Cameron had seen earlier. "It's hollow. His head comes right off. See?"

Cameron looked in. There was a furl of paper packed inside, and he tugged it out. Its texture was soft and fragile, like the wings of a moth.

"It's from another girl who worked for Mrs Ferguson," said Eve.

"I can't read it, it's too dark." He nudged the shed door, just enough to let in some light from the streetlamp. One side of the paper was a receipt for groceries addressed to a Mrs McDonald, while the reverse had been used for a message. The writing on the paper was cramped and faded, and it took him a moment to get used to it. He read the note aloud.

My name is Elizabeth Mearns, and this is my testament. I have been in service since I was seven years old. I was not born to this life, but mother said I must be strong and endure, and that in time father's fortune should rise again.

When I first entered the Mistress's household, I was summoned to her presence. "You shall do very nicely, my dear," she said. She had me kneel down, so that she might place a length of yarn about my neck. "A simple keepsake! Now you may never be lost to me." I thought it a kindness at first. Truly, it is a chain that binds me to her.

Ever since that day, I find on occasion I speak words and do things that I had no intention so to do. I have heard the servants gossip that I am suited only for Bedlam, should I not rouse myself from these fits. Yet I know somehow that it is the Mistress who is behind my illness, for it is her voice I speak with whenever the malady comes upon me...

"That's like what happened to you," said Cameron. The letter was clearly pretty old, like the toy that had hid it. How long had Mrs Ferguson been up to her tricks?

"Go on. Read the rest," said Eve.

All society believes the Mistress to be a good and kindly person, that I am fed and clothed well, and am most fortunate to have been spared the poorhouse. But yet, although she does not strike or openly torment me, I know in my heart that she is wicked.

On Sunday last, I found concealed within a trunk clothes fit for other children, but there are no other children here. I asked my Mistress from where the garments came, and what might be their purpose.

"So many been before, so many yet to come," said she, and she bade me tell her how long I had been in her employ.

"Five years this November, m'aam," I replied.

"Time indeed for some fresh blood," she declared, and sent me to my chamber.

Seven days have now passed, and she has not called for me. The kitchen maid brings me bread and water, but still will say nothing save for good day and to pass remark upon the weather.

At night, the drapes around my bed move most strangely, as if touched by hands I cannot see. Hellish eyes watch me in the dark. I fear I do not have long. I know she is hungry for my soul.

"That's all there is," said Cameron.

Eve sniffed sharply. "I think she keeps us till she gets bored, and then we get... used up somehow, and she finds someone else to do things for her, and to dress up like a doll."

"How long have you been working for her?" Cameron wasn't sure he wanted to know the answer.

"I don't know. She doesn't keep a calendar, and I don't get let out much. But I know I didn't always live there. I used to have a mum."

Cameron felt awful. He wanted to reassure Eve, to comfort her somehow, but he didn't know how. Her expression was as haughty as ever, and he felt he could no more reach out and hug her than he could hold a hedgehog. "Eve, you don't have to stay here, really you don't. Come with me."

"I can't."

"Why not? You got away this evening. We can leave here, run down the road. You don't need to go back."

"No, I can't. I tried it once, but she can pull me back anytime she wants. See..."

Eve tugged aside the collar of her dress. There was a length of what looked like dark wool running around her neck, tied off with a knot.

"Just like Elizabeth Mearns..." said Cameron.

"It was cut from a ball Mrs Ferguson keeps in a basket. If she ever wants me and I don't come at once, she winds some of the wool from that ball around a needle, and I can feel it tightening here." Eve touched her fingers to her neck, and Cameron saw the skin beneath the wool was red and irritated.

"But that's easy! We can get that off you in a second." He reached for a toolbox to find something sharp.

"No!" Eve yelped. "Idiot boy! You can't do that. Only she can remove it. If anyone else tries, it'll unravel me inside. All my guts and veins will come undone. She told me it's connected all the way to my heart."

Cameron didn't know if this could be true or not, but he could tell from the look on Eve's face she certainly believed it.

"I'm sorry. I don't know what to do."

Eve shrugged, in a curiously grown-up sort of way. "Can't be helped, I suppose."

Cameron looked down, feeling useless.

"What about you, what's your excuse?"

"What do you mean, excuse?"

"There's nothing stopping you from running away from Lady Ives, is there? I don't see any daemon-bond round *your* neck."

"No," said Cameron uneasily. "It's not like that. She's a real person. My grandma. Pretty much all I've got left in the world."

"Oh," said Eve. "I misunderstood. That must be good, having someone look after you?"

For the first time since he'd lost his dad, Cameron was starting to think things could've gone a lot worse for him. Grandma Ives didn't *have* to take him in. She could've said no, and then where would he have ended up? He realised he was grateful to the old woman.

"Yeah. I guess it's not so bad."

Eve craned her head towards the open shed door. "Listen, the opera's almost over. I need to go." She levered herself up off the compost.

Cameron caught her arm. "If I can't help you, if you can't get away, what's all this about? What was the point of meeting me?"

"I don't know," said Eve seriously. "I think I just wanted tell someone, that's all."

"I'll come back. I promise," said Cameron.

"You might, you might not." Eve brushed herself down, dislodging the dust and dirt of the shed. "Give me a moment to get down the road before you go. I don't want her finding out I spoke to you."

She dug in the pocket of her dress and, as if in afterthought, pressed a crumpled paper bag into Cameron's hand.

"Here. It's those rotten old toy cars. I don't see why she should have them."

Then she slipped out of the shed and was gone.

Cameron stared at the paper bag. It was a gesture of friendship, perhaps, or maybe it was just the only way the strange little girl could think of standing up to Mrs Ferguson.

"I will be back," he said. "I'll find some way to help, and I'll come back." But in the half-light of the shed, he wasn't sure how he could go about keeping his promise.

8. He's on the Beach

On the way back to the house, Cameron found his feelings of gratitude towards Grandma Ives faded, and were replaced by a dull throbbing sort of anger. He found the old woman in the lounge, listening to one of her jazz records. She was lying back in the squashy armchair, her feet propped up on a stool. Her fingers were pressed to her temples, and her eyes shut.

"Cameron, you're back," she said, hearing him enter. "There's stew in a pot in the kitchen. I'm afraid it may be a little cold."

"Fine, whatever. I don't want it anyway."

Grandma Ives opened her eyes. She peered at the boy in front of her, his hands jammed in his pockets, his face twisted defiantly.

"Well, don't have any then. It's not obligatory." Her eyes fell closed, slowly, like those of a drowsy lizard.

"It's all the same to you, isn't it? It doesn't matter either way."

On the record player, a saxophonist started a complicated solo that seemed to loop back and forwards. Grandma Ives said nothing.

"Why didn't you tell me Mrs Ferguson was a daemon?" demanded Cameron.

"I told you we were going to her for a resurrection spell. I hardly thought you'd think she was the local chemist."

"And what about Eve? Am I just supposed to ignore her? Did you know she's got some sort of string round her neck that'll pull her apart if she tries to run away?"

"Eve, from what I saw, is a most unfortunate young lady. I imagine her parents struck a bargain with Mrs Ferguson. She's not the first, and she won't be the last. Mrs Ferguson has been around a long, long time."

"So there's no way I can help her? She's just got to stay there, has she?"

"You've got to pick your battles, Cameron. Mrs Ferguson is not an easy opponent, and I dare say Eve has already lost."

He glared at the old woman. She had an answer for everything. "This is like when you sent me to Montmorency's, isn't it? You like dropping these things on me, and seeing if I cope."

Grandma Ives sighed and sat up, finally giving Cameron her full attention. "I told you the rules before we went. I made sure you knew them. I made sure you were safe."

"Yeah, well, maybe. You could've told me more."

"Weaver daemons like Ferguson have subtle powers of mind control. If you'd been worrying all the time about what form she would take, you might have lost focus and forgotten the rules. I couldn't take that risk."

"But I didn't though, did I? I was never going to drink that hot chocolate either." He didn't want to let on about the incident in the kitchen, where he'd come that bit closer to being ensnared in the daemon's web, but he felt that kind of proved his point. If he'd known Ferguson could take over Eve, he'd have stayed on his guard. "You've got to try and trust me."

"Cameron, I'm still getting to know you. Your father ran away from these things when I tried to show him. I didn't want to make the same mistakes again. Your father—"

"I'm not my dad."

He'd never have tried to take those toy cars for a start. And Cameron still couldn't believe his dad had known all about the daemon world, and kept it secret from him. He looked down, realising his fists were clenched into two tight balls, the nails biting into his palms.

"Just because he did something, doesn't mean I'm going to do the same."

Grandma Ives smiled. "Yes, dear. You know, I do believe that's true. I think you and I have much more in common." She glanced towards her record player. "For one thing, he never had much of an ear for music."

"I don't like this," said Cameron pointedly. "When does the tune start, exactly?"

"Oh, Cameron, you wound me. You simply don't know how to listen to it. We'll need to do something about that if you are going to help in the shop."

"And what shop would that be, then?"

"Why, my music shop, of course," said Grandma Ives. She saw Cameron was about to start another tirade, and interrupted quickly. "Alright, alright. I'm guilty. I haven't told you about that either. And I'm not going to tonight; I'm still exhausted from dealing with that *cratur*. Go have dinner. Please."

Cameron opened his mouth to speak, but thought the better of it. The old lady's face really was grey and tired. "Alright, ok." he said. "No more for now."

"Good lad." As he turned to leave she spoke once more. "Cameron? I am sorry about Eve. Sometimes you have to learn which things we can change, and which we can't."

"Yeah, but who gets to decide which is which?" he said. "That's what I don't understand."

He left her to her music.

That night, Cameron dreamt about the beach again. It was daylight this time, if you could call it that. Mist hung in the air, and the light was pale and sickly. He could just make out the Transit van, still parked up on the bit where the sands met the land.

It was strange, he thought, how sometimes you knew you were asleep and sometimes you didn't.

The sand beneath his feet, the smell in the air... it all seemed distinct and real, but somehow Cameron knew it couldn't be. He remembered the thing in the cloak that had tried to grab him as he hid in the back of the van. Whoever or whatever it was, he really didn't want to run into it again.

He had to try and wake himself up. But how did you do that? It felt like his eyes were open now, even if he knew they weren't, not really. He screwed his hands into fists and rubbed them in his eye sockets, but the scene in front of him didn't change. If only he could find a way to force himself out of the dream. But the real Cameron, the Cameron asleep in his bed in Grandma Ives' house, seemed to be a long way away. Trying to reach him was like trying to fight his way out of a balloon.

Ok, thought Cameron, *I'm just going to have to face it*. It had to be better to go looking for his fate than to be grabbed by those long white fingers, snatching their way out of the mist when he least expected it. He set off towards the van.

As he pulled himself up the cliff and onto the grass, he saw to his surprise that someone had spread out a picnic blanket, in spite of the clammy weather. A small figure sat cross-legged and composed, staring into the distance. It was Eve.

"Hey!" he called out. "What are you doing here?"

She looked up as he approached, a familiar disdainful expression on her face. "It's your dream. Why are you asking me?"

"I think if it was up to me, I'd have come up with something better."

"You don't dream what you want, stupid. You dream what you have to."

"Why would I need to dream this? It's happened, it's gone. I can't change it. Dad left his van here weeks ago."

"You're wrong," she said. "It's not just the past. That thing out there, creeping through the dunes... it's also the future."

"What's that supposed to mean?" he said desperately, hoping the white-fingered creature wasn't anywhere near.

She opened her mouth to reply, but no sound came out. Her fingers began to claw at her throat. He ran towards her, but as he got closer, she started to lift off the ground, as if the string around her neck was somehow pulling her up into the air.

He jumped and snatched at her shoes, but she was tugged away out of his grasp. Her hands flailed wildly and then she was gone, up into the mist and out of sight.

Cameron looked around frantically, searching for something or someone that could help.

There was now another figure, leaning against the side of the van. He was taller than Cameron, and dressed in blue jeans and camel desert boots. He had a small belly pushing out his well-worn T-shirt, and his sandy hair stood out in tufts from beneath his baseball cap. He used to say he wore it to keep his hair out of his eyes when he was working, but Cameron knew it was really to hide the bald spot he wouldn't admit he had.

"Dad!"

The figure didn't turn towards him. Instead he too started to rise from the ground, like a puppet being lifted from a stage.

"No, you can't. There's no string round your neck, Dad! Come back!" Cameron shouted.

But Malcolm Duffy was pulled upward and away, and out of Cameron's reach, without ever saying a word.

Cameron woke up. His pillow was hot and sweaty beneath his face. He picked it up and threw it out of the bed, resting his head on the sheet beneath. He shut his eyes. He wasn't even going to think about the dream. No, not at all.

9. How to Build a Resurrection Spell

"Not far now!" Grandma Ives stepped smartly around a large gull that was tearing at something on the pavement. It gave her a hard beady look, working out whether she'd make a better meal than a lump of cold pizza.

"They used to think those creatures were the souls of drowned sailors," she said to Cameron.

He glanced back at the bird. A couple of days ago he wouldn't have thought twice about a daft old superstition like that. Now he wasn't so sure. "Do you reckon it is?"

"I think they're just a nuisance," Grandma Ives sniffed. "Come along!"

They were going to Grandma Ives' music shop. They'd set out that morning, catching the bus to Elm Row, then heading down a long straight road called Leith Walk. The buildings were grey stone tenements with flats above, while down on the street, the walk was lined with small shops. Traffic hurtled to and fro, heading into the city or down to Leith and the coast.

Grandma Ives stopped at a row of railings, by a sign that said: *Scott & Forceworthy's Musical Bazaar*.

"Mind how you go, the steps can be slippy."

The stairs curved round as they descended, opening out into a paved courtyard. The shop window was bowed and draped with a length of velvet decorated with silver stars. In front of this make-believe sky, a tarnished brass trumpet hung by dark thread so it seemed to float in mid-air. Cardboard signs in the shape of musical notes promised:

The Latest Gramophone Records –
Hot Jazz, Swing, Big Band, Classical
Sheet Music and Sundry Musical Supplies
Everything the Budding Amateur Could Desire!

Cameron had to admit, the shop wasn't quite what he'd been hoping for.

"So who are Scott and Force-stuff then?" he asked doubtfully.

"Force*worthy*." Grandma Ives wrestled with the lock. "They were army buddies. They were in the Gordon Highlanders together."

The lock lost the battle, and Cameron followed her in. The shop looked – and smelled – to him almost like a museum: not the modern sort, with bright friendly signs and interactive displays, but the old musty forbidding kind, where curators glared at you for daring to touch things. The walls were lined with dark panelled wood, and every surface was covered in things for sale. There were cardboard boxes filled with strings, bows and valves, and row upon row of vinyl records. Wire racks stuffed with sheet music were dotted around the floor, and along the back wall hung a row of musical instruments: a violin, a flute, a clarinet... His heart skipped slightly as he spotted a guitar.

"Those are my predecessors, over there." Grandma Ives gestured to a picture by the cash desk. Cameron looked up. Two men in kilts and military regalia posed stiffly by a tree stump. The bottom of the photo said "Malta 1897".

She disappeared through a door concealed in a corner, and Cameron heard the sound of a kettle being filled. "Make yourself at home."

He picked up a pile of records from the chair behind the cash desk.

"I haven't heard of any of these..." He peered into a sleeve at the disc inside. It was thick, dark brown and brittle, like a hundred-year-old toffee. "Gran, you seriously need some new stuff. Have you heard of CDs? MP3s?"

"Em pee how many?" said Grandma Ives, emerging from the back room.

"M P *threes*. For computers and iPods."

"Those are 78 rpm discs. They stopped making them fifty years ago." Grandma Ives sounded more than a little proud. "You need a special needle on your record player to even play them."

"Sell many of them, do you?"

"Not a huge amount," she admitted. "My stock caters for specialist tastes. But it's not what the shop *appears* to sell that's really important. I believe the popular term is a 'front'."

A sudden absurd image of Grandma Ives as a gangland boss – wearing sunglasses and planning a bank job – flashed into Cameron's head. He laughed. "What are you, in the mafia or something?"

"Certainly not," she said. "Money comes in, money goes out. Ordinary human taxmen have a nasty habit of asking questions. This place helps me account for myself."

"What do you sell then, really?" he asked, wondering what secrets lurked among the musty boxes.

Grandma Ives smiled. "Now the human and daemon worlds are no longer close, those few who can access the parallel are at an advantage. We're the experts, you might say! There's not much understanding of daemon craft, of magic, left in the human world; just scraps of knowledge that were handed down. Those humans who are determined to dabble require daemon objects for their experiments..."

"And that's where you come in. They pay you to fetch them, right?" Cameron hadn't grown up trailing his dad around for nothing: he knew all sorts of rare things could be worth money.

"It works the other way as well," Grandma Ives nodded, her eyes shining. "Daemons sometimes need things from the human world. And the parallel is a resource in itself... There are all sorts of possibilities."

She seriously loves *her work*, Cameron thought. *Much more than Dad ever liked his.*

"I've had a happy little business, helping each side get what they want. And if the odd token of gratitude comes my way, all well and good." She lifted her nose slightly. "Coffee's brewed, I believe."

She made her way back to the internal door. "You can help me with all this if you want, Cameron. I'm getting too old to do everything myself. I need some fresh blood."

83

Cameron had to admit, he'd always wanted to do something with music. He'd been thinking more along the lines of starting a band, but there was still a guitar here he could maybe use to practise on. He went over to the acoustic, and gave the strings an experimental twang. It was way out of tune, but that could be sorted.

He looked around the shop again. Now he knew what Grandma Ives did, the dark and dusty interior seemed alive with possibilities. Somehow it was all connected to the mysterious world of the parallel – and that meant it was connected to bringing back Dad.

"Ok, then," he said. "I'm totally up for it. I'll help."

"Excellent!" Grandma Ives put down two mugs on the counter top. "I'm so pleased."

"One thing, though. What about ordinary customers? Do we get any of those?"

"Oh, now and again. But usually I find that if I don't bother them, they don't bother me."

It didn't take Cameron long to get a feel for the shop. Grandma Ives showed him where she kept the paper bags and how to turn the handle that worked the mechanical cash register, and then she left him to mind the counter: for the everyday customers, at least. She opened up the drawers of a tall wooden desk, and drew out a load of crumbly manuscripts that she said she needed to study in order to better understand the resurrection spell.

For half an hour, she said nothing but "Hmmm" and "But the application" and sometimes "Quite so". Meanwhile, Cameron counted the contents of the till

(£83.57), served precisely no customers, and became extremely bored.

"Oh, *c'mon*. Let's see," he said, stretching up on his tiptoes. He needed to be involved. After all, it was *his* dad they were trying to bring back.

"Not now," said Grandma Ives vaguely. "Watch the store, if you please."

"Who for?"

She sighed. "Oh, very well. Make it quick."

He scrambled over to peer at the document. The paper was a muddy brown, with dense paragraphs of spidery writing. A detailed line drawing showed a spear-shaped metal rod pointing towards a huddle of terrified people. At the other end crouched a bloated grinning goblin creature. Grandma Ives had put a yellow sticky above the spear, and another by a cylinder shape embedded at its centre.

"As I understand it, the formula for a resurrection spell is not complex. We'll need a source of energy, a conductor to transmit that energy, and a target to receive it."

"Energy and a conductor. Like making a circuit!" Cameron remembered diagrams he'd seen in science at school. "But we must be using magical power, not electricity?"

"Don't let's get ahead of ourselves." She turned her attention back to the scroll. "The first challenge is finding the means to execute that formula, which is where this comes in."

"*Machina ex Makaribus*," Cameron read. "What's that?"

"It means this shows a device built by the Makaris. They were a daemon clan of engineers that lived long ago. They farmed the humans they captured. The subjects were placed here." She tapped the people on the drawing. "Their life energy ran through this." She indicated the spear. "And it was either fed into a waiting Makaris daemon, or the excess stored up in a battery for later use." She thumbed the cylinder she'd also marked with a Post-it.

"Hold on. You say they *farmed* people?" A look of disgust ran across Cameron's face. "Isn't that a bit, you know, sick?"

"We take energy from the plants and animals we consume. The principle's the same."

"But people aren't animals!"

"And daemons aren't people," she said. "Or haven't you learnt that yet? We must deal with them on their own terms."

"I dunno..." He studied the intricate drawing again. "Making something to drain a person's life away... That just seems wrong."

"A tool is just a tool, Cameron. I could use a bread knife for much more violent purposes than slicing up a loaf for toast."

He looked up at her. "This machine wasn't exactly about making breakfast though, was it?"

"Just be glad that the Makaris were brilliant enough to build it," said Grandma Ives lightly. "For if we can track down two parts of their ancient machine – the battery and the conductor – we can put them to a much more benevolent use."

"To bring back Dad?"

"Precisely."

She started to roll the scroll up. "The battery I'm still to locate, then there is the matter of how and when to put the artefacts together. Mrs Ferguson holds the conductor."

"So *that's* why we went to see her. You still haven't told me what happened."

"She was a stubborn old goat, that's what." Grandma Ives spoke with a fair amount of venom. "The only way we'll prise the conductor from her eight hairy legs is by finding her something she desires even more."

"And what's that?" Cameron had a feeling it wasn't going to be good.

"I'm working on it." Grandma shoved the scroll into a drawer, and drew out another book. "And it would all go a good deal faster if you didn't distract me!"

Cameron ducked into the back room to escape her irritation. He was secretly pleased he'd managed to wangle some details of the spell out of her at last. The more he knew, the more real it became to him – and the closer he was to seeing Dad again. Unable to help himself, he wrapped his arms around his chest, and gave himself a tiny hug.

The kitchen area didn't hold his attention for long – a cupboard, a kettle and a tiny sink were all it contained – but he was intrigued to find a spiral staircase that led down to another level. The basement was filled with sealed-up crates and chests, and the air was cold and stale. Exploring, he found a claymore sword propped up in one corner – that might've belonged to the shop's original owners. On the rear wall, he discovered a locked steel door set in the damp stone blocks. Just how far below street level did the shop go?

He picked up the sword and swished it, scything a blanket of cobwebs from the roof. A muffled call from above disturbed him. He dashed up the steps two at a time, dusting himself down as he went.

"Sorry. I was downstairs," he said, only a little out of breath. "What's behind the metal door?"

"The broom cupboard!" Grandma Ives snapped. "Now, if you've quite finished poking about, could you deal with this customer?"

A girl with dark bobbed hair was leafing through the sheet music. Cameron hurried to the cash desk. After much thought, she chose a single score.

"Do you come here often?" Cameron said, putting the paper sheets in a bag. He blushed, realising it sounded like a cheesy chat-up line.

"It's a good place for out-of-print titles. My violin teacher's got obscure tastes." She leaned forward and ruffled his hair in an irritating way that made him feel awkward. "You're *so* the newest thing I've ever seen here."

Later, a student with a goatee beard and an army satchel drifted in. He yelped with delight after spotting a particular record.

"This place is the best," he enthused as he paid. "I'm gonna tell everyone on the retro forums about it."

Grandma Ives rose from her book, plucked a banknote out of Cameron's hand, and returned it to the man.

"Please *don't*," she said. "Here, a special discount. Keep it to yourself."

He took the money and the record, and left shaking his head.

"I get enough ditherers and dafties as it is. The last thing I need is a plague of students." Grandma Ives liked to reserve her attention for her "special" clients, as Cameron was about to discover.

Mr Hughes arrived in a seriously expensive black car. A broad-chested chauffeur stayed with it, while Mr Hughes eased his way down the shop steps, leaning heavily on his stick. He looked surprised to see Cameron sitting behind the desk, then his watery blue eyes registered Grandma Ives.

"My, aren't your shop boys young these days? I wouldn't have thought him old enough to be out of school."

Grandma Ives smoothly glossed over the question. "I hear the policemen are getting younger too. Age comes to us all."

"Not you, though, eh, Isobel? You seem to have stayed the same all the years I've known you."

"You're too kind."

They continued in this bantery sort of way for a while, although Cameron noticed Mr Hughes didn't ever smile. His eyes roamed about the shop, as though he was checking someone wasn't hiding behind a stack of records, taking notes.

Eventually he drew a brown paper package from his jacket. "A mere trifle, this time. You'll take care of it for me?"

"Gladly," said Grandma Ives.

"You'll have my payment by the normal method." With a last wistful look at the parcel, he bid "good day" to Cameron and to his "ever youthful grandmother".

"Does he have a thing for you, Gran?" Cameron said, after Mr Hughes' car had slunk its way back into the traffic, and vanished towards the city.

"I shouldn't think so," said Grandma Ives dryly. "I'm not made of paper."

Cameron grinned. "What is he, human or daemon? Human, I reckon."

"Human, yes, but not the most upstanding. He's a collector. Sometimes his passion for books is so great, those he acquires need to be hidden for a time, kept well out of sight."

"Do you mean they're *nicked*?"

"Do you know, I've never chosen to ask. Let's see what he's up to this time." She slit open the package, and drew out a small black book. The cover opened to reveal pages of handwritten script. "A Victorian binding of a medieval manuscript... It's all tales of death. Advice for the good soul on how to cross over."

Cameron leant over and touched the pages, feeling their dead-skin texture. He stopped at an illustration showing a strange forest scene: three empty-eyed skeletons in tattered robes posed and leered in front of three finely-dressed noblemen.

"*As you are, we were once. As we are, you shall be,*" said Grandma Ives, translating.

"Creepy... That's some awesome bedtime reading he's got there."

"People used to believe the dead could return, you know. They thought they would visit the living, and offer advice and warnings..."

"Do you mean like in a dream?" said Cameron suddenly.

"What?" She shot him a curious glance.

He'd been thinking about the beach dream last night. It seemed private somehow, and he wasn't sure how much of it he wanted to share. "I keep dreaming about the place they found Dad," he said eventually, and shrugged. "It's stupid, really."

"Not at all. It's very recent for you. It must be playing on your mind."

Cameron shook his head. "It's so real. It seems more than a normal dream. I even saw Dad, nearly spoke to him." He remembered how Dad had been lifted off the ground. Eve had been there too, not that she'd made much sense. "It's like he was going to tell me something, but he didn't get the chance."

Grandma Ives pursed her lips, as if she found the entire discussion a little distasteful. "It's just your imagination. Try to put it out of your thoughts."

"No one knows why he was there though," Cameron persisted. "That's the crazy thing. He didn't have a job on anywhere near."

"He was running, I should think," she murmured, looking down at her bony old fingers. "He was always running from something."

"What from? From *me*?" Cameron's words came out in an angry rush. "It's not like I ever gave him problems, did I? Mum left ages ago, so it wasn't her. His business never did great, but he'd have said if he was in trouble. Why would he keep it to himself?"

"There's only one way you'll know for sure, and that's to ask him." Grandma Ives brandished Mr Hughes' book. "The monks who wrote this, they believed life and death were not black and white – one thing or the other – but shades of grey. Your father's life, if it is grey now, will fade more into shadow as time goes on. The longer we leave it, the harder it will be to recover him."

"What are we waiting for then?" Cameron shoved his hands into his pockets.

Grandma Ives smiled. "I'm glad you're eager. There's plenty to be done. You will be my eyes and ears, not just in this world, but in the parallel as well. There are places you can go, and things you can do, that I'm no longer fit for. It's time we fully activated your Edinburgh Parallel inheritance."

Cameron's mouth had suddenly gone dry. He licked his lips. "I thought we'd done that, back at Montmorency's."

"No. That was just a test to see if your abilities were ready to emerge. Now you must learn how to shift to the parallel for yourself." She cocked her head, as if listening for something on the edge of hearing. She turned away, and when she turned back, the book she had been holding had vanished.

"Now you see it, now you don't. Let's see if you can bring it back!"

10. The Edinburgh Parallel Inheritance

Cameron stared at the patch of air where the book had been. He could feel his eyes twitching and burning. "No. It's no good. I'm gonna go cross-eyed."

"Don't just stare into space," Grandma Ives snapped. "Try to *feel* your way to the parallel."

"And how do I do that exactly?"

"When you went to Montmorency's, was there any kind of sensory disturbance that accompanied the shift?"

"Yeah..." He remembered the rush of sound. "It was like the noise from a radio that was off-station. Lots of songs all mixed up at once, you know?"

"That's good." A smile played across Grandma Ives' thin lips. "Do you recall any tune in particular? Try to remember, and to bring it to mind."

He shook his head gloomily. "No, I can't. It was totally random."

"Perhaps you need another stimulus." She went to her desk, and removed a dark wooden box from the middle drawer. Its lid was embossed with two gold letters: EP. "For me, Edinburgh Parallel has always been like a tune. I bring it to mind, and the parallel appears. The artist who made this copied it down as best he could."

Cameron felt a strange frisson run through him as he took the box. He lifted the lid. A hidden mechanism whirred, and a complicated tune began to play. There was a yellowing bit of paper stuck inside:

From Grandma to Cameron, with love.
I hope you find music opens up a world of
its own.

It's the present she'd tried to give me on my seventh birthday, that one and only time I met her, back before Dad died...

"You've been planning this a long time, haven't you? Even then you were wondering if I was ready."

She nodded, a strange expression on her face. "I hoped you'd be the one to keep the family tradition going. How does it feel when you hear the box play?"

He listened to the pings and chimes. "Jazz again. I like something you can sing, words you can think about." This music was so twisty; as soon as he thought he'd figured it out, it darted off in a new direction.

"The way to the parallel comes from *inside*, from who you are. Maybe you don't follow me that closely after all." Grandma Ives peered at him sadly, as if this was a colossal disappointment.

Cameron knew he must have the ability, from the glimpse of the parallel he'd already seen. He ran to the back of the store, and fetched the acoustic guitar. Eric had taught him a few chords; he hoped he could still play them. "Maybe I just need to find my own song?"

That evening he took the guitar and the music box back to Grandma Ives' house. Alone in his room, he listened to the box play over and over. As he listened, he strummed the guitar, and tried to find ways to get the chords he knew to fit the music. When he found his tune, it was *there*, and he knew it was his. It was as if some supernatural program had been quietly downloading inside his head, and suddenly – *ping!* – it was done.

He took a trip to Montmorency's to give his new skills a road test.

He stood in the aisle, and called the mysterious tune to mind. His fingers shifted unbidden by his sides, as if searching for the right chords. Swiftly, the shop changed around him. In contrast to the chaos of whirling shelves from his first visit, this time everything unfolded in an elegant dance, movements timed perfectly to the music that now ran through his head.

"Awesome." He grinned, and picked a couple of jars off the shelf. What on earth was Selkie Oil or *Bean Shìth* Freshener, and how would you use them?

Montmorency was amused to see Cameron's newfound confidence. "You've got the hang of it! You'd better watch out. She'll have you doing all sorts now." He steepled his hands together like a Kung Fu master dispensing wisdom. "So the pupil becomes the master."

Cameron laughed. "Who are you, Yoda now?"

"You think daemons don't watch TV? I do a lot of rentals to the daemon world, as it happens." He indicated a rack of battered DVDs behind the counter, and tapped his nose. "Not a word to your grandmother."

Glancing along the row, Cameron saw a familiar small black shape wedged between a cheesy-looking action movie and the wall.

"That's Mr Hughes' book! How did it end up here?"

"By a cunning sequence of underground tubes, lad. After that, it was mainly specially trained mice. And string."

"You're joking, right? Tell me you're joking."

"Am I?" Montmorency's bright green daemon eye stared at him unblinking. "Test passed I should say. Well done."

Grandma Ives, too, was pleased at Cameron's progress. It wasn't long before she began to send him out on delivery runs for the secret side of her business.

"This will be good practice for you whilst I do some research," she insisted.

She would disappear into the basement and emerge with a box – usually firmly sealed, to his disappointment – and give instructions on where to take it.

Cameron would slip the package into his old school bag and set off, eager to discover what he might find. Every time he came to trigger the shift, a thrill of anticipation would run through him. He never knew until that moment just how different the parallel place might be...

The rope ladder swayed and dangled alarmingly. *There's no reason,* thought Cameron, *why it should be any harder to climb up than it had been to climb down.* But the slightest shift of his foot on the ladder caused a sickening wobble, and any decisive move felt like it could trigger an avalanche.

His fingers dug back into the stonework around the shuttered window. Of course, it didn't help that the whole building to which he was helplessly clinging was suspended – impossibly – upside down in a deep dark shaft. Way above his head, near what should have been the tenement's ground floor, he could see the opening of the pit, and above it the bright blue sky. Dangling all the way down the side of the building was the ladder on which he stood, its rope strands turning as thin and spindly as a beetle's leg as they vanished into the distance. Far beneath him, at the building's roof, curls of smoke from the chimneys drifted lazily away into the endless darkness.

He placed one foot onto the more stable surface of the window ledge and clung to the ladder with one hand. (Did you still call it a window ledge when it was actually the window top, and everything was upside down?)

He knocked with his fist on the shutters. "Miss, miss? Can I come in? I've got kind of stuck."

The shutters flew open, shunting him off the ledge. For a few giddy seconds the rope ladder swung out into the void, then he and it *thwapped* back into the side of the building, forcing the air from his lungs.

"You still here?" said a bored voice.

"No thanks to you," Cameron moaned. He stopped. "Oh. You're different."

This didn't look anything like the daemon-woman he'd spoken to before. She'd been good-looking, with long red hair and an iridescent pair of wings that fluttered delicately on her back. This person's face was sallow and lined, and her wings were a cloudy grey, like those of a bluebottle. A curved pipe dangled from the corner of her mouth.

"Glamour costs, sweetie." She let out a puff of smoke. "And you ain't paying. What do you want?"

"I've got myself, um, stuck," said Cameron. He forced himself to smile, in what he hoped was a winning way. "I was thinking – is there any other way up? Maybe I could come in the window, and use the stairs?"

"No, you'll contaminate my stock! Flying's the best way." She cupped a hand to her ear. "What's that? You don't have wings? Too bad – so sad. You'd better get climbing." She took hold of the shutters.

"Hold up..." Cameron's palms were getting sweaty and he wasn't sure how much longer he could hold on. He certainly couldn't stay perched on this window ledge forever, like a pigeon with a bad case of vertigo.

He tried a different tack. "You do realise if I fall, and end up totally dead, this'll be the last time you trade with my gran?"

The woman sucked on her pipe reflectively. "No, I don't buy that, precious. Lady Ives is one resourceful mama. She'd find another goon. Nice try, though."

The shutters slammed shut.

Cameron groaned. How had he let himself get into this mess? This morning, when Grandma Ives had given him a package for Heave Awa' house, it had seemed like just another straightforward delivery.

"Strange kind of name," he had said.

"It's a sad story," Grandma Ives had replied. "Back in the 1860s, a tenement suddenly collapsed. The only survivor was a young lad who shouted to his rescuers to 'heave away'. The building that was eventually raised in its place was named after that. But I dare say you'll hear all about it. I'd take this myself, but I'm not as agile as I was."

"Simple swop, is it?"

"Oh yes." She opened her books, her attention already elsewhere. "Nothing can possibly go wrong."

The building was on the lower half of the Royal Mile, an ancient sloping street that started at the top of Castle Rock and ran all the way down to the Palace of Holyroodhouse. Wedged between two shops he spotted an arched doorway, above which rested the carved stone head of a young boy. A curling banner running above him was inscribed with the words "Heave Awa' Chaps, I'm No Dead Yet!"

The boy's face looked hopeful and just a little cheeky. *Good for you, mate,* Cameron thought. Now for the world-shift...

He concentrated, doing his best to ignore the whine of a bagpiper busking to a group of cold-looking tourists. Slowly, the rolling, strumming rhythm of *his* version of the Edinburgh Parallel tune rose within him, and the world around began to change as he shifted through to the parallel. The tourists melted from the street, like a bunch of snowmen caught by the sun, while the archway began to stretch wider and wider, until it straddled a space as broad as a building. There was a loud *glop*, and a hole swirled open between the legs of the arch.

The lids of the stone head blinked over pupil-less eyes. "Goin' doon, are ye?"

"You can talk!" said Cameron.

"It's aboot all I can do," said the head. A smile crept across his grey features. "Hiv ye heard ma story?"

"A bit..." Cameron was finding the head's blank-eyed stare a little unnerving. "The old tenement fell, right?"

"We called it a *land* back then."

"A land. Got you." Cameron nodded. He edged forward and peered curiously into the hole. It was like looking into the entrance of mineshaft. A rope ladder was anchored at the pit's edge. It ran down past what looked like the bottom of a wooden door, and then...

"You've *got* to be kidding me." He stepped back quickly. "There's a whole building hanging upside down in there!"

"Oh aye," said the head nonchalantly. "When the land fell, it jist kept on fallin'. Right on doon tae the parallel."

Cameron gulped. It looked like he was going to have to inch down this dangly ladder. "Heights are not my thing. Are you sure it's safe?"

"Safe as hooses. Nabody's broke their heid open for a year or two now."

"Cheers." Cameron glanced up at the boy. "Amazingly reassuring news there."

He tested his foot on the ladder. If he went quickly, and kept his eyes straight ahead, he'd probably not even notice a thing...

"Haud on, are ye no wantin' to hear ma story?"

"You go on and tell it," said Cameron. "I'll keep an ear open."

He gingerly made his way down into the darkness...

And that's how he'd ended up here, stuck on this ledge.

What would happen, Cameron wondered, if he didn't try to climb up the ladder, and instead world-shifted back from here? Grandma Ives had taught him there was always some kind of link between the parallel and the parts of the worlds it bordered: Edinburgh Humanian and Edinburgh Daemonic. A completely blind world-shift could be dangerous, which was why those who used the parallel often stuck to established crossing points, like Montmorency's. If he shifted back to Humanian from this far down, he'd probably end up buried deep underground, either embedded in the middle of a rock, or locked in some long-forgotten foundation of the city...

Cameron shuddered. No, that wasn't the way out. He thought again about the fairy woman. She'd opened her window, and called out to him encouragingly when he'd first climbed down into the pit. She'd pressed a bag of shiny apples and a couple of crystal spheres wrapped in paper into his hands, then purred and cooed as she opened Grandma Ives' box of goodies.

There were several battered paperbacks, a shoebox-sized mobile phone and a grubby set of kitchen mixer taps. The last seemed to particularly delight her.

"I'm sorry. I've got to ask. What do you want those for?"

She looked at him curiously. "This talisman can summon a great torrent of water from afar, can't it?"

"I guess you could say that." Cameron grinned uneasily. "It usually helps if it's plumbed in..."

"Why wouldn't you want something that could do that?" She sniffed at the taps. "And many, many human hands have touched it. It is ripe with contagious magic."

She had snatched it away from him greedily.

She'd certainly seemed happy enough to talk, back when he had something to trade, Cameron reflected. That now gave him an idea.

He thumped on the shutters again.

"Listen," said the woman, leaning out, "if you don't stop, I'm getting my scissors. It makes no difference to me if this ladder goes."

"No, no, hold up! I was thinking I could pay for a flight, you know?" He dug in his pocket. A torrent of change tumbled out and arced away, down into the pit. Some time later, there came the sound of a distant *splosh*.

Cameron re-tightened his grip on the ladder.

"Human money doesn't interest me, darlin'" she said. "Next?"

He dug through the contents of his satchel. There had to be something...

"Chewing gum, cereal bar. Really tasty?"

"Don't think so."

He rummaged some more, touching one of Eve's toy cars.

"What's that?"

"Nothing." He'd been carrying it around with the vague idea of taking it to a collectors' shop. He still wanted to raise funds for an electric guitar, but despite that, he'd never got round to putting his plan into action. Deep down, he knew this was because selling the toy cars would feel wrong, like a betrayal of his promise to Eve.

"That object has a sad story, I think. Its owner lost, long long ago..." The daemon woman's wings gave a quick flutter.

"How do you know?"

"That's my business," she said tartly. "The car I'll take – that or nothing."

Reluctantly, Cameron handed it over. At least he still had the others. Besides, if he got himself squished, there wouldn't be anyone to remember Eve and her problems.

"This I like." The fairy woman smiled. "It even buys you a wee bit of glamour..." She waved her hand, and her features smoothed. Her wings shone again as before. "There. What do you think?"

"You could make a fortune. Instant plastic surgery!" Cameron glanced down into the pit. His hands were feeling so tired and sticky now. "Do you think you could hurry it up?"

"You've no sense of occasion, have you darlin'?" She stepped onto the window ledge, and wrapped her arms around him. "Going up!"

His stomach lurched as they soared up and out into the light.

"You could've just eaten one of my apples, you know," she whispered in his ear. "They lend fire to the spirit, and make a timid soul strong."

"Oh, *now* you tell me!"

She placed him on the ground by the pit mouth, executed a neat loop in the air, and dived back into the pit with a laugh.

"Dinnae listen to her," said the head. "You get a different class doon there. She's all hoity-toity, airy-fairy..." A wave of greyness crept over him and his features stiffened once more as Cameron triggered the shift back to Edinburgh Humanian.

He looked in his bag. At least he knew what the apples he'd risked his neck for did, but what about the crystal globes?

"They're prognosticators. A sort of daemonic fortune teller," Grandma Ives explained when he returned to Scott and Forceworthy. "Not much good up here, I'm afraid. The weak magic left in the human world means they don't focus properly."

She unwrapped a globe and put it on the table. There was a brass circlet looped over the top like a carrying handle, and from underneath trailed a cluster of fine wires. Cameron reached out and touched one impulsively. There was a nasty clattering buzz, and a deep voice growled, *"By the Hill and the Fort and the Shattered Rock, I pronounce: old hearts shall seek to capture young, to add to their stock of days."*

Cameron's hair stood up on the back of his neck. "What was that?"

"That's your fortune," said Grandma Ives. "If you care to believe it."

He drew back his finger and sucked it as if he'd been stung. "It didn't sound like good luck to me."

"I shouldn't worry. These things really are worse than useless. Even if they get something right, you can't understand their predictions until well after the event."

"Sort of like getting a list of numbers, and not realising they're for the lottery till after the draw?"

"Very much so."

Cameron wasn't convinced. "It sounded spooky."

"Don't pay it any heed." She put the prognosticator to one side. It was later bought by a man with black-painted fingernails who insisted on calling it a "Mighty Daemon Orb".

"A rank amateur," she said after he left. "He'll foretell the end of the world with that, just because that's what he wants to see."

Cameron eyed the fat wad of notes she was counting into the till. "All that, just for a mouldy old set of taps..."

"A fair exchange then," Grandma Ives said smartly. "The prognosticator is only a novelty. Things that seem extraordinary to us are everyday to daemons, and vice versa; some ordinary human possessions can be very desirable to them."

"Like what exactly?"

"Oh, it varies. Things much used by humans sometimes take their fancy. They think objects take on hints of their owner's lives. The trick is to know what will satisfy which daemon! Fortunately I do, or I wouldn't have a business."

"But where do you get all the human stuff from?" Cameron remembered the clutter his dad had hoarded – all that well-used, broken-down stuff – and a thought struck him. "Is that how Dad got started clearing out houses? Was he finding supplies for you?"

"It may have been." She shot him an appraising glance. "I have other sources now."

There must've been a time Dad and Gran had been close... Then it had ended badly somehow, and his dad had been left with a career he didn't want and all the old junk, but none of the magic. "Why did you two fall out? You've never told me. Properly, I mean."

"Like I said, he ran away from the parallel. It wasn't the sort of life he wanted. Not like you, Cameron. It's in your blood, I can see that now."

"I dunno," he said thoughtfully. "I wasn't too keen on it this morning at Heave Awa' House."

She shook her head. "That was a fear of heights, not the unknown. When you found out about daemons, about the parallel, you didn't run or think you were going mad, did you? You started working on ways to explore. That's the *real* Edinburgh Parallel inheritance. It's not only the ability to go to the other place. It's the desire to do so."

It was true. He'd wanted to know what was down the pit. A shiver of excitement ran through him. It was like he'd just realised he was a little braver than he'd ever thought. "I do like it, going out there, finding something new. It's safe."

Grandma Ives frowned. "I wouldn't say it's safe at all."

"I mean it's *cool*."

"Cool?"

"Never mind," he laughed. "Do you think when Dad comes back – if we get him back – he'll make me give it all up?"

"Well, I hope not, because I'd be back to coping on my own." She reached forward and patted his hair, a little awkwardly. "I'm getting a bit long in the tooth for shinning down rope ladders. Now, if you have a moment, I need you to collect something else."

"Sure," said Cameron, getting ready. "Easy job, is it?"

"It should be perfectly straightforward. Nothing can possibly go wrong..."

11. Two Evils

Cameron looked up. He'd been lost in thought, going over the decision he'd made, and hoping it was the right one. He'd walked along Queen Street, down Heriot Row and round Moray Place. He was in the New Town now, although why it was called that, he didn't really know: it was still hundreds of years old. ("Everything was new once, Cameron," he heard Grandma Ives say, inside his head.)

He was nearly at the collection point...

The buildings he passed were mainly houses: elegant stone constructions built around stretches of trees and grass. They were much bigger than those near where he'd grown up. He glanced in at tall bookcases, squashy leather sofas and flat-screen TVs. In one huge room, there was space for a snooker table and piano. A white cat on a mantelpiece blinked at him, like a watchful sculpture.

At the end of the street he found a black-railed fence, beyond which lay a formal garden. A line of trees and hedges blocked much of it from view, but he could just see a path that lead away down the hill and out of sight. The sign attached to the gate read "Private Garden – For Residents Only".

This is the place, he thought. *I've got to remember everything Gran told me, and get this thing for Ferguson – and then everything starts to change. Then Dad comes back...*

Grandma Ives had taken up residence in the comfy swivel chair behind the counter. Cameron had sat crossed-legged on a threadbare rug beside her, and listened intently as she explained her plan.

"As you know, Cameron, we need a conductor for the resurrection magic, a tool to transfer life energy. I've long known that Mrs Ferguson possesses such a thing."

"What does she use it for, exactly?" Cameron couldn't imagine Mrs Ferguson trying to reunite someone with a lost relative.

"There are some daemons that pass unnoticed in this world, for their appearance is basically human," said Grandma Ives, the red light from the electric fire reflecting in her eyes. "Mrs Ferguson is not one of them. You've seen how her true form manifests?"

Cameron nodded. "A spider-thing that can grow a body from a curtain. You'd spot that if it went running down the street."

"So," Grandma Ives continued, "she uses the conductor to transfer her life energy and entire identity into something less conspicuous... "

"Can it do that, then? I thought it was only built to steal life-force?"

"She's adapted it. Now it works for her like a two-way channel, so she can leap in and out of her chosen target whenever she chooses."

An image of the fake Mrs Ferguson, smiling cheerily in her flower-print dress, popped into Cameron's head. "The avatar, you mean. Mrs Pretend-Old-Lady herself!"

"Indeed. The avatar gives her eyes and ears, and a means to draw supplicants and sacrifices to her. It is how Ferguson has been able to cling on to this world so long, while most of her Weaver daemon sisters have long since scuttled away."

"So why does she need Eve?" Cameron rubbed his knuckles against the rug's bristly tufts. "Does she just get her kicks bossing a wee girl about?"

"I had wondered much the same myself." Grandma Ives nodded. "Perhaps she needs a servant because the avatar has become so frail. The more she uses it, the faster it wears out and breaks down. The human form simply cannot contain the spirit of a daemon for long."

"So what happens then?"

"She has to make another."

"How does she do that?"

"That she did not share with me."

Cameron remembered the letter Eve had shown him, written by her predecessor. The receipt on the other side had been addressed to a Mrs McDonald. He hadn't thought much about it at the time, but now he realised it could be significant. "So Mrs Ferguson hasn't always been Mrs Ferguson?"

"She's played at being lots of different people. Every so often Ferguson has to move on, to create a new face, find another house and start again. But she yearns for stability – and that is her weakness."

Grandma Ives leant forward in her chair. "If we can find something to extend the avatar's life – so allowing her to use one avatar for longer – she has promised to lend us the conductor."

Cameron's eyebrows shot up. "You think we can trust her?"

"I agreed a very detailed contract. Her code of conduct demands she observe it."

"Still, it's not going to be simple, is it?" If Ferguson could solve the problem easily, she'd have done so by now, Cameron could see that. "What do we have to get?"

"I must confess, at the time I agreed, I had absolutely no idea."

"You mean you kept a straight face while she ranted and raved, and said you'd come up with something, no problem?"

"It was the only way to persuade her."

Cameron boggled. Grandma Ives could be a pretty cool customer sometimes.

"Over-confidence has always been my downfall." The old lady frowned. "But after a good deal of research and a great many favours, I believe I may have the answer. I have discovered there is a daemon called the Temperatori. In much the same way Weaver daemons like Ferguson have ability with thread, so the Temperatori has a natural affinity with time. If anyone has a means to slow the avatar's decay, it must be this creature. I've made an arrangement with Mr Hughes. In return for storing some of his more dubious acquisitions, he's given me something that will appeal to this daemon. Will you take it and exchange it for me?"

Cameron shifted awkwardly. He could tell she was proud of her discovery, but there was still one huge flaw in her plan. He took a deep breath.

"Gran, it's great you've managed to work this out, but I can't do it. We'll have to find another way."

"Whatever do you mean?"

He knew she wouldn't want to hear this. "I told you about Eve, how she can't leave Ferguson. You convinced me I couldn't help her, and maybe I can't – but I don't think I can help the creature keeping her prisoner."

Grandma Ives rubbed her forehead. For a moment, the old and tired look she'd had after her confrontation with Mrs Ferguson returned. "If we don't make the trade for the conductor, there is no way for the resurrection magic to work. Do you follow me, Cameron? Our quest stands or falls here."

"I'm not sure Dad would want to come back, if he knew it meant helping her," the boy said slowly. "He was always honest, you know. Big Joe used to say that's why he never had any money. He didn't just look out for himself."

A tight feeling crept into his throat. Was he really going to turn down his chance – his one and only chance – to get Dad back?

"The choice is yours, Cameron." Grandma Ives seemed to have read his mind. "He was your father. You must do what you think best."

All last night Cameron had tossed and turned, unable to sleep. He even started to long for another dream about the beach, if only so he could scream up into the sky, and ask his dad what he should do.

In the morning he had dragged himself bleary-eyed into the living room, his hair standing up madly in all the wrong directions. Grandma Ives was sitting with a fresh pot of coffee, studying yet another crumbly old document.

Cameron had poured himself a cup. The coffee was black and fiercely strong, but he was starting to get a taste for it. "Gran, tell me – is there any chance Mrs Ferguson getting her way could be a good thing? Any chance at all?"

The old woman thought for a moment. "If Ferguson gains a permanent avatar, I suppose her need for a human servant would be reduced... She might be persuaded to let the child go, although I couldn't guarantee it."

"And if we don't do anything, what happens then?"

"Things shall go on as before. When the avatar fails, she will replace it. When her servant starts to bore her, she will seek another."

"And there's nowhere else we can get another conductor for the resurrection spell?"

"Ancient life-transferring daemonic machines don't exactly litter the street, Cameron," she said dryly. "Not even in Edinburgh."

"So we take a chance or do nothing," said Cameron. "I risk helping Ferguson, and maybe I get dad back – or I don't help her, and nothing changes. Dad can never come back at all. That's the choice, isn't it?"

"It's called picking the lesser of two evils." Her grey eyes swept over him. "Well, Cameron, what's it to be?"

"It has to be better to do *something* than nothing, hasn't it?" He knew now what he was going to do, what he *had* to do. "We've got to take the chance..."

Taking a deep breath, Cameron tried the handle on the gate of the private garden. It rasped in protest.

"You can't get in that way."

He looked round. There was a boy leaning up against one of the flashy cars parked across the road. He wore a battered leather jacket, and his fair hair hung down towards his shoulders in tangled clumps. The strange thing was, Cameron hadn't remembered passing anyone else as he walked down the street.

"Yeah, I can see that," said Cameron. "Don't s'pose you've got a key?"

The boy sauntered over to join him. "Do I look like I'd have a key? You think I belong round here?"

His clothes were well worn, like he'd scavenged them from junk stores; his jacket a couple of sizes too small. It was a studenty sort of look, thought Cameron, but he didn't reckon the boy was at uni. He was probably only a couple of years older than Cameron.

"Maybe not, I guess."

"You got one?" said the boy, moving closer still.

"No." Cameron glared back at the boy. There was something about him that seemed oddly familiar...

"Then how were you going to get in?"

"I dunno. I was just going to try my luck."

The boy's green eyes narrowed, and he sniffed a long drawn-in snort, almost as if he was smelling out the truth of Cameron's words. "Hay fever," he said, by way of explanation.

"It's the middle of winter!" said Cameron.

"Ok, then, I'm allergic to Christmas trees. Happy?"

Cameron was starting to feel awkward. He didn't like the way he was being stared at. It reminded him of the power games his old enemy Sneddon used to play at school.

I'm not at school now though, am I? he thought, with a rush of pleasure. He'd learnt such a lot since then. His fingers drummed by his sides. Gran would be mad if she found out what he was going to do...

"I'm really happy actually," he retorted. "Totally ecstatic. Bye!"

He triggered the world-shift, transferring himself to the parallel.

The cars faded, and the paving stones became greasy cobbles. The broad windows of the buildings darkened, like a row of sad watchful eyes. In the human world, the fence had been not much higher than the average person, but now it stretched up as tall as a house. At the very top, the spiked tips of its bars curved round and in, like jagged fingernails clawing at the garden enclosed in their grasp.

But the boy was still there.

He hadn't vanished as Cameron slipped into Edinburgh Parallel. He'd followed him through...

"Yeah, I can do that too," he said.

Cameron knew now why the boy had seemed familiar. His green eyes reminded him of Montmorency. But while Montmorency had turned out to be pretty sound, the boy seemed harder and more challenging.

"Ok, so you're a daemon. So what?" To Cameron's surprise, he found himself pushing his shoulders back, and pulling himself up straight. He was almost as tall as the boy when he tried. "I've met plenty of your lot, and compared to an offal-eating curtain, you're not all that."

The side of the boy's mouth twitched, as if he found this funny. "Maybe not. Maybe I'm just different."

He drew his foot back and aimed a vicious kick at the gate, which shook so hard it made the whole huge fence vibrate and sing.

"Hey, what did you do that for?" Cameron stepped back. He glanced around, hoping the noise hadn't drawn any unwanted attention.

"Experiment," said the boy, giving him a pointed stare. "Some things give way to pressure."

Cameron said nothing.

As the thrumming sound died down, the boy tested the gate again. "And some don't."

He turned back to Cameron. "So, are we finding a way in – or not?"

12. The Best Tracker in Town

"Short of flying over, no one's getting in that way," said Cameron quickly, eyeing the towering barrier.

"I don't fly," said the boy. "I can't bend the bars right now either. What else?"

"I don't know, do I?" Cameron glowered back.

The boy shrugged amiably. He was watching Cameron in a slightly bored sort of way, as though mildly curious what he might get up to next. Cameron couldn't figure him out. A moment ago he'd seemed threatening, now he was acting as if Cameron was some kind of mate.

Feeling exasperated, he shifted back to Edinburgh Humanian, where the fence was at least a more manageable size. Cameron reckoned he could easily pull himself up the gate, wedging his foot against the crossbar where the lock was fitted. Getting over the top would be trickier due to the row of club-shaped spikes.

He started to walk the length of the fence.

Looking round, he saw the boy had followed him back, and was still idly watching. Trying to ignore him, Cameron continued his investigation.

Further down the street, he noticed that a branch from one of the trees in the garden projected out over the fence. It had grown with a downward slant and looked fairly substantial.

He jumped up, trying to grab at the branch. It was just out of reach.

The boy ambled over. He stretched out his arms above his head, but he too couldn't quite touch the bark.

"If you gimme a bunk, I can get it."

"Hold on," said Cameron. "When did we decide to become a team?"

"We didn't," said the boy. "But we're both going in there, right? So you help me, and I help you, and everything is full of win."

"I s'pose." Cameron couldn't really argue with his logic.

"Good. So gimme me a bunk up."

"Why don't you give me one?" said Cameron. He was clearly the lighter of the two.

"Sure, if you want." The boy looked Cameron up and down, as if gauging his strength. "If you go first, you've still gotta lift me."

"Ok, whatever," said Cameron crossly. He knotted his hands together, forming a step. "Get on with it, then."

"Awesome." The boy gave a half-smile, pleased to have won the point. "Here we go."

He planted his boot on Cameron's palm and pushed up, grabbing for the branch as he did so. For a moment he dangled, then with a grunt and a swing of his legs he managed to pull himself up and onto the branch. He arranged himself in a sitting position, one leg either side of the bough.

A hand appeared by Cameron's head. "Come on then, Shorty."

Reluctantly, Cameron put his hand into the boy's and was tugged up into the air. He grabbed for the branch with his free hand. There was a moment of confusion as he scrabbled around, then he too was sitting in the tree.

"Problem solved, eh?" said the boy.

"Cheers," said Cameron, only a little grudgingly. "Yay for us."

The boy shunted along the bough, shifting to a standing position as he reached the trunk. Then, with one agile motion, he dropped down into the garden below.

Cameron paused for a moment, taking advantage of his new viewpoint. He could see properly down into the garden. A gravel path wound round several leafy terraces, finally reaching the river near some kind of building.

He pulled a scribbled map from his pocket. There was meant to be something about the river that appealed to the Temperatori; the way it was constantly flowing, yet never the same drop of water twice.

"Here be Temperatoris," he murmured. The water was the place to go.

Copying the movements of his mysterious helper, Cameron dropped down into the garden, wincing only slightly as his feet hit the frozen soil.

The boy was scuffing about, kicking up stones from the ground. "Ok. Where now?"

Cameron scowled. He still didn't know how this interloper might affect his plans. "*I'm* going to the river. I don't know where *you're* going."

"River's good," the boy shrugged. "How's about a race?"

"A race!" Cameron snorted. "What are you, five?"

"What's the problem?" The boy's green eyes blinked slowly. "Are you very, very ancient or something? Or are all humans just a tiny bit feeble?"

Cameron could tell he was being provoked. Then again, maybe he *had* been spending too much time with his old gran lately. He'd been ever so sensible and responsible as he trekked around the city, taking packages to and fro, his mind always on the greater goal...

"Ok, you're on." He checked his satchel strap was secure – it would be disastrous to lose its contents now. "Last one there's a—"

Cameron never finished his sentence. With a crunch of boots on gravel, Morgan took off, loping away in great strides.

You wee cheat, Cameron thought, racing to catch up, his legs pumping. Soon enough he was neck and neck with his challenger.

"Not bad," said the boy out the corner of his mouth. He wasn't even a little out of breath. "Now let's see what you've really got..."

He banked sharply at the next bend, then with a whoop of delight, he put on a fresh burst of speed, accelerating down the path.

Cameron slowed to a trot, his mouth open. There was no point competing any more. What was this boy, anyway? Some kind of daemon road-runner?

He wiped his hand across his forehead. As he neared the end of the path, he got a better look at the building he'd spotted from the tree. Shaped like a Greek temple, it had a disc for a roof supported by three columns, although in overall size it wasn't much larger than an upended ice cream van. A carved marble figure of a man stood in the open central space. It was set a little way out into the water, linked to the shore by three stepping stones.

Cameron spotted the boy crouched by the river's edge, his fingers trailing in the water. His head kept turning from side to side, and he was sniffing at the air. Cameron breathed in deeply too, filling his lungs. He could smell frosty soil and a smoky odour like a bonfire left to smoulder. There was something else too, something sweet, like newly cut grass or pollen from the flowers... But that couldn't be right, could it? It was far too late in the year.

As Cameron approached, the boy shook his head sharply, as if trying to clear it, causing his tangled blond hair to fly out in clumpy strands. "Something round here reads wrong. It's like the seasons are all mixed up."

"Yeah, I get that too." Cameron shivered. *Could this be a sign I'm getting close to the time daemon?*

"You don't run too bad for your species." The boy stood up, brushing his palms on his dark jeans. "Morgan."

"Sorry?"

"Morgan. It's my name."

"Oh. Oh, right. I'm Cameron." Cameron shook the boy's outstretched hand.

There was an awkward pause, and Cameron tried to keep the conversation going. If nothing else, he needed to know what the boy was up to. "So, Morgan, do you usually break into gardens on Tuesday afternoons, or what?"

"Yeah, all the time. That's my schedule. Every Tuesday regular," said Morgan. "Just like it's yours. What are you doing here, Cameron?"

"I asked first."

"OK, fair enough," Morgan grinned. "I've been following you, mainly."

A chill ran through Cameron. "You're kidding, right?"

"No joke."

"I've never seen you before."

"Course not. I'm subtle. Best tracker in town."

"Why would you follow me?" said Cameron, still not quite believing him.

"For your sweet human smile and good temper?" Morgan's grin grew even wider.

He had oddly sharp teeth, thought Cameron. "Yeah, very funny."

"Maybe I heard Lady Ives found herself some new blood? Someone to fetch and carry things that shouldn't leave one world for the next, but do. Fairy fruit and fortune-tellers are no biggie, but when I saw you trying to break in here, I got interested. Wanted to see what you were up to."

"You're a psycho stalker, that's what you are," said Cameron angrily.

Morgan laughed. "Not a stalker. Seriously I'm not. I'm a free agent, that's all. Looking for an opportunity."

"You can take your opportunity and get—"

"Easy, easy! Before you say something you regret, why don't you wait and see? I helped you get in here, I might help you again."

"Yeah, right." Cameron eyed Morgan suspiciously. "What's in it for you?"

"I dunno yet. I just follow my instincts."

"I don't need your help."

"Hey, your loss," shrugged Morgan.

Cameron turned around and walked away, towards the temple-thing on the little island. He wasn't freaked out any more, just annoyed. Perhaps he should head back to Scott and Forceworthy, but he'd have to find a way into the garden again if he came back tomorrow, and there was nothing to say Morgan wouldn't be hanging around then too.

He stepped across the well-worn stones that led over to the monument. Up close, he could see a carved snake wrapped around the statue's chest, and the marble man was seizing it by the neck. A single word – *Chronos* – was engraved into the statue's base.

Cameron glanced back to the shore. Morgan was still watching. It was as if Cameron was a performing seal, and Morgan was waiting to see if he'd come out with an amusing trick.

Fine, Cameron thought, *if he wants a performance, that's what he'll get.*

"Hello, Chronos, if that's your name," he said loudly to the statue. "How's the snake-hugging working out for you?"

The statue didn't reply.

"What's that, Mr C? The snake just started following you about one day, and now you can't shake it? Sounds like a total drag."

Over on the water's edge, Morgan's expression shifted from one of vague confusion to annoyance.

Cameron jumped up onto the stone balustrade that ran around the temple, and walked along it, holding his arms out for balance. Across the other side of the river, he could see another steeply-raked garden, just as empty as the one he'd come through. High above him, a bridge carried traffic and pedestrians over the Water of Leith, to and from the busy city.

"Hey! Has anybody seen a TEMP-ER-A-TOR-I?" His voice echoed across the valley.

Morgan hurried towards him across the stepping-stones. "Was that 'Temperatori' you shouted?"

"Yup, so what if it was?"

"That's not a good word."

Cameron ignored him. He looked again at the statue's base. *Chronos*. "Chronometer" was another word for watch. He'd seen it written on those chunky sorts you got with lots of dials, and he *was* searching for a daemon that could manipulate time...

"What do you reckon this temple-thing's for?"

Morgan gave it an impatient glance. "I dunno. Garden ornament?"

"Bit big, isn't it?"

"Is it? Humans like strange things in their gardens. Gnomes, plastic toadstools, cats..." He lifted his head, and sniffed the air. "Listen, if there's a Temperatori nesting here, you want to clear out fast. I can tell you this much: this place is a crossing point. I can scent it."

"You *smell* Edinburgh Parallel?" Cameron almost laughed. What must the parallel smell like?

"Yep, course I can smell it," said Morgan. "What do you do, slip a ring on your finger or something dumb like that?"

"Nah, it's like music for me."

"Music. Nice." A flicker of interest ran across Morgan's face. "What sort?"

"Like a guitar riff. I just sort of listen, and it comes to me," said Cameron. "Like this..."

Moss and pondweed crept up the pillars of the temple, as they shifted into the parallel. It was as if the water level often rose and fell, leaving the stone a dark mottled brown. The Chronos statue vanished, and in its place now rested a perfect white egg. A hammer hung from the roof on a rusty metal chain. There were words inscribed along its length: "Those who seek the Temperatori must speak through me."

"That looks like an invitation." Cameron reached for the hammer, but Morgan grabbed him by the elbow.

"Listen, I'm not saying *don't*," said Morgan, "but if this is a Temperatori egg, most of my lot wouldn't go near it. Those things are unpredictable. You've gotta be sure you know what you're doing. Do you?"

"No," said Cameron honestly. "No, I don't." Thoughts of his dad, of Grandma Ives and of Eve flashed through his head. They were all relying on him in different ways. "But if I don't do anything, if I just walk away and do nothing, that's probably even worse..."

"Worse than what?" Morgan growled.

"Than risking – this!" Shaking himself free of Morgan's grip, Cameron hoisted the hammer back as far as its chain would allow, then let it swing.

There was a loud crack.

Cameron and Morgan watched as a million fault lines ran across the egg's surface.

13. The Temperatori

A clawed hand poked its way through the surface of the egg. It groped about in the air, discovering its environment. The hand was as smooth and pink as a baby's, but from each immaculate finger projected a rancid yellowing nail. Abruptly, the talons clacked together, forming a single curved blade. They sliced down, tearing the shell as easily as Cameron might rip open an envelope. Sharp fragments of shell flew towards them.

"Woah!" Cameron instinctively took a step backwards.

Morgan said nothing, but ran his hand swiftly down his jacket, brushing away the debris.

Freed from the confines of its egg, the creature stretched and stood up. It was the size of a full-grown person, but more like a bat in appearance, with filmy wings that hung between its body and arms. A belt slung around its midriff displayed a curious assortment of objects, among them a clock face, a pair of shears, an old-fashioned egg-timer and what looked like a coil of leather. Although newly hatched, the creature's wings seemed tattered and worn. Skin hung in folds around its face, but the eyes that peered out from the hollows above its snout were a bright and inquisitive blue.

"It's like it's young and old all at once," breathed Cameron, fascinated.

Morgan nodded. "Like the seasons all mixed up."

The creature cocked its head, and responded in a fluting tone. "From the egg I rise, to the egg I go. Where this circle begins, no one can know."

"It's speaking in verse," said Cameron. He addressed the creature. "Do I need to speak in rhymes to you? I'm here to make a bargain. You've got something I need. Can you understand me?"

The Temperatori took a number of jerky steps towards him, descending from the plinth where its egg had rested. "Poetry is a word mirror, reflections I adore. I am Temperatori, time eater and deflector. You, human, speak plainly. You've woken me – what for?"

"Careful now," Morgan said to Cameron in an undertone. "Don't trust it."

"Since when did I take advice from you?" Cameron hissed back. "You don't understand. I've got to do this."

He reached into his satchel and produced the packet from Mr Hughes. "Temperatori? I've been told you have a powerful talisman – something called a time funnel? I'd like to make a trade for it."

The creature's claw went to its belt. It unhooked the egg-timer contraption, and held it out. The two lumpy glass bulbs were filled with glowing sand, and wrapped around them was a framework made of small white bones. It looked to Cameron like a skeletal hand...

"In a hundred years an ocean, may crush a rock upon a shore – but start this funnel's motion, and rock shall be sand no more." The Temperatori turned the device upside down. Slowly, ever so slowly, particles of sand drifted down from the top bulb into its empty partner below. Their descent was so gradual, individual grains could be seen suspended in the air.

"Formed from my bone, Temperatori's claw – this defeats erosion, and will deaden time's roar."

"It's made from the bones of its own hand! That's where it gets its power." Morgan nudged Cameron. "That's some serious time voodoo."

Cameron studied the creature. "How could it, though? It's still got both claws. Did it just grow another?"

"Maybe. Old and young all at once, you said. I reckon you had something there. This dude doesn't do cause and effect like the rest of us."

"That's mad, chopping off your own hand to make an egg-timer!"

"That's dedication – if you're a time-obsessed bat-thing." Morgan gave a low whistle. "You'd better have something pretty good to swop for it."

The creature had been following their discussion, its head flicking from boy to boy. It re-attached the time funnel to its waist, and eyed Cameron suspiciously. "On my belt it will rest, there it shall stay – until Temperatori knows, how you would pay."

Carefully removing the brown paper wrapper, Cameron held out a book to the daemon. He was going to have to give this his best sales-pitch...

"Temperatori, this is a book of dark days, written long ago by a great human adept. It's a record of all his deeds, from when he first got his magic to the day his bottle-daemon evaporated, and took the adept's last breath with it. It's a life preserved on paper, very rare and full of secrets. Would you take it in exchange, perhaps, for the funnel?"

The creature shuffled forward eagerly, and snatched the book from Cameron. It held it under its snout and sniffed. Then it leafed through the pages, running its claw down their dark mottled surface.

"It's um, written in the adept's own blood," added Cameron. "That's supposed to be good, apparently—"

The daemon seized a wodge of pages, tore them from their binding, and stuffed them into its maw. It chewed on them thoughtfully.

A look of disgust spread across its face. "This thing tastes of dust, there is no time here. Those who annoy me, shall be made to fear!"

It spat the mangled mass of paper to the ground, and raised its clawed hand in the air.

Cameron spoke quickly. "Ok, ok. The book wasn't a hit." *Thank you so much, Gran*, he thought. *What happened to all that research?* "We can work round that, right? There must be something else you want?"

Morgan had been watching this exchange with a wary fascination. Now he turned a little pale. "So, Cameron. Awesome to meet you. I think I'll be going?" He flashed a grin at the Temperatori. "Bye, then. Nice, um, egg and that." He turned round and made a dash for the shore.

The creature moved like lightning to block the exit to the temple.

Its piping voice took on a sterner tone. "If you wake me up, I must be fed. Deny me what's mine – you'll end up dead!"

It stretched out one claw so its sharp talons rested just under Morgan's chin.

Morgan stood very still.

"Easy! No need to do that," said Cameron urgently. "No need at all. Just tell me what you want."

"Dry paper cannot feed me, it is for time that I ache. If my time funnel you seek, then your *days* I must take!"

It reached down to its belt again, its yellowed nails moving along the line of tools. They selected a blackened strip of leather and unfurled it into a nasty looking whip. The handle appeared to be made from the dried head of a snake.

"What are you going to do?" said Cameron. A sick and anxious feeling was rolling round his stomach. None of this was going as he'd hoped...

"From a part of your life, I will take my cut. As the day vanishes, my belly will glut."

Cameron backed away. "You want part of my life for your time funnel? I don't think so. That was never going to be the deal."

The creature growled. It flexed the claw held under Morgan's chin, and its talons criss-crossed the boy's flesh. A network of red lines appeared on Morgan's neck, from which sprang numerous tiny drops of blood.

Morgan winced. "Cameron, mate, just listen to what the nice bird-bat-time-daemon wants..."

"I thought you told me not to trust it?"

"Yeah, but that was before it decided I needed a shave!"

The creature spoke again, and this time a wheedling, sing-song note entered its voice. "A young heart you have, full of days to come; while I, though a hatchling, am old. What it is to you, but one day from your sum? Will you notice its loss, from your total, all told?"

A young heart... Cameron remembered the message from the prognosticator: *old hearts shall seek to capture young, to add to their stock of days.* The Temperatori must be the "old heart" and that meant he was the young! Cameron swore. What good was a prediction, if you had to be in the middle of it to understand what it was about? Couldn't the globe have said something *useful*, given him some kind of clue to help him get through this?

"So let me get this straight," he said, thinking on his feet. "You want to take a day from me – one day, no more?"

The creature's head rocked up and down in a strange approximation of a nod.

"What does that mean? If I was going to live till I was eighty, would I now die one day earlier?" Cameron guessed he could cope with that, if he had to.

"One day full of potential, I shall strip and re-shape, to make build-stuff for my shell. Twenty-four hours, from your stockpile deducted, will nourish and amuse me as well."

"I've got to risk it..." said Cameron. What choice did he have?

He glanced over at Morgan to see if he had anything to say, but Morgan's eyes were almost crossed, staring down at the Temperatori's claw. It would've been comical if it hadn't been so serious.

Cameron pulled himself up straight. "Ok then, take it. Just one day. I've got plenty, right? I can afford to lose one."

"The funnel for a day, then, our deal is done?" said the Temperatori.

"Yes."

"Then I take my day –" A look of immense cunning crept into its baby-blue eyes, as if it had thought up a particularly vicious plan. "– but which one?"

"What do you mean, 'which one'?" Cameron felt uneasy. What had he agreed to?

The creature lurched forward, its interest in Morgan forgotten. It started to circle Cameron, and as it did so it recited: "This whip can strip days, from past and future alike. From your childhood I could pluck, the day you mastered your bike..."

It moved closer, staring at Cameron, as though measuring him up. It licked its lips then continued: "No, no, that's too trite; how about I consume, the first great song that you write? Or I take from your days, your very first kiss? So many experiences, life-shaping, to miss."

Its breath stank of stale water and decay. Cameron gagged. How could it know about his music, that he wanted to write songs? And who exactly was he gonna get to kiss? It was like the creature was looking up and down his entire life-line, all the things that had been and were yet to come.

He thought about making a break for it, but that hadn't done Morgan much good. Besides, he still had to get the time funnel somehow.

"Just get on with it," he said.

The creature stopped circling, and raised its whip. "Or here's one whose removal, would make you feel sad – I could take from your future, *what really happened to Dad?*"

Cameron's eyes opened wide in shock. "I've changed my mind, I want out!" he yelled.

Morgan, who had been rubbing at his neck ruefully, rushed forward. He grabbed for the creature's arm. It hissed furiously, and cuffed at him with its other claw. He staggered back, and the creature seized its opportunity. It struck down with the whip, the unfurled coil hitting Cameron and Morgan both.

For an instant, time seemed to freeze. Cameron felt light, lighter than he'd ever felt before, as if he was floating up out of his body and away. For just a moment he was removed from everything – then with a sickening lurch, like being in a plummeting elevator, he was back in his own skin.

The creature's stomach bulged, the folds of flesh much tighter than before. Making a contented crooning noise, it reached up and tugged upon the steel chain from which the hammer hung. There was a creaking, grinding sound of ancient machinery juddering into life, and the temple began to shake. Like a film running in reverse, the Temperatori walked backwards up to its plinth and crouched down. The shattered pieces of eggshell twitched in their resting places, and lifted up into the air.

Cameron struggled to speak. "Hey! Hey, we had a bargain! The time funnel, remember?"

The fragments of shell were circling in a miniature whirlwind, twirling round and round the creature. They came together with a *whoosh*, and in a matter of seconds the shell re-assembled, as perfect and white as before. On its very apex sat the egg-timer device that had hung from the creature's belt.

The time funnel!

Cameron struggled to his feet. He felt dopey, as if he'd woken up suddenly in the middle of the night. He lurched towards the funnel, but the temple floor was shaking violently now. He looked around wildly. The hillside beyond seemed to be sliding steadily upwards – or was he just seeing it from lower down? That was it – the building was sinking! Suddenly, the damp-sodden pillars made a terrible sort of sense. The building had sunk beneath the river many times before.

Cold muddy water started to flood in, pouring over the low wall that ran around the temple's circumference, and filling the floor of the central space.

Morgan, who had been clutching at his head, now came to his senses. "Come on. Let's get out of here!"

He sprang for the stepping-stone causeway and the safety of the shore, but Cameron wasn't going to leave the time funnel behind. He sloshed through the water, hauled himself onto the plinth, and pressed his body up against the egg. He stretched to grab the time funnel, but it was just beyond his reach.

"Morgan?" he called. The boy was out of sight. There was no one to give him a bunk up now.

He pushed himself up on tiptoes, and stretched again with all his might, until he thought his arm might slip from its socket. His fingertips scrabbled, and finally latched on to a piece of bone. With a scrape, the funnel slid down the egg and into his grasp.

Turning back round, he saw that the floor of the temple had been completely submerged, and the water was now lapping at the sides of the plinth. The temple was sinking fast, and if he didn't move quickly, he'd risk being trapped when the roof met the surface of the water. He jumped from the plinth.

The water closed over his head.

He tried to kick out with his legs, but to his horror he couldn't make any progress.

He flailed his arms, never letting go of the time funnel, but he was sinking, down, down to the bottom of the temple. The water was murky, and he could no longer tell which way was up. A rushing sound filled his ears, and for the second time that afternoon, he had the eerie sensation that he was no longer quite inside his own body.

Suddenly, he felt a hand on his shoulder. Next an arm wrapped around his chest, grasping him tightly. At last his head broke the surface. The descending roof was almost on top of them, but Morgan back-crawled furiously, pulling them through the gap between two pillars and out on to the river.

Back on the shore, Morgan shook himself like a dog. Water flew from his long hair. "I thought humans could swim. I'd have dived in sooner."

Cameron spat muddy water and coughed. "Of course... I can... swim!"

It had always been one of the few sporty things he really enjoyed. Not only that: swimming was part of the best memories he had of his mum. When he was little, back before she left, they used to go swimming every week. It was their ritual. Afterwards they'd sit in the warm café that echoed with the excited shouts and cries from the pool below, him with a chocolate milkshake, her with a cup of tea. He even remembered the day he'd learnt to swim by himself, it was...

She had...

They'd...

"That's it. That's what it took," Cameron said quietly. "It cut away the day I learnt to swim, and then it sank its temple under the water. It nearly killed me."

He felt his body shaking. He wanted to be with Dad again, but not like that. Morgan had got him out just in time.

"Thanks. Thank you. I mean that."

Morgan shrugged. "I said I might be useful."

Cameron's teeth chattered. The river had been freezing.

Morgan looked at him quizzically. "You're cold."

"No, I'm not. I'm really, really, warm..."

"Don't be daft." Morgan held out his leather jacket. "Here, take this."

It was still dry, Cameron noticed. He must have taken it off before jumping in.

Morgan started to prise the time funnel from Cameron's numb fingers.

"Hey!" Cameron objected.

"You can't get the jacket on holding that, can you? Look, I'm putting it in the pocket."

Cameron felt the jacket being pulled around his shoulders. It was odd, really, the way Morgan kept helping him, but Cameron was grateful. If he'd been in the Temperatori's garden all alone... He didn't want to think about what might've happened.

"That whip-thing," he said quietly, "it got you as well. What day did it take?"

"I dunno. I don't feel any different. Maybe it's

something from my future." Morgan glanced up at the darkening sky.

"Either way, I'm sorry I got you involved."

"Don't kid yourself, Shorty. I involved myself." A lopsided grin spread slowly across Morgan's face. "You still chilly?"

"Me? I laugh in the face of hypothermia."

"You'd better come with me. I know just the place to sort you out..."

14. The Daemon Drink

"And there you go!" Morgan thumped a pair of battered metal tankards full of blue frothing liquid on the table.

"What's that?" said Cameron.

"Wolf's Boon." Morgan swigged, and shivered. "Ah! That's the stuff. I can feel it doing me bad all the way down. What's the matter?"

"I asked for a Coke," Cameron said awkwardly. He didn't want to appear uncool in front of his new friend, but Wolf's Boon didn't look or smell very appealing.

"No Coke. It's all daemon drinks here." Morgan wiped a dod of foam from his top lip, and looked at Cameron expectantly.

Grandma Ives probably had some rule about not eating or drinking in the parallel, but her advice hadn't exactly been much help today. *Oh, what the heck...* He took a sip. The coloured liquid was thick and rich, and surprisingly sweet.

"You know, it's alright."

Morgan grinned. "What did I tell you? Wolf's Boon's for the win."

Cameron settled back in his chair. There was a fire roaring in the grate behind him, and his clothes were drying out nicely. His mobile didn't look like it would ever recover, though. There was water sloshing about behind the screen. There'd been messages on it from Amy too... He'd kept meaning to reply, but recently he'd found himself ignoring them.

A pang of guilt shot through him. The more he got involved in Edinburgh Parallel, the harder he found it to talk to her. With every day, his old life in Cauldlockheart seemed further and further away. Amy would never believe in stories about Temperatoris and time funnels, or that he could bring back Dad. She'd just think he'd gone mad.

He took another mouthful, and glanced around the place Morgan had brought them to. Leaving the Temperatori's garden, and sticking to the parallel, he had led Cameron to an unmarked wooden door on a side street. Once inside, they had climbed down a spiral staircase for what felt like days, finally coming out into this stone-built room. It was filled with benches and tables, and numerous groups of different daemons were sitting talking over their drinks. To Cameron's surprise, everyone seemed to be getting along fine.

"What is this place anyway?" he asked.

"You don't know about old Kitty?" Morgan nodded towards the fat woman working the bar. She was laughing as she poured a glass of something green and sparkling for a short daemon in a suit woven out of moss.

The barwoman caught Morgan's eye, and shouted over, "You all richt there, pet?"

Morgan was instantly all charm. He winked, and yelled back, "All the better for seeing you, Kitty!"

"That's the spirit!" The woman turned back to her mossy friend.

"She's the best landlady in town. No one's allowed to beat up, kill, eat, bewitch, drain, possess or injure anyone else in here."

"That's good to know."

"Not unless you spill someone's drink, and don't buy them a replacement. Then all bets are off. But that's just manners, isn't it?"

Cameron glanced back to the barwoman, who was now pouring a pint of something frothy and blood red. "What's she famous for?" he hissed.

"Ok, the story goes that Kitty was so *thirsty* that when she died she took over a tavern halfway to heaven." Morgan jerked his thumb towards the ceiling. "At least, that's what the humans think..."

"But really, she ended up –" Cameron pointed downward "– here?"

"Nothing's really ever lost in this mad old city. People used to fall into daemon lands all the time. Kitty's been hangin' around since before the world-split, and now there's no way back for her."

Cameron gawped. "That was *years* ago... How can she still be here?"

"Dunno." Morgan set down his tankard, and stared at the foamy dregs a little sadly. "Some people just don't know when to let go."

The bar really was an extraordinary place. Cameron had been trying to work out which types of daemon he could recognise. The tall thin model-like couple standing decoratively in the corner had to be fairies, with their glamour all turned up to the max. The cloak draped over a chair that crumpled and contorted its way into a spidery face could only be one of Mrs Ferguson's Weaver daemon sisters. It had given him a bit of a shock when it first materialised, but once he saw that it seemed to content to gnaw on a hambone, he was able to relax.

"So," said Morgan idly, "what you gonna to do with that time funnel? Piece like that could be pretty valuable. Lady Ives must be pleased to have you as her new delivery boy."

"I'm not her delivery boy." Cameron was a little indignant.

"No?"

"I'm..." Cameron hesitated, searching for something suitably impressive. "I'm her second-in-command."

"Really?"

"Yeah," said Cameron, growing in confidence. "Her business is all going to be mine one day. She told me. She's training me up to take it over."

"Ok, ok. You're a major player! I respect that." Morgan's green eyes sparkled with amusement. "So this time funnel... it's a business deal thing, is it?"

For a moment, Cameron glanced down at his tankard. He saw no reason why he should explain to Morgan about his dad, but he didn't want to lie to him either. "Something like that," he said casually. "We've got a client that wants it. What's it to you anyway?"

"Like I said, I'm a free agent. I've got to keep my nose out for opportunities." Morgan stretched out his arms, and made to lean back and cross them behind his head. Unfortunately, he clipped another daemon's tankard, and knocked it clear from his grip. The tankard clattered to the ground, and its contents sloshed across the floor.

A hush fell across the bar, and all eyes turned towards Morgan.

"Idiot mongrel! Look what you did!"

The tankard's owner was an old man with a heavily weathered face, his long grey hair poking out haphazardly from beneath a dirty red bonnet. He shook his gnarled hand to clear the droplets of spilt drink.

Morgan leapt to his feet, his face a picture of concern. "I'll buy you a replacement. I'll buy you two, how's that?"

"That disnae matter..."

"Four then! Can't say fairer than that."

"Fair?" The old man glowered. "What do I care about fair?"

A bell clanged loudly, and Cameron's eyes darted to the bar.

"Hoose rules, Mister Red Cap, hoose rules!" Kitty called out sternly. "Let the laddie make good."

"You heard what the lady said." Morgan grabbed Cameron's shoulder, and pulled the boy out of his chair. "Come on, Shorty. I'll need you to give me a hand."

Slowly, the buzz of conversation returned, and the bar's patrons shifted their attention back to their drinks.

"What's the matter?" Cameron grumbled as he was dragged across the floor. "You just need to get him another, don't you?"

"Oh yeah, easy. Two problems with that..." Morgan executed a sharp swerve as they approached the bar, pulling them through an archway that led to a wood-lined snug. He patted his pockets frantically. "Problem one. Got nothing left to trade."

He reached forward and snaked his hands into the leather jacket Cameron was still wearing, rummaging through its pockets as well. Cameron yelped, retreating from Morgan's scrabbling fingers.

"Problem two. Old Red Cap's always looking for a fight. There's a reason his hat's stained that colour, and it doesn't involve clothes dye. You hearin' what I'm sayin'?"

"Oh!" Cameron peered anxiously back through the archway. "What are you going to do?"

"Nothing." Morgan finished scrabbling, and instead gave the wood-panelled wall a sharp kick with the heel of his boot. There was a mournful creak, and the bottom panel swung aside, revealing a dark space beyond. "Just as well I know another way out, eh?"

He dropped to his knees and wriggled through, his broad shoulders just fitting through the gap. Cameron followed closely behind. As his eyes adjusted to the gloom, he saw he was at the bottom of another spiral staircase. An arrow chalked on the dank and dripping wall pointed upwards, beside which someone had scrawled: *To the dog.*

"To the dog?" Cameron said, bemused.

"You read my mind." Morgan swivelled round, having pulled the hidden door closed. "And fast! Old Red Cap's dumb, but he won't wait forever."

The boys dashed up the stairs. As they climbed, the spiral got tighter and tighter, until Cameron found himself squeezing his way between the damp stone walls. Abruptly, the spiral came to an end, leaving him staring at a blank curved wall.

"There's no way out – it's a dead end!" Cameron felt uncomfortably wedged in, with almost no room to breathe. *This must be what baked beans feel like... just before they get eaten.*

"Give the wall a push!" Morgan's breath was hot on Cameron's neck. "Hurry up, I heard something behind us..."

Cameron shoved, and the curved wall slid sideways. He stumbled, and fell on his back onto the street. Above him, absurdly, was the famous statue of Greyfriars Bobby, the faithful Edinburgh dog of legend. He'd pushed his way through the crowds of tourists that surround it often enough. The sad face of the little terrier peered down at him. He must've fallen out the statue's cylindrical base!

Morgan squeezed his way out the curved door, and swung it closed. "Always have an exit strategy, that's what I say!" He patted the little dog on the head. "What's up, mate?"

"What – about – Red Cap?" Cameron panted.

"He'll never get through. Too big and too stupid. Even if he does, wee Bobby won't open for him." Morgan laughed heartily. "Good times, eh, Shorty?"

Cameron pulled himself to his feet. Thanks to Greyfriars Bobby, he knew where he would be when he shifted back to Edinburgh Humanian. The landmark clearly existed in both locations, although he doubted its base hid a handy secret passageway back in his world.

He glanced up at the sky. It was properly black now, and the evening's frost was starting to creep its way across the pavements. How long had he been hanging out with Morgan? Even laid-back Grandma Ives might be starting to worry...

"Listen, I have to go. But it's been good – as good as being nearly drowned and chased by monsters can be." Cameron started to zip up his jacket and then stopped. "Hey, I forgot. This isn't even mine..."

Morgan stepped back. "Keep it."

"Seriously?"

"Why not? It's too small for me anyway."

Cameron felt a grin starting at the corners of his mouth. He had a sneaking suspicion that the jacket might suit him. He reached for his wallet, checking for some money for the bus. He had a fiver, but it had gone all damp, and he didn't have any change. It must've all fallen out of his pocket down under the water.

"You haven't got a loan of a quid, have you?" Cameron looked up. "Morgan?"

The street was empty. Morgan had slipped away.

Grandma Ives gave Cameron a hard look when he made it back to the shop, taking in everything from his mud-streaked hair to his creased and dirty clothes. "Good gracious! What happened to you? No, hold on. Let us have blankets, a hot drink, and the heater turned up full! I shall order a taxi back to Observatory Road."

"It wasn't as easy as you said it'd be," said Cameron blearily, as she fussed about him. He'd had a miserable, shivery walk back to the shop. The bus had been a non-starter; the driver had taken one look at him, and driven off.

"So, tell me. Did the Temperatori like the book?" Grandma Ives was eager for news.

"Oh yeah, it ate it up –"

"There, what did I tell you?"

"– and spat it out."

"Oh dear." Grandma Ives' face fell.

"It took something from me too. The day I learnt to swim. Maybe more for all I know."

"Ah." Grandma Ives rubbed her temples. "Now I think of it, there *is* another word for Temperatori that *could* translate as 'day-eater'. But I didn't imagine it would be quite so literal."

"Are you sure you didn't know?" said Cameron darkly. "You knew all about Mrs Ferguson, Montmorency... You usually know everything. Maybe that's why you sent me. You couldn't risk it snatching some of your precious knowledge."

"That was never my intention, Cameron, truly it wasn't."

The old woman's features seemed to radiate a mixture of distress and concern, and instantly Cameron felt bad.

"Sorry. It's been a long day."

"Apology accepted." Grandma Ives raised an eyebrow. "Of course, you may always learn how to swim again. So no great harm was done."

"It wasn't just the swimming I lost. That wasn't all it was about," muttered Cameron. He didn't elaborate.

"Nonetheless, you succeeded? You found the device?"

Cameron nodded. He delved into the pocket of Morgan's jacket, took out the time funnel – and noticed at once something was wrong. The glass bulbs were still intact, but the skeletal claw that had been wrapped around them was missing.

Frowning, he felt in the pocket again. Next, he tried the others. Nothing! It *couldn't* have fallen out, there was no way...

He thought again of Morgan, his fingers scrabbling through the jacket pockets. He'd been full of questions about the funnel. He'd told Cameron he was a free agent, looking for an opportunity. He'd tracked Cameron to the garden in the first place...

He couldn't have! He wouldn't!

"Gran, I need to tell you—"

She waved him to silence, taking the funnel from his hands. She turned it over, so that the sand-filled sphere was now in the air. Instead of the spookily slow descent he'd seen before, the grains poured swiftly from one bulb to the other. Without the Temperatori's claw to hold them, it was just like ordinary sand.

"I can see how this might be used, but I can't seem to activate it..."

Cameron stared down at his canvas trainers. The water had turned them an unappealing green. He didn't know how to tell her that the time funnel was useless, after all he'd gone through to get it.

"Maybe it's because I'm not a daemon," Grandma Ives mused. "Natural magical ability has to count for something! Ferguson will probably be able to trigger it in an instant."

She put the funnel down, and turned her attention back to Cameron. "Sorry, my dear. What was it you were going to say?"

"Nothing. Nothing at all."

"Oh, don't look so miserable! Some hot food and clean clothes and you'll be fine. This is a triumph, you know. Our greatest success so far!"

Cameron watched the tumbling sand. The top bulb was almost empty. It'd be great for boiling an egg, he reckoned, but not much use apart from that. Mrs Ferguson wouldn't be taken in for a second. And if Mrs Ferguson was unsatisfied, they'd never get the conductor – and the resurrection spell could not be made.

He cursed himself. How could he be so stupid? This was *his* fault, for trusting Morgan, for thinking he'd found a new friend. He'd been too busy enjoying himself, and having a laugh. He'd lost focus on the one important thing. Now the whole plan to bring back Dad was going to fall apart.

He had to take action.

He had to track down Morgan, and make him give the rest of the funnel back.

15. Morgan

Grandma Ives stood in the entrance hall of the house on Observatory Road, pulling on her gloves. "I might be home late tonight, Cameron. Indeed, I may not be back at all, but you are not to worry. Our plans are moving on apace, and I have a little research to conclude."

She adjusted her hat in the mirror. A small flicker of pleasure played around her lips as she got the angle exactly right. "Will you be alright on your own?"

"Yeah, I'm good. I'm used to it, remember?" It was a real bit of luck, Cameron thought, her going out. Usually he'd be desperate to discover what she was up to, but today he had other plans.

"Oh, and the time funnel must be taken to Mrs Ferguson. Would you run and fetch it?"

Cameron's heart sank. "No, don't do that..."

"Why ever not?"

"I just don't think you should," he said, aware of how lame that sounded.

A look of sympathy ran across Grandma Ives' face, and he cringed inside.

"Oh, I *see*," she said. "Don't be concerned. I noticed how that beastie behaved last time. There's no need for you to come."

"All I meant," said Cameron quickly, "is that we haven't put together the rest of the spell. Just suppose we can't? I mean, there's no point giving her something we don't have to, is there?"

Grandma Ives considered for a moment, and then smiled. "You make a good argument. We must take care of our assets. You know, Cameron, sometimes you think very much like me!"

"Thanks," he said, uncertain that this was a compliment.

"Now, what are you going to do with your day of leisure?"

"I dunno. Hang about, watch TV."

"Ah, the idleness of youth. Good day to you, dear. Wish me luck."

Cameron waited until he heard the garden gate clang, then he dashed up to his room. He'd already scoured Morgan's jacket for clues. In the end, the only thing he'd found was a folded square of paper stamped with a crescent and the words "Admit One".

There was no point going back to the Temperatori's garden, Cameron reasoned; there was nothing left to interest Morgan there. He didn't like the idea of running into a still infuriated Red Cap, so Kitty's Tavern was out too.

There was nothing else for it. He'd have to ask for help.

He tugged on his trainers and, on a whim, pulled on Morgan's jacket as well. He checked his reflection, and rubbed the tarnished metal buckle by the neck.

"C'mon. Let's go find your owner..."

"Joined the Hell's Angels, have we?" Jack Montmorency looked up from his paper as Cameron clattered into his shop. "I've got a magazine here for you, lad. A part-work for wasters learning the guitar. You get a free book of tabs with issue one."

"Awesome," said Cameron, not really listening. "Jack, if I had to find someone, could you help?"

"Who are we talking about, exactly?" said the shopkeeper cautiously. "I'm not treading on your grandma's toes. I know what I do best, and I stick to that. That's enough for me."

"It's nothing to do with Gran." Cameron already had his story worked out. "It's a mate I met in the parallel. I, um, lent him something, and I need to get it back."

"Neither a borrower nor a lender be, my old man used to say. There's lots fallen out over less."

"We've not fallen out. He just doesn't know I need this thing back, and I can't exactly text him, can I?"

"Well..."

"C'mon, Jack. You get loads of people coming in here. You see things. You know stuff. You're connected. You're The Man."

"Hmmph," snorted Montmorency, but Cameron could tell his flattery was working. "Go on, then. Just this once. Who is it you're looking for?"

"Morgan."

"Never heard of him."

Cameron's face fell. "Awww, don't let me down! You're my only hope! He's a big guy, bit older than me, kind of scruffy, long hair..."

"And your granny knows you're hanging out with this lout?"

"Never mind Gran," said Cameron firmly. "Do you know him?"

Montmorency screwed up his face. "No, lad, you'll have to give me more to go on."

Cameron sighed. "There isn't much else. Just this bit of paper..."

"The old half-moon, eh? That takes me back." Montmorency whistled as he examined the ticket stub. "You'll be wanting the Alhambra Cinema, by the shore at Leith."

"Great! I *knew* you could help. Thanks, Montmorency."

"A pleasure. Now, about this magazine..."

"Can you hold on to it? I'm a bit short..."

"I don't know. Come in here, beg for information, and you won't even spend a quid." Montmorency grumbled, pretending to be offended. "I'll keep one behind the counter for a week. No longer, mind."

"Cheers." Cameron grinned. "I'll be back."

"Bye, then. Have fun with the werewolves."

Cameron stopped dead, halfway out the door. He ducked back into the store. "Did you say werewolves?"

"Uh-huh."

"That's *werewolves*, as in howling, and chasing, and turning into a wolf when the moon is full?"

Montmorency laughed. "Blimey, you don't know much, do you? A daemon werewolf is like a proper wolf, but bigger, stronger and devilishly quick. But that's only when he wants to show his wolf side. He doesn't have to. The ones that come up through the parallel tend to keep it to themselves."

"So I should be ok, then? I'm not going to get bitten or anything?"

"Why would you?" Montmorency scratched at his temple. His sticking-plaster covered glasses lifted up, and just for a second, Cameron caught a glimpse of his daemon eye, shining bright and green. "I mean, you said this guy was your mate, right?"

"Yeah," said Cameron uncertainly. "That's what I said."

Cameron found a seat on the top deck of the bus. As it chuntered down Leith Walk, he made a point of peering into the basement of Grandma Ives' shop. The lights weren't on. Wherever she had gone, it clearly wasn't there.

Were-WOLF, Were-WOLF, Were-WOLF!

The bus tyres rumbled over an uneven stretch of ground, causing the word to bounce around in Cameron's head.

If Morgan truly was a sort of super-wolf, he probably had really heightened senses... That'd explain how he could sniff out things in the Temperatori's garden, and the way he'd tracked down Cameron too. Morgan had helped him, maybe even saved his life, by dragging him out of the water. Then again, he'd also nicked the claw from the funnel, for what reason Cameron couldn't tell. Images from all the horror films he'd ever seen came back to him, of wild and terrible creatures that emerged every full moon, human flesh cracking open to reveal the wolf beneath. But films weren't true, were they? He'd learnt recently that real life could be even more strange and complicated...

The bus dropped him in the centre of Leith, and Cameron spent a frustrating couple of hours trying to find the Alhambra. The closest he came to any cinema was the multiplex in the big shopping centre, and that just didn't feel right. He didn't reckon the parallel touched there at all.

Realising he was cold and tired, Cameron spotted a chip shop and decided to treat himself. As he was leaving, a warm paper bundle clutched in his hands, he noticed an old couple sitting at one of the plastic tables outside. They were wrapped up like a pair of Christmas parcels, the woman feeding a steady stream of chips into her mouth, her husband more interested in his cup of tea.

They look like they've been about a bit, thought Cameron. It couldn't hurt to ask...

"Excuse me... do you know where the Alhambra Cinema is?"

"The Alhambra?" The woman looked up from her fish supper. "Do you no mean the Vue? It's over at Ocean's Whatsit."

"No," Cameron persisted. "Not that one. Definitely the Alhambra."

"The Alhambra's been closed forty years."

That'd explain why I can't find it, thought Cameron. *Thanks, Montmorency!*

"I'm on a... on a field trip, for school," he improvised. "I'm finding out how people used to entertain themselves in the, uh, old days."

"No that old, son." The man lowered his cuppa. "That's where me and the missus met."

"Sorry."

"Aye well, so am I."

Cameron felt his cheeks colour. "I didn't mean that..."

The woman laughed. "Take no heed, he's just sendin' you up. Go down Constitution Street, and take a left. It's the boarded-up building along there. Dinna try and go in, though. It's no safe."

"It's ok. I'll just take a picture and go." Cameron popped a celebratory chip in his mouth. "Thanks."

The building was where the old woman said it would be. In fact he'd passed it twice that afternoon. At street level, a thick layer of billposters was papered over the chipboard. Up above, a row of tall thin windows were painted over from inside, and gave no clue as to what lay behind.

What's Morgan doing hanging out here? It looked so gloomy and rundown. Cameron couldn't see any way in, but just because there was no route in the human world, didn't mean it would be the same in the parallel... He brought the Edinburgh Parallel tune to mind, and slipped into the other place. As he did so, the plasterboards dissolved, revealing a v-shaped lobby decorated with chequerboard tiles. Above the entrance, an elegant red and yellow sign swirled into existence:

THE ALHAMBRA
Brings the Pearl of the Cinema
To the People of Leith & the City of Edinburgh

Beneath was a turnstile, like you'd get at a railway station, and a wooden kiosk.

Cameron glanced back into the street. The other buildings had faded into grey, while the Alhambra seemed to exist in a bubble of vivid colour. It clearly had been a grand and important place, once upon a time.

He clacked through the turnstile, and went in.

Peeling gold pillars stretched up to an arched roof decorated to look like the night sky. Tiny bulbs had been set in place of stars, and a few still glowed dimly, but most were dull and black. The walls were lined with posters for films Cameron didn't recognise. *I Know Where I'm Going!* said the banner across one: it showed a woman gazing defiantly out to sea.

"Good for you," muttered Cameron. "I wish I did."

He leaned over the counter of a little stall that was meant to sell sweets and refreshments. The air smelled damp and more than a little mouldy. The popcorn had probably gone off.

"Morgan? Hello? Anyone here?"

He shivered. It was odd to be in a place that was meant to be full of happy people, chatting and laughing, but now seemed utterly deserted.

"Do you have a ticket?"

He turned round. There was a girl in the lobby, not much older than him. She was dressed in what had once been an usher's uniform, made of tattered red velvet. The gold piping along the arms and collar had long since faded. Her skirt was short and ragged, exposing her legs.

She looked at him curiously. "I said, do you have a ticket?"

"No. Sorry. Should I have? Listen, I'm trying to find—"

She tapped her fingers against a printed notice on the wall. "Rule number one: 'All Patrons must have a Ticket.'"

"If there'd been someone at the gate, I'd have bought one."

The girl strolled across the lobby towards him. She frowned.

"That smells like lies to me. I don't like lies."

"Wait a minute." He dug in his pocket, and triumphantly pulled out the square of paper he'd shown Montmorency. "Yeah, I do. See?"

A twitch of irritation shot across the girl's face. She snatched the ticket, and tore it in half. "That's used. Not valid."

"Well, maybe. But this isn't really a proper cinema any more, is it? Be fair," said Cameron hastily. "I'm looking for Morgan. Have you seen him? Big guy, blond hair. Used to have a jacket just like mine."

"Oh, I don't think we can let you see Morgan. Not without a ticket. Can we, lads?"

She stuck her fingers in her mouth and whistled. A door opened in the panelling by the refreshment stall, and three more figures emerged. The first was burly, with blunt heavy features. He wore an usher's uniform, similar to the girl's, but he'd cut off the sleeves to show his tattooed arms. The next had a thin sharp face, and dressed in a pinstripe suit with absurdly large lapels. The third wore a set of oil-stained overalls, and shuffled awkwardly. None of their clothes seemed to fit well. In fact, it looked like they'd dressed up in whatever they'd found lying about the old cinema, in the staff lockers or the lost property.

Cameron held up his hands. "I'm just looking for a friend. I'm not trying to make trouble."

"You're not going anywhere," growled the one in the cut-off usher's uniform. He lifted his fists and studied them idly, as if trying to work out which was his favourite to hit things with.

"Easy, guys," said Cameron, backing away a few steps. "Just tell me what you want."

"Run," said Usher Boy.

"Yeah, run," said Overalls.

"Fast as you can," added Pinstripe Suit. "When we catch you, we'll show you what we want."

"That clear enough for you?" said the girl. She smirked.

In the low lights of the hall, the eyes of all four glowed green. Their teeth seemed unnaturally sharp and white.

Cameron was certain now. They were werewolves. Every single one.

16. Werewolves of Edinburgh

Every fibre of Cameron's being was telling him to run like crazy, but that was exactly what the werewolves wanted. Could he make it to the door and back out into Edinburgh Humanian? If this lot were anything like Morgan, they could outpace him easily...

"Awww, look. The human cub reckons if he stays still we'll get bored and go away." The girl's voice was heavy with sarcasm. "We're not cats, you know. We're *wolves*..."

She lurched forward, her face contorted into a snarl.

Instinctively, Cameron darted backwards, away from her grasp. His back thumped into a bubblegum vending machine, which fell to the ground with a crash. Its glass globe shattered, sending hundreds of brightly coloured gumballs scattering across the floor.

"Excellent work, dude!" said the one in overalls. "I've been wanting those—"

"Save it!" the girl snapped. She scooped up a handful of gum. "It'll be something sweet for dessert—"

A startlingly bright flash of torchlight arced across the lobby.

"Lola, Eddie, Grant, Half-Tail – back off!"

Cameron shielded his eyes against the glare. Someone in a long dark army trenchcoat was hurrying down the stairs at the back of the lobby. All four werewolves looked most displeased to be disturbed.

"He's just a human. Can't we have a bit of fun?" said the girl.

"He's not just a human," replied Morgan amiably. "He's Cameron, and he's alright." He nodded to Cameron. "You ok there?"

"Me? Never been better." Cameron gulped.

"You're not Alpha Dawg, Morgan. You can't boss us around!" sneered Pinstripe Suit.

"We're only having a laugh," said Usher Boy.

"A laugh? I'll tell you what'd make me laugh," said Morgan. "Wouldn't it be a shame if it wasn't only Half-Tail here whose name matched his looks? How about Cut-Face, No-Ear or One-Eye? Sounds good to me."

"That's not funny," said Overalls.

"No? Makes me smile." Morgan's voice was soft and dangerous. "I could help. If you did want new names."

The girl stamped her foot in annoyance. "You think you're so clever, Morgan..."

"I don't need to be clever, Lola. I just need to stay one step ahead of you."

Lola spat on the ground. She shot a contemptuous look at Cameron. "You'd better hope your *friend* is here next time we see you, or else..." With a flick of her head, she led her gang across the lobby and out onto the street. There was a shimmer as they world-shifted, moving across into Edinburgh Humanian. As they faded from view, Cameron caught a glimpse of them outside in the late afternoon light. Their clothes didn't seem so bizarre now. A bit punky and out of the ordinary, sure, but nothing madder than you'd see on the streets every day. Nobody would think to look at them twice.

"Thanks," Cameron said. "I guess that's the second time you've got me out of trouble."

"Them?" laughed Morgan. "They're nothing. Their bark's way worse than their bite. Actually, I lie. Their smell is worse still..."

"I'll take your word for it," said Cameron.

"C'mon, then. Do you want to see my pad?"

Morgan's pad turned out to be in the old projectionist's booth. Cameron followed him up three flights of stairs, past the red-carpeted rooms meant for the public, to a door marked "Private".

As Morgan tugged the door open, a small pink shape scurried out, and scampered into the distance, squealing furiously.

"That was a piglet..." said Cameron incredulously. "Why do you have a piglet?"

"I don't now. Just ignore it."

"How do you ignore a pig?"

"With difficulty. Noisy little rasher." Morgan scratched his lank hair. "Come in. Mind your head. It's a bit cramped."

Two colossal projectors – bulky steel machines bolted to the floor – stood facing a shuttered hatch in one wall, taking up most of the space. A hammock was strung jauntily between them. Piles of film cans were scattered everywhere, some of which Morgan seemed to have adapted into furniture. A tape deck stood balanced on three cans, with a stack of CDs beside by it.

"Hey, I've got this." Cameron noticed a disc on top of the pile. "They're pretty good."

Morgan grinned. "Human music rocks."

He pulled a stopper out of a brass tube that jutted like a periscope from the floor. "See. I can keep an eye on things from here."

Cameron looked down the tube, and saw a distorted view of the entrance hall they'd left. "Are we right above the lobby? There's got to be some sort of lens hidden in the ceiling..."

"I dunno how it works, I just use it. That's how I saw you coming." Morgan ducked under the hammock, and unlatched the covered window in front of the projectors. "This is useful too."

Cameron peered through into the auditorium below. It was all one large room, more like a theatre than a cinema, with lots of rows of seats on three different levels. Dotted around, he saw odd piles of possessions and clutter, and many blankets strung between the aisles, screening them off into smaller sections. It was like a city of tents. He jumped as a flash of light from somewhere on the ground level shone in his direction, and several pairs of green eyes flared into life in the gloom.

"Werewolves in a cinema," breathed Cameron. "You've got to admit that's pretty random."

"The guy who ran this place way back was one of us," said Morgan, shutting the window. "He had a real old-school urge to stare at the moon, but he didn't trust himself to do it. He used to practise watching the movies, every moonlit scene. Convinced himself he

162

could take on the real thing. Bad move. Went wild. Lots of people got hurt. The pack had to drag the dude back to Daemonic. I don't think they ever let him out again."

"So the cinema shut down in normal Edinburgh, but it still exists in the Parallel?"

"Pretty much. It fell through the cracks. Lots of things do."

"And you're a werewolf too, right?" Cameron asked.

"Yup," said Morgan.

"Why didn't you tell me yesterday?"

"Why would I? Do you tell everyone everything about yourself?"

"No—"

"Do all your human buddies know you found the parallel? Did you call them up and say, 'Hey monkeys, guess what? I've been hanging out with daemons.'"

"No, I s'pose not," said Cameron, remembering the way he'd been avoiding Amy, not sure what to tell her about his new life.

"Well then. It's no different." Morgan went and rooted in a locker by the door. He came back with two sticks of beef jerky. "Hungry?"

"No, I'm good. I had chips."

"I'm starved." Morgan pulled the wrappers off, and tore into the dark strips of meat.

"You're not like the guy who ran this place, then?" Cameron persisted. "You don't have to... have to turn all teeth and hair whenever there's a full moon?"

"Nah... The moon only pulls on you like that when you're a kid. When you're new," said Morgan, between mouthfuls. "Most of us learn to control it. We're not allowed up into the human world if we can't. The pack's pretty tight on that."

"Why's that?"

"We've got to keep it quiet, haven't we? One of your lot might notice something, and we don't want that."

"Cos then you'd have to kill us?" Cameron licked his lips nervously. "That Lola looked pretty bloodthirsty."

"She just wanted to scare you for kicks. Probably." Morgan looked thoughtful. "No, it's the other way round, mate. We're in danger from you. You don't get wild wolves in Scotland, do you? They were wiped out years back. The pack thinks your lot would do the same to us if they found out we're still about. So we gotta hide, and be careful."

Cameron felt awkward. "We're not all like that, you know."

Morgan shrugged. "Hey. Ancient history as far as I'm concerned."

"If a person did get bitten, though, would they end up like you?"

"Not like me, no. I'm pure werewolf." There was a touch of pride in Morgan's voice. "I'm either wolf or human shape, nothing in between. Bitten humans turn out strange. They never change all the way, just become a mix. They don't control it well." He paused in his chewing, and grinned. "What's with all the questions? Do you want me to bite you?"

"No!" said Cameron, startled. "Why would I want that?"

"I dunno. Humans get strange ideas. Look, it's a full moon out there tonight. No problem at all... But you didn't come here to discuss my pedigree, right? What do you want, Shorty?"

"You know fine." A wave of irritation ran through Cameron. Why was Morgan playing games with him? "You stole part of the time funnel. You took the Temperatori's claw. I want it back."

Morgan turned away, and started digging through a pile of clothes resting on the film cans. "Yeah, well, I took half the risk. Reckon it's mine. Might be worth a bit 'n' all."

"You don't understand," Cameron said. "I have to have it."

"Well, I have to have it too, so we're stuck, aren't we?"

A plastic bag dislodged by Morgan's rummaging fell to the floor. He looked down and made a move to grab it, but Cameron got there first. Inside were several egg-timers of various sizes, all in different states of disrepair, their glass bulbs torn from their stands.

Cameron glared at Morgan. "You've been trying to fix it, haven't you?"

"Didn't do me much good though, did it? I reckoned all the power was in the claw, but there must be mojo in your half too. Something special in the sand." He threw Cameron a small, squareish lump. "Here. Catch."

"What's this?"

"It was gonna be my dinner. Nice couple of ham sandwiches."

Cameron squeezed the blackened square in his hand. It had no give at all. "It's like a rock! You'd snap your teeth off if you tried to bite this..."

"That's what the claw did when I tried to test it. It seems to age things up, or run them backwards in time till they're something else completely."

"That explains the pig," grinned Cameron. "It was in the other sandwich, right?"

"It'll be sorry it ran. Won't last a minute with the wolves out there." Morgan scowled. "It's like the claw bones are the power, and the glass bulbs are the control. You gotta have both to work the time funnel."

"Yeah, well, you should've nicked them too, shouldn't you?" said Cameron smartly.

"I don't know how Temperatori magic works, do I? Anyway, I had to leave something in the pocket or you'd have noticed, even with your rubbish monkey senses." He looked at Cameron curiously. "Any chance you'd cough up your bit?"

"No way. You need to give me the claw."

"Stalemate then, innit?" Morgan shrugged.

Cameron felt his hands clench. He had to make Morgan understand how vital it was for him to have the time funnel. Everything rested on that deal with Mrs Ferguson...

"You've got to listen to me. I really, really need you to give me that claw back. It's way more important to me than it is to you."

"Oh really?" said Morgan. He yawned massively, exposing his white teeth. "Stopping you drowning's not enough, then? Why do you need it so bad?"

"It's complicated."

"So? Complicate me."

Cameron took a deep breath. He realised he hadn't told anyone else this. No one at all. His words came out in rush. "My Dad died. There was an accident, or maybe... maybe something else, I never found out for sure. But my gran, Grandma Ives, said she could bring him back. If I helped her, and we got the things we needed, he wouldn't have to be dead any more. Do you see? Things could go back to how they were. How they should be." He paused for a moment, letting the awful truth come to the surface. "I have to know if it was my fault – if I could have stopped him, or helped him somehow. This is the only way I'm ever going to know."

Now it was Morgan's turn to look awkward. "Hell, Shorty. I'm sorry," he said gruffly. "Do you reckon she can do that, then – bring him back?"

"She says she can. And I believe her."

"Resurrection magic is big bad stuff," said Morgan doubtfully. "I've not heard of anyone doing it successfully, not for hundreds of years. Why would she risk it?"

"Why d'you think?" began Cameron, but he stopped. He hadn't heard Grandma Ives say anything good about his dad, not in all the time he'd known her. Her enthusiasm seemed to be all for Edinburgh Parallel and her business, and for Cameron helping her to keep running it.

"She probably started on all this just to show off," he said thoughtfully. "She's a bit vain. Likes to impress people with how much she knows. But really, I think she's doing it for me."

Morgan started to pick at his teeth with a finger. "Yeah, well, that's all very sweet, Shorty, but I've got to live too. 'Honour the dead, but feed the living', don't they say? I'd help you, honest I would, but I've promised that funnel to a certain lady, and it doesn't do to disappoint her."

"So you're not going to give it back?" said Cameron.

"No," said Morgan. "Sorry. I can't."

Cameron stood up. "Then I guess I'd better go."

Morgan put a hand on his shoulder. "Look, mate, the chances of your old nan putting that spell together are low, I reckon. Even if she could, what are you going to get out of it? He might come back wrong. Way wrong. Scary wrong, perhaps."

"I've got to try. He's my dad," said Cameron, knocking Morgan's hand away.

Morgan stared at his displaced hand, glaring at both palm and back as though it didn't quite belong to him. Then he shook his head, and shoved the hand in his pocket.

"I'm sure he was great, your dad. A real wise old dog. But everyone's got to grow up one day. Maybe you need to move on."

"Go to hell," said Cameron quietly. "You don't give a stuff for anyone, do you?"

"I'm sorry, Shorty, it's not my problem... Hey, you can keep the jacket though. I've got a new one."

"Like I'd want to!" He started to pull the jacket off. How daft he was, thinking it made him look tough and grown up. How stupid he'd been, even starting to like Morgan. "Here, take it."

Morgan ignored him. He was staring at his hands again. They were shaking slightly, Cameron noticed,

168

like he'd had one too many cups of Grandma Ives' viciously strong coffee.

"I'm gonna change," said Morgan.

"You can change all you like," said Cameron. "You'd still be useless."

"No, you wee twit. I mean *change*. Go wolf."

Cameron started. "How do you know?"

"How d'you know you're gonna sneeze?" snarled Morgan. "I just know, don't I?"

He began scratching at his sides, as if his skin was itching beneath his clothes.

"You said you could control it, that it was no big deal!" shouted Cameron.

"I've been on top of it for years. I don't know what's happened. It's like I just don't have it any more..."

"Just like I used to be able to swim..." said Cameron. "The Temperatori! That's what it took from you. It got the day you learnt to control your wolf side!"

"Great, I'm so glad that mystery's solved." Morgan's voice cracked as he spoke. "It's gonna be a big relief to me when I'm living out the rest of my days in Daemonic."

"You mean they'll make you go back?"

"I said they would, didn't I?"

"Can't you just stay here, in your room, till it's over?"

Morgan shook his head wildly. "If the change is forced on me, it's gonna be bad. I don't know what I'll do." He gestured towards the auditorium, beyond the hatch. "If I make enough noise, that lot'll come running, and it'll be no more parallel for me. No more Edinburgh Humanian. No more playing human. No more rock music. No more fun. Ever." The strain was starting to show on his face. "You need to get out of here."

"Wait. How long have you got?" Cameron said urgently.

"Ten minutes. Twenty tops."

"It's ok, Morgan," said Cameron. "Hold on. I've got an idea..."

17. What Lies Beneath

The door to Scott and Forceworthy burst open in a fury of clattered keys, letting in an out-of-breath Cameron and a grim-faced Morgan. The inside of the shop was dark, and Cameron hastily reached for the light switch.

Still no sign of Grandma Ives, thank God. Cameron didn't know how he'd explain bringing a soon-to-be-wolf-shaped visitor back to her precious store.

He and Morgan had sprinted up Leith Walk, Morgan racing ahead at times, then stopping to clutch at his sides and groan. Halfway to Grandma Ives' shop, Morgan had staggered right into a tough-looking lad, almost knocking him over.

"Eejit!" the lad had said, as he regained his balance.

"Eejit yourself," retorted Morgan, a murderous look in his eyes.

Cameron could see a fight was brewing, and that wasn't going to do anybody any good. "Sorry about my mate," he said. "He's not feeling well."

"Oh yeah? He'll be feeling a lot worse if he doesn't watch himself."

"He ate a dodgy curry," Cameron improvised. "He's been puking every colour of the rainbow. Believe me, it's gross. It's been shooting out of him like a fountain. You should probably keep back."

The lad now looked a little pale himself. "Just get him to mind where he's going."

Now, in Grandma Ives' shop, Morgan paced back and forth like a caged beast. "What good does this do me, eh? What's your bright idea?"

"Well, you're away from your tell-tale buddies; that's a start. And there's a basement here, quite deep down. I thought the further I could get you from the moon, the better it might be. That makes sense, right? And I can lock you in down there. What do you think?"

"Show me. Quickly."

Cameron led the way through the back room, and down the stone spiral steps to the vault where Grandma Ives stored her excess stock.

"Ok, ok. Location is good," said Morgan, looking around. "Might even help a bit. But I could get through that in a second." He tried to gesture towards the wooden door at the top of the stairs, but his arm went wild, knocking a box from the top of a teetering stack. Its contents scattered across the floor.

"*By the Hill and the Fort and Shattered Rock, I pronounce: old hearts shall seek to capture young, to add to their stock of days...*" A fortune-telling globe rolled from the spilt box, and came to rest by Cameron's foot, where it squawked away like a neglected parrot.

"What good are you? That's already happened!" He aimed a savage kick at the prognosticator, and sent it bowling across the floor to the opposite side of the room.

Morgan was prowling round the cellar, his movements jerky and uncoordinated. More boxes fell victim, as he staggered about. He came to a stop by the metal door on the far wall. "*That's* what I need. I couldn't get through that, even in wolf form. Put me in there, and I'll wait it out."

Cameron swore. "I've never got it open! Gran wouldn't tell me what's in there; she came out with some guff to put me off. I don't know even know where the key is."

Morgan slumped to his knees. "You'd better find it quick. Find it, or get out. I've not got long now..."

Cameron thought furiously. If Grandma Ives had the key, there was nothing he could do. But if by some stroke of luck it was kept in the shop, where would she put it?

Think, think, think!

Got it! The desk near the counter, where she liked to study her ancient books and scrolls! Its top drawer was stuck fast. She'd always said the catch was broken. What had she got in there? He'd need to break it open...

He looked frantically around the basement for something he could use. His eyes caught on the Claymore sword in the corner, the one that had belonged to the shop's first owners all those years ago. Just the thing!

Offering thanks up to the ghosts of Scott and Forceworthy, he dashed towards the sword, seized it, and brandished it in the air.

A stabbing pain gripped him. Morgan had lurched back into life, whipped across the room, and grabbed Cameron by the shoulders. His nails dug in fast, somehow sharper and more terrible than they should've been.

"What's the big idea?" he snarled. "Bring me back here, then run me through with this thing?"

"No! Get off! What do you think I am?" shouted Cameron. "Come on, Morgan. You've got to trust me!"

Morgan glared at Cameron, but he slackened his grip. "Whatever it is you're gonna do, you'd better hurry." With a yell of frustration, he swiped at a nearby packing case, gouging five deep marks into its surface.

"Just hold on! I can sort this."

Carrying the sword, he ran up the stairs, taking them three at a time. He dashed to Grandma Ives' desk. He wedged the tip of the sword into the gap between the drawer edge and the wooden surround, and pushed. Almost immediately, he met resistance. He slid the sword from side to side, hoping it would snag on the hidden latch that was holding it closed, but the drawer did not give.

Damn! He told himself now wasn't the time to be subtle. Stuffing the sword tip in the gap again, he grabbed Grandma Ives' ledger from the desk. It was a heavy leather-bound book she'd been using for years. He raised it high above his head, and swung it like a club at the hilt of the sword. It connected with a thump, causing a huge cloud of dust to rise up from the book. At the same instant, the sword was driven home. There was a crack of splintering wood, and whatever had been holding the drawer closed gave way.

Cameron seized the newly freed drawer and scrabbled through the contents. A tin of coins, a paper-knife, a pack of cards and – yes! – a bundle of keys. But which one? A rat's nest of string and paper labels hung from it.

"Come on, come on!" he yelled. There couldn't be much time left now...

174

What had she said, when he'd asked her about the door downstairs? She'd called it... a broom cupboard?

There it was! A label saying just that. He grabbed the key, shaking it free from the tangle, and vaulted back down the stairs. He ran straight to the door, and plunged the key into the lock.

With a protesting squeal of un-oiled cogs, the mechanism clicked round, and Cameron dragged the door open.

"I've got it! Morgan, I've got it!" he shouted triumphantly.

Behind the door, a greasy set of steps lead down to another room, its walls unplastered and rough, and clearly older still than the store built above it. At the very top of the stairs, by Cameron's feet, stood a dust-covered suitcase. He grabbed it and threw it out of the way. Years in the damp foundations of the building must have softened its fabric, for when it hit the ground it burst open like a colossal puffball, scattering a load of paper and documents across the basement floor.

"Morgan, come on, get in here!" Cameron glanced round the basement. "Morgan?"

The spot where he'd left his friend was empty. He made his way round the room, threading cautiously through the stacks of boxes. Slung over a chest and crumpled into a heap was Morgan's long coat. Not far from it, a discarded pair of biker boots.

"Morgan?"

A low growl answered him. Cameron crouched down behind the nearest box. His hands instinctively grabbed around for anything he could use as a weapon. The only thing he could find was the prognosticator he'd kicked earlier. He picked it up, being careful not to touch the trailing wires that brought it to life.

Another long, low growl reached his ears. Carefully he raised his head over the stack of boxes. There, in the corner, Cameron saw him: a huge white wolf, sleek and powerful, its green eyes blazing.

He gulped. The wolf had definitely seen him. There was no point hiding.

Cameron had no idea how Morgan might behave now that he was a wolf. Would he still know him? Or would he be more animal than person? He decided to take a chance.

He moved out from behind his cover. The wolf's head followed him curiously.

Cameron held out the fortune-teller globe.

"Here, look at this," he said softly, "this shiny ball. I bet you'd like this, wouldn't you?"

The globe gave one of its disconcerting shrieks of static, as Cameron rolled it about in his hands. The wolf growled again.

Taking hold of its handle, Cameron swung the globe back and forth, the wolf watching intently. Gracefully, on its massive paws, it crept closer.

"Good boy, good boy. You're interested, aren't you? Now – fetch!"

He turned round, and hurled the globe through the open metal door. It bounced down the steps, buzzing and clattering madly, and vanished into the darkness.

Like a streak of lightning, the wolf dashed after it.

Cameron threw himself at the door, and slammed it shut, swiftly turning the key in the lock.

From behind the door, he heard a scrabble of paws as the wolf turned round and raced back up the stairs.

The wolf crashed into the door, causing it to ring like a beaten gong. Again and again it tried, thumping the full weight of its body against the obstruction. There was a terrible blood-curdling howl, and then finally, silence.

Had Morgan run head first at the door, and somehow knocked himself out?

Cameron backed away from the door, praying it would hold, his heart beating wildly. His feet scuffed through the papers scattered on the floor from the mouldy suitcase. A folded scroll cracked apart like an autumn leaf as he trod on it. He looked down.

A face he recognised stared back. It took Cameron a moment to place it. It was a photograph of his dad, but much younger than when he'd known him. Gathering together as many of the documents as he could, Cameron dumped them into the bottom half of the suitcase, and carried it up the steps. He glanced back at the cellar door, but all was quiet.

My baby's gone and left me,
And all I do is cry,
He's bin a dancin' devil since
He got the moonlight in his eye.

He always was a wicked dog,
He always loved to roam,

But he's a dancin' devil since
He got the moonlight in his soul...

...sang a scratchy voice. Cameron had clicked on the record player behind the counter, but he wasn't sure he appreciated Grandma Ives' choice of disc. Still, it had to be better than listening to the mournful yowls that filtered up from the room below.

He started to set out the contents of the suitcase on the desk. He was most interested in the photographs he'd found. There were a good four or five of his dad. There he was, wearing stupidly flared trousers and a purple tank top, a grin plastered all over his face. Another showed him younger still, riding a bike in the back garden of the house on Observatory Road. Cameron smiled, laughing at the clothes and his dad's haircut. It was shorn so close to his head that his ears stuck out like jug handles. No wonder he'd always kept it shaggy. Cameron would tease him something rotten, if only he were here...

Everyone's got to grow up one day... Maybe you need to move on.

Morgan's words sounded mockingly in his ear. The more Cameron thought about them, the more they irked him. His dad wasn't an old sweatshirt, something you grew out of and threw away! That wasn't how you treated *people*, was it? Looking at this hoard of pictures, it seemed like even frosty old Grandma Ives clung on to the past.

He dug further into the pile. He passed title deeds for the shop, then birth and death certificates for family members from years back, with names he didn't recognise. Then, more photographs. These were much older, small and square in shape, and shot in black and white. He saw a family, posed as stiff and formally as Scott and Forceworthy in the picture that hung behind the counter. The father had a long beard, and was dressed in a sober suit. His wife had a kind but tired face, and wore a dark dress that bunched up around her shoulders, so she looked more like a crow than a person. Before them sat four children: three girls in long dresses and a boy in puffy shorts. There was something about the face of one of the girls that reminded him a little of his grandma. She was smiling slightly, but she seemed a bit aloof as well. It couldn't be her though, could it? It was far too long ago.

He moved on to the next picture, another of the same family. They were dressed in black now, and Cameron noticed the young boy and one of the girls had vanished. They all wore sombre expressions – all except the little girl with Grandma Ives' face. Her jaw was set, her arms pressed rigidly to her sides. She seemed more angry than sad.

He turned up one further photograph of the girl, old enough now to be called a woman. Her mother was the only other family member pictured. She seemed pale and fragile, her hair turned to a coiled turban of silver. She looked up at the daughter by her side, but the girl did not return her gaze.

What had happened to the family in between the photos? Had three children and the father all died? How long was it before the mother joined them?

179

Sudden death was more common back then, he knew. People had larger families as not every kid was expected to survive.

He wondered who the young woman was. Could she be his great-grandma, Grandma Ives' mother? By the time of the last photo, she looked so cold and hard. He imagined she must've been strict. Perhaps that was why Grandma Ives had told him she didn't like to think about her childhood. Instead, she'd wrapped the memories up and put them away, buried them along with everything else.

Cameron's stomach rumbled. A raid on the tiny kitchen netted him a packet of biscuits and a can of Coke. Biscuit in hand, he wandered to the front of the shop, and lifted the blinds. It was early evening now, and people were hurrying home from work, or off to meet friends and family. Up in the sky hung the moon, full and yellow and bright, and utterly unaware of the mischief it could cause.

He sighed. There was no way he could go home, not with Morgan like he was, locked away down below. He had to hope Grandma Ives' research trip would last the night, and his absence wouldn't be noticed. He had to hope the door would hold, no matter how often or how hard Morgan threw himself at it.

It was going to be a very long night.

Click, spluff! Click, spluff! Click, spluff!

Cameron woke to the sound of a jammed record. Sitting up, he unglued his face from a photo that had stuck to it as he slept, slumped over the desk.

7.17 AM.

He really hadn't meant to sleep at all, but sometime after two, he must have drifted off.

Rubbing his eyes, he made his way down to the basement, taking in for the first time the chaos they'd caused the night before. Upturned boxes lay everywhere, and the floor was strewn with stuff. He hoped there hadn't been much broken. To his relief, the metal door stood fast. He pressed his ear against its surface, but he couldn't hear anything.

"Morgan? Morgan? Are you ok?"

"Just let me out already!" grumbled a voice. "And can you get my coat? I'm kind of naked down here..."

Grabbing Morgan's trenchcoat from the chest, Cameron unlocked the door.

"Cheers. Proper vintage, this is," said Morgan, wrapping the coat around him. "I'm glad it didn't get shredded along with the rest."

"Yeah, I'm kind of glad too."

Morgan stretched stiffly. "It's crazy cold down there. Stinks of rats and dead spiders. Not the best place to grab a bit of shut-eye." He padded across the basement and pulled on his boots. His hairy legs stood out absurdly between the boot tops and the bottom of the long jacket. "How do I look?"

"Like a sort of mad flasher," laughed Cameron.

"Human though, right?" said Morgan. "That's something."

"Morgan, do you reckon you're always going to change now?" asked Cameron. "Every time we get a full moon, I mean."

"I dunno," said Morgan thoughtfully. "I learnt to control it before, so I guess I can again. Ask me next time Mother Moon shows her fat face. For now, I'd better get home. Don't want to startle the locals." He paused, and looked away, as if he didn't want to meet Cameron's gaze as he spoke. "Thanks, Shorty, for what you did to help. There's not many would've."

Cameron shrugged awkwardly. "It's no big deal."

"It was, though," insisted Morgan. "Reckon I owe you now. If there's anything I can do for you, you just gotta ask."

"But there is something. You know there is," said Cameron.

A pained expression crossed Morgan's face. "Yeah. I reckoned that's what it'd be. You can have the Temperatori's claw, even though it's gonna cost me." He started to climb up the stairs.

"Morgan, hang on! That's not why I helped you..."

"Yeah, I know," said Morgan. "You're a good guy. I get that."

"Where will I find you?" Cameron called after him. "Back at the cinema? I'm going to need it pretty soon."

"I'll find you." Morgan shot a grin in Cameron's direction, but to Cameron's eyes it looked a little forced. "I'll track you down. I'm good at that, remember?"

Grandma Ives turned up a little after nine o'clock, clutching a bag of pastries from the bakery above. Cameron fell on them ravenously.

"I thought you must be here," she said. "You made an early start."

Cameron hadn't long finished clearing things up. "I couldn't sleep, so I jumped on a bus and came down here instead. I've had a bit of tidy. It was getting kind of mad downstairs, so I sorted it all out."

Grandma Ives arched an eyebrow. "How very industrious of you. But let me tell you my news. I've been to see the Augur of Calton Hill."

"The Aug-*what*?"

"The Augur... a sort of wise man or seer. He divines hidden truth using the city's birds."

"Wow. What's that like?"

"Rather too much squawking and feathers for my tastes. And he insisted on playing a reel on his fiddle every time I asked a question, so you'll understand why my visit took so long. But I found out two most important things."

She reached into her coat pocket, and produced a dirty-looking map. "Firstly, I know where we can find the energy source for the resurrection spell, or at least I will once I decipher this."

Cameron took the map from her, and unfolded it. There were several hills he recognised, and he could see the castle, but much of it was unfamiliar. "It's Edinburgh, isn't it, but a long time ago?"

"Yes. Back before the Nor' Loch was drained and the New Town built, back when everyone lived clustered about the castle. The Augur's reference points are a little dated, I'm afraid. He hasn't left his cavern in quite a while."

She tapped her finger at a yellow squiggle that had been added to the map. "The Augur divined for me the daemono-voltaic battery's location. It still exists, even all these years after the Makaris built it. We must acquire the battery, and re-unite it with the conductor."

Grandma Ives put the map to one side.

"Secondly, I now know for certain where and when the spell must happen. We must go the crags at Arthur's Seat on the anniversary of the world-split. For on that night, the daemons believe, all things turn to their true nature."

A shiver ran through Cameron. "Their true nature... what does that mean?"

"The human and daemon worlds, so long pushed apart, try then most keenly to reconnect into the whole they once were." She clasped her bony fingers together and wiggled them, as though enacting this. "The dual-world, in which magic and reason could intermingle."

"And that's important, for the spell to work?"

"Very. I have no great magic myself. My weapon is knowledge, it always has been. If I am to perform the spell successfully, the conditions must be right. At that precise time and place, the Augur assures me, even here in the human world of science and reason, a taste of the old magic will be possible."

Cameron felt his heart beating fast. "When is it? When do we have to be ready?"

"Mitchell and Astredo, the world-splitters, certainly knew the significance of dates." She looked at him gravely. "It's the winter solstice. The shortest day. December 22nd."

Cameron glanced down at his watch. The green figures said: *Dec 20*. Only a few weeks ago he'd been walking back from Amy's – the fireworks for bonfire night exploding over his head – and waiting for Dad to come home. The days had shot past since he'd come to Grandma Ives'! He hadn't even noticed how close it was to Christmas.

"December 22nd... But that's only two days away!"

"Indeed," said Grandma Ives, and there was a sparkle in her eyes that Cameron could have sworn was excitement. "We're going to have to make haste!"

18. Aulder and Bartie

Grandma Ives moved over to the desk, and rummaged through a drawer. To Cameron's relief, she didn't seem to notice the broken compartment – he'd wedged it closed with a tiny wad of paper. She returned with a pencil case and a street map of Edinburgh.

"Now, if we can transcribe the markers on this," she indicated the Augur's old map, "to its modern equivalent, we should be able to get started."

She produced a length of string and a set of compasses from the pencil case, and began to work. Her eyes flicked back and forth between the maps, searching for points of similarity. Recognising the tapering shape of Castle Rock, Cameron spread his fingers and touched the same place on both. She nodded, and made a tiny mark.

"So, will I have to watch out for these Makaris daemons when we go for the battery?" Cameron recalled the scroll she'd shown him back when she'd first explained the spell. The story of the daemon clan that lived by farming people was hard to forget. "I don't want to end up anyone's lunch..."

"That's not very likely. The Makaris died out centuries ago." Grandma Ives smiled grimly. "Once the world-split restricted travel to a select few, they starved for lack of prey. Their magnificent devices were broken up, or forgotten, their skills lost to time. It was a sad end for such an inventive race."

"I suppose." After his run-ins with werewolves and a Temperatori, Cameron found his sympathy for hungry daemons was limited. "You reckon this battery is still good, though, even after all this time?"

"I don't see why not. Don't forget, Mrs Ferguson's conductor still functions, and it was once part of the same machine. The battery should still work as a storehouse of life energy. I shall channel power from it through the conductor, and so resurrect your father."

Scenes from the TV hospital soaps he used to watch played through Cameron's mind, of white-coated doctors running to revive a dying patient. "All clear!" they would shout, pressing a paddle to the victim's chest. A colossal charge would rush through and jump-start the patient's heart.

"We're going to zap him back to life, then. Like on *Casualty*."

"Almost. The energy will be magical, though, not that of human science."

Another more disturbing image snuck into Cameron's head. In place of the sterile whiteness of a hospital, he now saw Frankenstein's laboratory; a bolted-together corpse lay upon a slab, waiting for the lightning strike that would jolt it into motion...

A sick feeling rose up in his guts. All this time he'd been focussed on the goal of bringing his dad back, he'd stopped himself considering the practicalities of how it might be done.

"Gran..." he said slowly, "we're not going to need Dad's... body, are we? What was buried, I mean. I don't think I could face that."

Grandma Ives dismissed his worry with a flick of her head. "We're not trying to create a zombie, Cameron, we're going to re-invoke life." Her attention returned to the map.

"So where does all this life energy go, then?" Cameron persisted. "If it's not into him, how can he come back?"

"Oh, Cameron. So many questions!" The old woman gave Cameron an exasperated look. Then, as if noticing at last how troubled he was, she reached forward and ruffled his hair. "We shall need an icon, shan't we? Something that represents the essence of your father. We can make it from things he owned, things we associate strongly with him. You can help if you like."

Her hand was cold against his scalp, and he shivered. "Ok. I guess I can try to do that."

"Good lad."

He thought of the few of his dad's possessions he'd been able to keep. Grandma Ives had always said they'd go back to Scott Street and finish sorting things out, but they never had.

"There isn't much to choose from—" he began glumly, but Grandma Ives interrupted by tapping sharply at her teeth with a pencil.

"First things first! We must have the battery. Allow a scale of one inch to twelve daemonic furlongs, so that's 360 divided by twelve, that's..."

"Thirty."

188

"Of course. How terrible to be old and slow of wit. Gah!" She lifted her compasses from the old map, and planted its tips down on the new. "Good gracious!" she said. "What on earth is it doing there?"

In the run up to Christmas, Princes Street was transformed. White lights picked out the branches of the trees that swept down the hill from the castle. By the gothic space-rocket shape of the Scott Monument, a huge Ferris wheel spun. An ice rink had been set up in the gardens nearby, and people circled round, bumping into each other and laughing hysterically. Everywhere shoppers rushed, counting down the days left to buy presents. Cameron made his way briskly through the crowds.

Grandma Ives' calculations had pinpointed the corner where a huge department store now stood.

"It's Aulder and Bartie. An Edinburgh institution." She had sounded a little indignant. "Everyone who's anyone shops there."

"Perhaps they're like you," Cameron had suggested. "Maybe they sell things between the worlds. Maybe we're going to have to pay for this battery-thing somehow..."

"I'd know about any competition," she'd insisted. "Whatever is going on there, it's nothing to do with trade."

They decided to investigate separately, and then meet in Aulder and Bartie's cafe to compare notes. Cameron arrived first. From the other side of the road, he stood back and examined the rambling bulk of the department store.

It looked less like a shop, and more like a castle built to please a lunatic king. Two huge towers stretched into the sky, and from their top, numerous cheeky gargoyles gibbered and pouted. Carved antlers jutted out of the stonework, and beasts of the forest capered and leapt. Down on the street, swarms of people filtered in through arched doors, ushered by smiling attendants. Yet more shoppers staggered out, bent over with the weight of their purchases.

He was just figuring out from which entrance to make his attack, when he saw a familiar face amongst the people scurrying along the street. She'd cut her hair since he'd seen her last, a severe choppy fringe replacing the long dark mane. Her brown eyes were ringed with make-up, and she had her iPod on, her mouth just moving along to the words.

Amy.

Oh hell, he thought. *Not now.*

"Cameron Duffy! Don't even *think* of moving or I'll take you down so hard you'll be seeing stars."

"Hey, Amy," he said helplessly. "How's it going?"

"Don't you 'hey Amy' me!" She swung one of her shopping bags at his head. "I thought you were dead! Or your grandma had eaten you, or you'd found God and gone to the moon!"

"Is that what people do in Amy World?" Cameron dodged and laughed. "Get religion and go and live in space?"

"Well, you'd better have an A-one explanation, or we are so not friends!" She threw her bags down on the pavement, ignoring the chaos she was causing for the other pedestrians, and hugged Cameron so tightly he thought he'd stop breathing.

"It's good to see you, Cam-boy."

"It's good to see you too." And it was, he realised. He'd got so caught up believing he could never explain his strange new life to her, he'd almost forgotten how much he liked Amy, how well they got on. These past weeks, he just hadn't allowed himself to miss her.

But now really wasn't the best time for a reunion.

"What are you doing here anyway?" He struggled out of her grasp.

"They do let us out of Cauldlockheart without a pass, you know? I'm doing my Christmas shopping, aren't I? Mum gave me a list, as if I couldn't remember." A huge smile spread across her face. "She gave me fifty quid too."

"And where are you going to spend that, exactly?" With a sinking feeling, he realised he already knew the answer.

"A & B, of course! You should *see* the stuff they've got..."

Cameron hung back. "I'm not sure you want to go in there. I mean—"

"D'you not want me to see the present you're getting me or something?" She scooped up her bags, grabbed his arm and dragged him towards the door. "You'll get it all wrong if I don't help you."

That was the other thing about Amy, thought Cameron. She was unstoppable.

Like a hurricane.

They found themselves in a large atrium that rose up through the centre of the store. Balconies circled above, and arched doorways led off to other departments. Dominating the space was a huge wooden Santa Claus that almost reached the domed roof. He was dressed in dark green robes, and wore a wreath of holly round his head. In his cupped hands he clasped a lantern that sparked and glittered.

"That's one big Santa!" Amy threaded her way past a display of toys to take a closer look. "Imagine sitting on his lap. You'd need a crane. Shouldn't he be wearing red, though?"

"Green is more traditional, I assure you," said a man smoothly. He had slicked-back hair, and wore a neat pinstripe suit. His eyes blinked from behind a pair of horn-rimmed glasses. "Mr Hairtman, store manager, at your service. We're very proud of our festive display. He's been with us every winter since Aulder and Bartie opened. That's nearly one hundred years this Christmas."

"Well, I hope you got him a birthday cake," said Amy straight-faced.

"We'll certainly be celebrating one way or another." Hairtman removed his spectacles and studied Cameron. "And what do you think of our centrepiece?"

"I dunno. He looks kind of sad," said Cameron. He wasn't quite sure why. A woollen beard hid much of Santa's face, and the rest was blank and expressionless.

A tiny twitch of annoyance played around Hairtman's mouth, then quickly vanished. "Perhaps it is you who needs some winter cheer? Here you are – two vouchers. Free ice cream in the café!"

Amy took the tokens smartly. "I *knew* this was going to be a good day!"

"And if I could direct you somewhere...?"

"Food Hall, please. I need a tin of shortbread for my nan."

"Very good. We do magnificent shortbread. Go through the doorway, past the perfumery, up the escalator, past ladies' fashion, turn left, up the escalator, past the lighting department, up the escalator – ah, but I'm sure you'll find your way." He smiled broadly. "Enjoy your visit!"

"Free ice cream," said Cameron scornfully as they headed off. "How old does he think we are?"

"Well, I'll have some even if you don't. I'm not proud." Amy prodded a finger into his ribs. "C'mon. Let's shop."

Half an hour later, after following Hairtman's directions, they still hadn't found the Food Hall. Cameron wasn't sure if they'd missed a turning, or if it was just because Amy kept stopping and getting distracted.

"Don't think I've given up finding out what's going on with you." Amy ran her hand over a T-shirt. "I *know* you. There's stuff you're not telling me."

"I broke my phone," he said truthfully. "It got kind of soaked, and stopped working."

"And 'she' doesn't have one?" Amy paused, midway through clacking hangers. "Grand-ma Ives," she added in a silly drawn-out voice. "Is that *really* what you call her?"

"Yeah, I do and yes, she does." Cameron squirmed. "But she doesn't like strangers, so she'd never let me ask you round."

"She runs a music store, but she doesn't like strangers? How does that work, exactly?"

"It's kinda... exclusive?"

"She sounds like a proper mentalist. And how come she's letting you skive off school?"

193

"She's teaching me at home." It wasn't really a lie; Amy didn't need to know *what* he'd been learning. "She thinks I need more time..."

"You should be with your friends..." Amy sighed and shook her head, as if to clear the thought away. She held up a checked dress. "What d'you think? Too cow girl? Will I try it on?"

Cameron rubbed the back of his neck. He was getting distracted from his quest, and unless he could put Amy off for a bit, he'd have nothing to show for his investigation. "How about I meet you at the café? You'll be ages, and there's something I've got to look for."

"That'd be my present, then?" Amy fixed him with a stare. "Ok. You get one *Get Out of Jail Free* card. But no disappearing!"

He held up his hands. "Would I dare?"

She went off to join the queue for the changing room.

Cameron wasn't sure what he'd do if Amy and Gran ended up in the café at the same time. They'd probably fight like cat and dog – either that, or sit down together and discuss his faults over tea and scones. He wasn't sure which'd be worse...

His head throbbed, and not just with the effort of coming up with a string of lies and half-truths for his old friend. The air was hot and stuffy, and shoppers dawdled round, getting in his way.

Ducking behind a large stack of hatboxes, he found a little nook against the wall. The Humanian shop seemed ordinary enough. If the battery was here, it had to be in the parallel. He tried to concentrate and bring the Edinburgh Parallel tune to mind, but it was difficult to blot out the plinky-plonk version of Christmas songs that played endlessly over the shop's speakers.

He pushed his fingers into his ears *hard*, and tried again.

All around him, the store began to transform. The top of a display stand, just visible from his hiding place, gave a shake and started to stretch upwards. Its central column thickened into a sturdy trunk, its four arms lengthening into branches. As he watched, the little metal nodules that had held the clothes hangers in place swelled up and shed their silver casings, turning into a row of green buds.

Beneath his feet, the thick brown carpet rippled and grew lumpy and irregular, its pile now resembling a tufty blanket of moss.

He peered out from behind the hatboxes into the murky yellow light. Throughout the department, twisted tree-like shapes now stretched from floor to ceiling. Where the clothes had been, swathes of material in dark greens, browns and reds hung like tattered curtains from the branches. The piped music had gone, and in its place he could hear a rustling, creaking sound, like wind blowing through leaves.

He breathed in. There was a definite scent of pine needles.

"Woah..." This was *way* more interesting than some old clothes shop!

He moved to examine the nearest cloth hanging, which was stained a deep cherry red. A pale grey human figure drifted past him, and lightly brushed his hand.

"Sorry," he said automatically – then he did a double take.

The figure wasn't just grey. It was practically transparent! And it wasn't the only one. The forest room was full of them – human-shaped spectres flitting between the trees. They were so faint he hadn't noticed them at first in the dim light. He dodged to the side as another drifted past.

To his surprise, he didn't feel frightened or unnerved. The figures touched and pulled the tattered drapes with their ghostly hands. There was something about their slow caress of the material that reminded him of...

They're like Amy when she's out shopping! But did that mean the ghosts were really... people? From the human world?

Click. Click-click-click. Click. CLUNK!

A ratcheting sound drew his attention. In the ghost-filled forest, it seemed oddly out of place. He scanned for its source.

At the far end of the room, he saw a pair of bowed trees, their branches knitted together into an arched doorway. Grafted on to the centre of this arch was a strange metallic device. As each ghostly figure passed beneath it, a cogwheel clicked round another place.

Cameron counted the ghosts. One – two – three – four – five – *CLUNK!* A glinting needle on the end of a mechanical arm jabbed down, striking the spectre underneath on the back of its neck. For an instant the human ghost twitched and burst into colour, like a butterfly stuck with a pin, and Cameron caught a glimpse of the person it must truly be in Edinburgh Humanian. Then that image faded, and the ghost moved on, even paler than before.

The probe retracted, awaiting its next victim.

The entire process had taken only a second, but Cameron found it horrible to watch. He remembered the life-sucking Makaris. Grandma Ives had been sure they were all dead, but still... If their ancient battery really *was* hidden in this crazy indoor forest, he couldn't help thinking someone had found a way to feed it.

He had to see if he was right. Returning to the hatbox alcove, he shifted back to Edinburgh Humanian. It didn't take long to find the spot where the probe was in the parallel: here in Edinburgh Humanian, it was the doorway to the next department.

Lurking nearby, he kept a close eye on the people that passed through. One, two, three, four... A red-haired old man and his son approached. The son went through first.

That's five... Cameron watched intently. As the man walked through the doorway, his shoulders sagged, and his pace began to slow.

"C'mon, Dad. We've got loads to get yet..." The younger man paused, noticing something was wrong. "What's up?"

"Someone walked over my grave, I think." Cameron saw the father's face had turned a little grey. "Can we go get a cuppa? I'm worn out."

"Again?"

The old man smiled uneasily. "Must be too much shopping."

I was right, thought Cameron. *The door probe is targeting every sixth shopper. It's spiking them – and draining them somehow.* But why, and what could he do about it?

A trio of teenage girls surged past him, chattering happily.

"Just can't leave me alone, can you? I thought we were meeting at the café?" Amy tapped his shoulder, and waved two more or less identical checked dresses at him. "I can't decide which, so I'm gonna get both. I need to pay, then we can get that ice cream."

She stopped, seeing the look on his face. "Come on, I wasn't *that* long."

"It's not that." He glanced up at the doorway. A man fiddling with his mobile wandered through. *The group of girls were three, so he must be number four...*

Panic seized him.

He grabbed Amy's arm. "Amy, hold up—"

Amy shook herself free. "You *are* a loon. The checkout's through there, or do you think I'm just gonna nick this?"

"No. Just put it down and go." Cameron scanned the room. Was there another way out, some way to avoid the probe? How could he make Amy understand?

A woman with stringy blonde hair hurried past.

She's number five...

"Look, there's a fire exit over there. Go out that way."

"Yeah, right. Because shops *love* it when you do that." Amy started again towards the doorway.

Cameron plucked the clothes from her hand and threw them over his shoulder.

"Hey!" She stared at him as if he'd gone mad. "What's up with you?"

He practically danced on the floor with frustration. "You know that thing I haven't been telling you? This is it!" He took her arm again, harder than he meant to.

"Listen to me – I can see things you can't! That doorway isn't safe—"

"Get off, Cameron Duffy!" Amy looked angry and hurt. "God! They always said you were different. I never listened—"

"I'm trying to watch out for you—"

"Just *don't*. You can't drop me for weeks, ignore me then boss me around, and expect me to take it."

"Amy, I—"

"Save it," she snapped. "I know you've gone through some bad stuff. But it's maybe time to come back to the real world, yeah?"

She grabbed the crumpled clothes from where they had landed, and stalked towards the doorway...

That's it – she's definitely going to be sixth! She's going to get caught and drained...

In desperation, Cameron ran up behind her, and gave her a little push. Amy gasped, and stumbled. She turned round and stared at him, a shocked expression on her face.

"I wouldn't put up with that if I were you, love." An older woman turned to Cameron. "You should be ashamed of yourself, shoving lassies about. I've a mind to call security." Her hand went to the back of her neck as she bustled through the doorway, as though she'd been nipped by a tiny insect.

Cameron didn't care. He was just relieved Amy had missed her turn. He looked at his friend, preparing himself for the full force of her anger, but when she spoke, her voice was surprisingly soft. "I think I'll go now. You call me when you get yourself sorted."

"Amy, I—"

She held up a finger. "Not before."

"Amy, I am sorting things out, that's what I'm doing here!" Cameron shouted after her. "Two days more, that's all it's going to take. I'll put it all back like it was, you'll see!"

But Amy did not look back.

19. The Internal Forest

"Girl trouble?" said Morgan.

The werewolf was leaning nonchalantly against a nearby display, picking at his teeth with a fingernail.

Cameron whirled round and glared at him. "Do you have to just *appear* like that?"

"It's a knack, I guess. Told you I'd find you." Morgan sounded a little smug. "What's going on?"

"Amy's a friend. Was a friend, at least. You saw that probe thing above the doorway? I was trying to warn her, but she wouldn't listen."

"She's just human, isn't she? It's not like she understands."

"Amy's plenty smart – she might have. I should go after her..." Cameron hesitated. He knew Amy wouldn't be happy if she caught him following her, not in her current mood. He sighed. "I should've told her about the parallel right away, when I had the chance."

"If she can't see something, she can't see it. You can't make her something she's not." Morgan glanced around. "Come here a minute." He shambled closer and sneaked his balled fist into Cameron's jacket. "There – that thing I promised you."

Cameron peeked inside, checking the missing part of the funnel really *was* in his pocket this time. The bare white bones of the Temperatori's claw glinted back at him.

He opened his mouth to thank Morgan, but the werewolf's eyes narrowed.

"What's with the secret agent act?" Cameron whispered.

"Not an act. I don't want her to see." Morgan jerked his head in the direction of a girl some distance away across the floor. Her raven-black hair was tied in pigtails, and though she looked only a couple of years older than Morgan, she wore dated, frumpy clothes that might have belonged to a much older woman. Her eyes were wide with pleasure as she browsed, as if she was drinking in every detail.

"What's up with her?" Cameron couldn't shake the suspicion he knew her from somewhere. "She seems a bit... strange."

"Hasn't got out much recently. She's just had a new lease of life."

The girl started to stroll towards them.

"We're good now, aren't we?" said Morgan out of the corner of his mouth.

"Yeah, we're good."

"See you about then." Morgan nodded curtly, and started to move off.

"Hey, hang on," said Cameron. "Don't just vanish again!"

"Not a good time, Shorty."

"What about the door-things? I've lost track how many people have gone through."

"It's alright. *She's* protected." Cameron watched the girl wave a careless hand in the air as she neared the doorway. There was a faint crunching sound.

202

The girl glanced back, and smiled a curious half-smile in Cameron's direction. She clicked her fingers smartly.

"I'm gonna have to go." Morgan's angular features were unreadable.

"She snaps her fingers, and you come running?" Cameron was incredulous. This didn't fit with what he knew of the wolf boy at all. "Who is she?"

"Someone I used to do a bit of work for. It was a bad deal though. I'm trying to get out of it... Listen, good luck with the resurrection spell. You're gonna need it."

He loped off in the direction of the dark-haired girl, like a reluctantly obedient dog.

Who is she? Cameron had no time to puzzle over who the girl reminded him of. He had to return to the parallel and continue his mission...

Starting again from his hiding place in the nook, Cameron studied the department.

There was no movement apart from the drifting ghosts, and he was about to set out when a creaking sound drew his attention. A door concealed in the trunk of one of the bigger display-trees was sliding open. Cameron spotted the silhouette of a pair of antlers, and for a moment he wondered if a stag could have found its way into the indoor forest. The antlered head swept from side to side, testing the air, then the animal stepped out into the yellow light.

This creature walked on two legs, not four – and its body was clothed in dark overalls. *It must be a daemon!* Cameron craned his head, trying to get a better look. The daemon moved through the trees with the grace of a dancer. As it neared the doorway the girl had passed beneath, its head nosed upwards. It stretched a three-fingered hand to the mechanism and cuffed it.

Click... Click... F-TONK! A cluster of tiny cogwheels fell to the ground.

A snort of frustration blew from the daemon's nostrils. It produced a small box from its overall pocket and spoke gruffly: "Winter God feed-line down in Department Three. Human spirits flowing freely, life energy untapped. There's been interference."

Cameron's heart thumped. *What's a Winter God?* He shifted in his position behind the stack, anxious not to miss a thing. His shoulder brushed the topmost hatbox, and to his horror it started to slip. He grabbed the striped container by its sides and steadied it, but the daemon's head had already swung in his direction.

Cameron froze, scarcely daring to breath.

For an agonising few seconds, the daemon blinked and snuffled suspiciously – apparently looking straight at him – then the great head swept on.

"No sign of the attacker. I'm going to recce. Out." It returned the box to its pocket, and moved on.

Cameron breathed out, listening to the retreating clop of the creature's hooves. It seemed this daemon had pretty poor eyesight. That meant he had a good chance to follow it – and find this Winter God, and hopefully the battery. He waited a moment to let the daemon gain some distance, then snuck out from his hiding place.

The next department was similar to the first, filled with twisted display-trees, and thronged with ghosts. He entered the forested room cautiously, but to his surprise there was no sign of the stag-daemon. Perhaps it had already moved on?

Another mechanical probe was suspended over the doorway that led on, but here too it looked as if the mysterious girl had worked her magic, for a curl of smoke was drifting up from the mechanism. Cameron was grateful to her, whoever she was. Amy had likely continued this way, so she'd probably been safe.

As he passed under the smoking probe, he found he had a choice of directions. He chose right on a whim, and crept through a glade with a central water feature assembled from basins, pots and pans.

He peered in at a shoal of silvery fish. "Must be the kitchen department," he whispered as they darted away.

Again, there was no trace of the stag creature. It must've gone the other way, or perhaps it had disappeared into a hidden door? Cameron turned the corner – and found himself by a familiar stack of hatboxes.

He stared at them in amazement. He could even see the one he'd knocked out of place. It was definitely the same pile, but how? He hadn't had a chance to double back.

He remembered how he and Amy had got lost on their way to the Food Hall. The parallel version of the store was just as confusing. There was something about this place...

He set off again. This time at the crossroads he picked left, and found himself threading his way through a domed room filled with giant multicoloured flowers, their heads pushed flat to the roof, their roots burrowing into the carpeted floor.

Got to be a florist's... He reached out and stroked a furry leaf, but its edge was surprisingly sharp. He was sucking the blood off his finger as he turned the corner – and found himself in the clothes department again!

"This is totally mad!" he said aloud. The pathways in the store were as tangled as a ball of wool left to a hyperactive kitten. He wondered if Grandma Ives was getting lost too. She hadn't warned him what to expect in the parallel store, but then again, she hardly ever did...

He glanced at the spot where Morgan had met him. The wolf boy didn't rely on his eyes alone – he was always sniffing something out. Perhaps he could take a tip from Morgan? What could his other senses tell him?

He closed his eyes. Everywhere he had been in the forest, he had caught the sound of wind in the trees and the scent of soil and pine needles. But now he could tell there was something else too, just on the edge of his hearing... He tried to focus.

Ebb and flow, rise and fall, the circle must always turn... a voice breathed in his ear.

"What's that?" Cameron's eyes flicked open and he whirled round, but there was nobody there. He forced himself to close his eyes and focus once more.

Winter, summer, ice and snow, sun and rain, cycles round and round again... the voice whispered in his other ear.

Where was the sound coming from? "What do you want? Who are you anyway?"

I am the morning, when you rise and it is still dark.

I am the soft white blanket that comforts and kills.

I am the red of the berry, and the blood, and the robin's chest.

I am cold and I am fever.

I am feast and I am famine.

I am the darkest night before the new dawn.

Cameron shivered, as if an icy breeze had just blown down the back of his neck. "You're Mr Surreal, that's who you are – and you're in my head. I'm not sure I like that." He tried to make himself sound more confident than he felt. "Why should I listen to you?"

There was a distant, deep laugh. *I can lead you through this twisted forest to winter's heart. And there you will find what you seek...*

"You've got the battery?" Hope leapt in Cameron's chest.

Lodestone of life energy, forged by the Makaris, now forced into my hand... I would be free of it...

If the voice had the battery – and it sounded like it did – he had no choice but to follow it, no matter what sort of creepy things it said. And *anything* had to be better than walking round in circles.

"Ok. Where do I go?"

This way... This way... The voice now came from in front of him.

Cameron gritted his teeth, and followed the sound. "I'm listening! Keep talking!"

This way... This way...

He moved carefully down a grand staircase, its banisters twisted round with leaves and holly. "Keep going, whoever you are!"

Soon, soon, come to me soon...

Cameron walked forward, his eyes still closed and his arms outstretched, searching for obstructions. The ground beneath his feet felt different now, no longer the spongy give of mossy carpet. Suddenly, his foot slipped sideways. He struggled, but somehow kept his balance. He took another step... and fell flat on his bum.

His eyes blinked open.

He was back in the central atrium. He'd fallen on a slick of frost that coated the floor, thickening to ice as it approached the Santa figure. Except it wasn't Santa any more... Now it looked like a sleeping giant, with dark brown skin the texture of withered leaves. Tendrils of holly grew all over it. An immense pair of silver manacles bound the creature's wrists, which were in turn chained to the floor.

"No wonder Santa looked sad," Cameron breathed. The giant's cupped hands rested on its knees, and where Santa had cradled a lantern, it held instead an iron cylinder that glowed a fiery orange-red. A cable pulsing with bursts of colour connected to the cylinder's top. "And I'm pretty sure you've got what I've been looking for—"

A wrinkled hand thrust itself in front of Cameron's nose.

"So glad you could join us," said Grandma Ives, offering to help him up.

"Gran! You made it. You didn't get lost!"

"The advantage of going on a quest inside a department store is that it's easy to procure supplies." She dug in her shopping bag and produced a ball of wool. "A traditional defence against labyrinths, but none the less effective."

"I like your footwear." Cameron saw she'd equipped herself with a sturdy pair of hiking boots to guard against the slippy floor. "What else did you get?"

"This unwieldy package is a folding ladder. I had one of the assistants in the Humanian store carry it down for me."

"How did you manage that?"

"I can be quite persuasive when I need to be."

"Yeah, I've noticed." Cameron grinned.

She pursed her lips. "I shall overlook that. Now, if you help me stand this ladder up, I'll stay at the bottom to brace it. You run up and disconnect the cylinder. I've bought a motorised screwdriver too, in case it proves troublesome."

"So if that's the battery," Cameron took a quick glance up at the cylinder as he helped to open the ladder, "does that mean the Makaris are here as well?"

"No, I told you. They're long gone." Grandma Ives shook her head. "The battery's been scavenged by the Cervidae – these stag beings."

"And we're just going to *re-scavenge* it, are we?"

"What was once abandoned cannot truly ever be stolen. Hurry up!"

Together they leant the ladder up against the side of the giant. It didn't quite reach the creature's waist. Cameron was going to have to clamber onto, and then along, its outstretched arms in order to reach the battery.

"Did I ever tell you I'm not great with heights?" He tested his foot on the bottom rung, remembering Heave Awa' House.

"You're going to be fine. Fine and quick."

"Who is Mr Big anyway?"

"Something very old and very powerful. Probably best not disturbed, so go lightly..."

"It's a bit late for that. I'm pretty sure it spoke to me." Cameron closed his eyes for a second, and searched for the mysterious voice, but it had gone silent. "Kept going on about the winter and the cold. What's that about?"

"Now's not the time," she snapped. "Hurry up and get the battery—"

"Unfortunately, that will not be possible." A figure in a smart suit stepped from a shadowy corner of the atrium.

"It's Hairtman, the manager!" The voice was the same, but everything else about the man had changed. Soft brown fur now lined his face, his nose was splayed wide, and his eyes had become large and wet. A magnificent pair of antlers jutted from his forehead; a calculator and a mobile phone dangled on ribbons from their branches. The daemon snuffled suspiciously.

"I recognise you both. You, old dotard, had my staff run ragged answering questions and fetching ladders." Hairtman's stag-like head swung balefully from Grandma Ives to Cameron. "And you, boy-calf. Lost your doe? How was your ice cream?"

"We never got it." Cameron moved quickly to stand by Grandma Ives. She gave him a small smile, as though grateful for his company. "This store's a maze. You need better signs."

"Humans have always got lost in the woods." Hairtman held his furry arms aloft, taking in the surrounding store. "These twisting aisles are our pathways, the displays our shrubs and trees. Only those who belong can see their way safely through it."

"What he's trying to say is that people are *supposed* to get lost here," said Grandma Ives sourly. "Isn't that right?

They're meant to become tired and confused. It lowers their defences, makes them easier to drain."

"Quite so. That is Aulder and Bartie's purpose."

"But why? What do you get out of it?" Cameron was playing for time. He had the missing part of the funnel hidden in his pocket, and the glowing battery was so tantalisingly close... He didn't think he could bear it if they had to leave empty-handed. "You're not like the Makaris, are you? You don't live on people."

"Of course not." Hairtman rolled his dark eyes. "My tribe is strictly vegetarian."

"They don't consume the life energy they steal. They've been pumping it into that thing." Grandma Ives waved a hand at the sleeping giant, crouched in its circle of ice. "A nice way to treat your customers, I must say."

"Come now," said Hairtman. "Only every sixth visitor is subject to the probes, and even then we tax them lightly. Take too much energy and the humans become insensible, and that is bad for business."

Grandma Ives pulled her cardigan straight with a series of brisk, angry gestures. "And what's this frosty lump going to do with all the power you're forcing into it, hmm?"

"Soon he will wake, our Winter God, our lord of the dark and the snow." Hairtman swung his antlered head upwards, gazing at the dark figure that towered above them all. "Nourished by our gifts, he shall chase summer away, and it will be winter always."

"So that's your plan." Grandma Ives looked appalled. "But how will people live in the never-ending cold?"

"I'm not unreasonable. We will hold special sales for them, all stock reduced—"

"People won't go shopping if they're freezing to death!" shouted Cameron.

"You're quite mad," added Grandma Ives.

"Am I?" A more wistful tone crept into Hairtman's voice. "And if in time the humans perish and their cities fall, and the forests spread their green arms around the world again, what should I care? My ancestors made their homes in the forests well. We will do so again."

Grandma Ives tutted. "You? You couldn't live in a proper forest if you tried. You're as soft as a pet rabbit."

"Have a care, Madam." The stag-daemon's hoof reached up to touch his antlers. "A knife long sheathed is still a knife..."

Hairtman's mood was changing, from boastful pride to something more sinister. Cameron shot a warning glance at his gran, but she took no notice.

"Is that what you believe, hmm?" She brandished an angry finger at Hairtman. "It's a long, long time since your tribe left Daemonic for the parallel and Edinburgh Humanian. Look at you, look at this grand department store you've created... Don't you see? You're now utterly part of the world you are hoping to destroy!"

"It's not a store, it's a trap," hissed Hairtman. "An old, old trap whose teeth are about to snap shut." Hairtman opened his mouth wide, and bellowed a great stag-like roar. All round the atrium, lift doors started to ping open. More Cervidae emerged, their hands holding lengths of rope and hide.

Grandma Ives drew herself up to her full height. "Cameron, I believe our day at the shops is over. Time to go." Grabbing her grandson by the shoulder, she executed a swift turn in her hiking boots.

"Seize them!" Hairtman roared, gusts of steam jetting from his nostrils. "Take them to the nearest door probe! Let it drain them completely..."

As one, Cameron and his grandmother ran towards the exit, but the deer-people surged forward, blocking their path.

"I shall not go quietly!" Grandma Ives set her jaw and swung her handbag fiercely.

The Cervidae snorted and ducked, but continued to edge forwards, the circle around the two humans growing tighter by the second...

Desperately, Cameron turned back to the sleeping giant and focussed. "What are you waiting for? Why did you call me here, just to do nothing?"

You must do something for me... whispered the voice in his head.

"Oh, you're back now, are you?" A Cervidae grabbed at Cameron's wrist. He yelled out, and flung the electric screwdriver at it.

"Do *what* exactly?" he shouted to the giant.

"Cameron, now is not the time to commune with seasonal spirits!" There was an edge of panic to Grandma Ives' voice. "I could do with some assistance!"

The totem you carry. The Temperatori's claw. You must touch it to my bonds. Set me free...

Cameron's hand went instantly to his pocket. A shudder of revulsion ran through him – the claw seemed alive, and was scrabbling wildly like a seaside crab dredged from a rock pool. Seizing it by its wrist joint, he

213

drew it from his pocket, just as another Cervidae made a lunge for him. He swiped at it with the wriggling claw. Its dark eyes widened in alarm, and it shied back, giving him the chance he needed. He dashed across the floor towards the giant, slipping and sliding furiously. Out the corner of his eye, he saw Grandma Ives surrounded by a group of Cervidae – her handbag had been torn from her, and they were closing in fast.

"Do something – quick!" he gasped, touching the claw to the huge silver chain. There was a sudden howl of wind as time accelerated. Manacles and chain together dissolved instantly to powder, and fell to the floor in a hail of sparkling sand.

The giant's eyes snapped open, and complete and utter darkness fell upon the store.

20. The Winter God

Cold swept through Cameron, a cold more bitter and terrible than he'd ever felt before. It was still dark... or were his eyes just closed? He rubbed at them, forcing his eyelids apart. Tiny particles of ice came away on his fingertips.

He was standing on a plain by the edge of a forest, the ground thickly blanketed in snow. In front of him, the land rolled downwards to meet an ice-bound loch, and then thrust up to form a vast stony crag. A smoky orange light flared at its top, and he could just make out the shape of a building, a sort of crude wooden fort, caught in the flickering glow.

In his hands, the Temperatori's claw had turned dead and rigid once more. The last thing Cameron remembered was touching it to the giant's chains... *the giant!* He turned round as quickly as he could, each step plunging him knee-deep into the snow.

Against the snow-covered landscape, the giant stood out vividly: as tall as an electricity pylon, his body a rich and muscled brown, shot through with leaves and tendrils of brilliant green holly. The silver manacles were gone, but he still held the glowing battery. As Cameron watched, the giant lifted his arms in a colossal stretch, and let loose an echoing cry that sent the birds shrieking and squawking into the air.

He lowered his vast head and stared at Cameron.

Cameron gulped. He felt like a mouse caught in the gaze of the world's hugest cat. "Wh-where are we? Wh-what happened to the store?" His questions stuttered out through chattering teeth.

"All winters are my domain. For a hundred years, the Cervidae bound me to the present. Now I am free again; we have but taken a step from one winter to another."

Cameron looked again at the outline of the rocky crag and the distant building at its top. *A hill. And some sort of fort...*

He was still in Edinburgh, but many, many years ago! Back before even the familiar stone castle that watched over the city had been built. How long ago was that? Four hundred, five hundred years – perhaps more?

A chill worse than the bitter cold ran through him as he realised what this meant. No one he knew had been born. There was no one he could turn to. Nowhere he could go.

"W-why have you brought me here?" He looked up at the giant. "H-Hairtman said you were s-some sort of god..."

"Do I appear as a god to you?"

The giant's voice was deep and calm, and to Cameron's surprise, he found he wasn't scared, not really. Being stuck centuries from home was terrifying, but the giant himself seemed peaceful.

"You're c-certainly pretty big," he said eventually.

The giant laughed. "I need to be, to carry winter on my back."

"At Aulder and Bartie you were Santa Claus..."

"You still do not know me? Time was, human and daemon alike would celebrate my rise and fall, and that of my sun-kissed brother. Feasting and carnivals would welcome us and the seasons we brought in." The giant's features rippled, rearranging like logs floating upon water. "Who is this Santy Claws?"

"Well... he comes once a year, and brings stuff." *This is so bizarre*, thought Cameron. *I'm explaining Santa to a time-travelling giant.* "You're meant to leave a bit of food for him and his reindeers. My dad used to get me to put out a tot of whisky and some biscuits." He paused. "That was a long time ago. I grew up. And Dad's not here any more..."

"A midwinter offering," the giant sighed. "Perhaps, then, I am not entirely forgotten."

"S-Santa doesn't bring the cold though, presents are more his thing." Cameron stamped his feet, trying to keep his circulation going. "H-Hairtman said you were going to make it winter always..."

"Hairtman and his tribe are forest-daemons gone mad." An eyebrow the size of a small tree-branch rose up the giant's forehead, and a note of anger crept into his rumbling voice. "They've forgotten the circle of birth and death, the true nature of all things. They believed the power they placed in my hand would warp me, make me so strong I could resist my yearly death at the hand of my summer-brother."

"Your brother kills you every year?" said Cameron incredulously.

"And I in turn rise and slay him, yes. It is fitting. I would no more break the cycle than I could swallow the sun."

"And I thought my family was weird." Cameron's face was turning numb. Perhaps the cold was getting to him. "Please. Go on."

"You shattered my chains, but the last of the Cervidae's magic still binds me." The giant turned the palm that bore the cylinder upside down and shook it hard, but the battery held fast. "I cannot cast this object aside, but it is in my power to gift it away, if I can find one to take its burden. Are you that one, Cameron Duffy?"

"Yes, I am." Cameron licked his chapped lips. "It's what I came looking for. Grandma Ives says I've got to have it, so I can get Dad back. It's all a bit... complicated."

"I am an old god, and not familiar with this grimoire ivy you consult." The giant scratched his head, setting the holly that grew over him rustling and crackling. "The only ivy I know creeps and creeps and creeps, and then it kills. Do not trust it."

"*Ives*, not ivy. Grandma Ives." Cameron almost laughed. "She's a person, not a plant, and I do trust her."

"A person may have more than one face, an object more than one aspect." The giant brought his palms together. The battery collapsed between them, closing in on itself like a telescope until it was no bigger than a tin of beans. "I make a gift of the battery to you now, but be warned. It is good for things to die, to lie fallow. It is good for new things to take their place. Winter, summer. Life and death. All must exist in balance."

Cameron's heart was beating fast. The parts of the resurrection spell were so nearly complete. All he could do was focus on the battery. He *knew* it wouldn't be long now till he could see Dad again...

Holding the shrunken cylinder by his fingertips alone, the giant placed it gently in the boy's grasp.

"Thank you," said Cameron. "You don't know what this means."

"It may be you who does not know what it means." The giant shook his head. "But take it, and go with my blessing."

"What will you do now?"

"The winter's solstice is nearly upon us. Dark nights will soon turn once more to aching light, and my reign will end for another year. Winter's wolves shall do their work..."

His voice grew softer as he spoke, and Cameron noticed the giant seemed to be fading. He could just make out the outline of the trees behind him, and the first few flakes of a new snowdrift starting to fall.

"Hold on! What about me?" he shouted. "How do I get back?"

Do you see the fire that burns on top of the hill, in Eideann's camp? The voice echoed in his head once more.

Cameron nodded.

Can you smell its smoke and feel its heat?

"It's too far away..." He stared towards the distant glow. "No, wait – I can!"

The thick smell of smoke was all around him, its grey curtains twisting before his face. Hot air sent tingles juddering through his frozen limbs. He turned in amazement to face the giant, but somewhere in the turn, the world about him changed...

He was back in the store. A hand pushed him hard between the shoulder blades. He staggered and looked round, expecting to come face to face with one of Hairtman's tribe, but instead he saw a fat and angry woman, her face contorted with fear.

"Don't just stand there, move! Can you no hear the fire alarm?"

The regular dull wail of a klaxon filled the air. He'd not only been returned to the Humanian version of Aulder and Bartie, but it seemed the fire had followed him back from ancient times.

"Sorry," he stammered, trying to get out of the fat lady's way. All around him shoppers pushed and stumbled, heading for the exits in a tide of barely concealed panic.

"Gran! Grandma Ives!" Cameron searched desperately for her face among the crowd. Could he hope she'd escaped Hairtman? He had the battery and the claw – he couldn't lose her now...

A flash of bright green eyes and the swirl of a long army trenchcoat grabbed his attention. "Morgan, is that you, mate?"

"Crazy good this, isn't it?" Morgan grinned down at him from a balcony, his teeth glinting in the smoky air.

"It's totally mad! You've got to get out of here!"

"A parting gift, Shorty," Morgan shouted. "You've got to stay away from me from now on..." He vanished into the darkness.

"Keep moving, son!" said a burly guard in uniform. "You're causing an obstruction!"

"You don't understand – I'm looking for my gran. She's old, and needs help—"

"Let's leave the rescue expeditions to the professionals, shall we?" The man took hold of his shoulders, and propelled him kicking, struggling and swearing towards the exit.

Out on the street he wriggled free, and pushed away through the crowd. At last he spotted her – she was resting up against a lamppost. Her mane of silver hair had fallen out of its bun, and her cardigan was torn where Hairtman's lackeys had grabbed it.

"Gran! You're ok! I got the battery!"

She took him in her arms, and hugged him tightly. "Well done, my boy, well done. I knew it! I knew we could do it somehow."

Cameron laughed joyously, pulling himself free. "What happened to old Antler-Head? How did you escape?"

"When the sirens started, Hairtman went berserk. He couldn't decide whether to threaten me, or rush about and save his precious store. I transited back to Edinburgh Humanian in the confusion, and became part of the crowd pushing their way out."

"You'll never believe what happened to me. That Santa-thing in there—"

She raised a finger to her lips. "Explanations later. Let's make haste and away before the police arrive, and start to ask questions..."

They threaded through the dazed horde of people heading out from the centre of town just as the fire engines appeared in a rush of sirens and blue lights. Cameron glanced back at Aulder and Bartie. Flames were blazing from the roof now. They leapt and darted in the night sky, brighter and more gaudy than any Christmas decoration on Princes Street.

How had the fire followed him and allowed them both to escape? He remembered the giant's words, "Winter's wolves shall do their work." *Winter's wolves*... In his mind's eye, he saw Morgan's smile through the smoke.

21. Old Friends

"...fire swept through the store yesterday evening, devastating much of the landmark building just days before Christmas. Hundreds of shoppers were evacuated onto Princes Street, many required treatment for smoke inhalation and minor injuries. The shop manager, Mr Joe Hairtman, along with five staff members whose identities have yet to be released, are still thought to be missing..."

Cameron sat watching breakfast telly, a bowl of cereal on his lap. The jubilant feeling of the night before had faded. What had really happened to Hairtman and his crew? Had they slipped away through the parallel? Or were they caught up in the flames, and burned along with the store?

Forest daemons gone mad, the Winter God had called them. He couldn't help thinking the Cervidae weren't entirely bad, despite the way they'd acted. They'd got so caught up trying to resurrect their forests they'd gone crazy, shut away in their twisted and confusing little world...

He pushed the soggy flakes around his bowl. Cameron understood what it was like to become obsessed with bringing back something – or someone – nearly everyone else insisted was gone. *But I'm not like the Cervidae*, he told himself, *I'm not. I'm not trying to hurt anybody.*

He got up and moved through to the kitchen. Grandma Ives was at the table, examining the daemonic battery. She'd been at it half the night, consulting old books and poking at it with strange tools.

"I thought it might need to be charged, but it seems primed and ready." She took a reading from a dial. "Perhaps our horned friends did us a service keeping it active."

"You know the life energy in there is stolen," he said, remembering the door probes. "Is it really ok for us to use it?"

"We can't give it back. Besides, if you want your father returned, we have no choice."

He was surprised she could remain so calm, seeing how close they'd come to adding to the battery's charge. If the fire hadn't distracted the Cervidae, she'd probably have gone first... Cameron wondered again if Morgan had started the blaze, and if he'd been right to. Was it really the only way out for them all?

"Gran, what do you know about werewolves?"

"They prefer to work by stealth rather than force, but they've plenty of raw muscle to call upon, should they need it. They're not the most sociable of creatures, at least outside the pack. If they do bond, it tends to be with just one other. Rather like Alsatians in that respect." She unclipped a jeweller's eyepiece from her glasses, and looked up. "Why do you ask?"

Cameron shuffled. "I sort of know one. I was starting to think he was a friend, but he keeps *doing* things... I never know if I can trust him."

"Cameron, a person's species won't tell you that. Only your heart and your head can, and even then, they may be misled." She glanced away. "Still, you'd better not risk getting bitten. Human-werewolf hybrids rarely turn out well."

"I guess." He dug in his pocket, and produced the Temperatori's claw. "Here. You'll need this."

"Where did you get that?"

"Found it in my jacket." *That's almost true*, he thought. "It's part of the time funnel. It must have, um, fallen off."

He lifted the hourglass bulbs from the shelf, and wrapped the finger bones around them. The claw snapped shut, grabbing the glass spheres, and the sand began to glow as it had done in the Temperatori's temple. Cameron turned the funnel upside down, and the sparkling grains began their impossibly slow descent.

"Well, that would explain why it seemed to be inert." Grandma Ives glared at him. "Any other misplaced artefacts I should know about? No magical talismans left in your trouser pocket, and accidentally put through the wash?"

"That's it. I'm all out." Cameron grinned sheepishly.

"Just as well you found out before I took it to Mrs Ferguson! The deal might have been scuppered. She'd seize the slightest chance to weasel out—" She broke off, clutching at her chest in a fit of coughing.

"Are you ok?"

"Still a little wheezy. From the smoke, you know."

"Maybe you should stay in. I can go—"

"No!" She spoke so forcefully Cameron was taken aback. She paused, collected herself, and continued in a more reasonable manner. "No time, remember? The spell must be ready by tomorrow night, for the

225

anniversary of the world-split. I shall go to Mrs Ferguson, and return with the conductor. There's no sense in delaying any further." She swept to her feet.

"I'll get on with finding things for the icon, then," offered Cameron. "Then we'll be ready sooner..."

"The icon?"

"You know, you explained it... the icon that represents Dad during the spell."

"Of course! How stupid of me. *The icon*." She clapped her hand to her forehead. "My mind is addled from staring at Makaris texts. Yes, of course."

He looked at her curiously. "And you'll put in a good word for Eve, like you said? You'll see if Mrs Ferguson will release her?"

"Oh yes, yes... the poor little child. Certainly, I will speak to her." She moved to the door.

Cameron watched her go. These were big, important things she was forgetting; not just the icon, but how she'd agreed to stand up for Eve. "Gran, are you sure you're ok?"

"Not really, dear." She turned around, and smiled. "But I'll be right as rain quite soon."

Cameron spent an awkward half hour poking about in his room, looking at the things that were connected to his dad. A scratched and battered wristwatch felt right – Cameron had rarely seen his dad without it – and he had some snapshots too, photos of him and his dad together. *Would they be ok*, he wondered, *or would the magic get confused, and not know who it was meant to target?* He sighed. The trouble was, most of Dad's stuff was still in the house on Scott Street. When he'd come to stay with Grandma Ives, they'd mainly brought things from his old bedroom. He hadn't known where to begin with the rest. But if the spell needed the icon, and the icon represented his dad, it was important to get it right.

He had to go back to Cauldlockheart.

He stuffed his old keys and some money in a pocket, scribbled a note to Grandma Ives, and set off to catch the bus. He meant to get off at Waverley train station, but he stayed on, watching the tenements bump and shudder past as he headed down towards the coast.

It wasn't just the icon that was on his mind. He had decided to go see Morgan too. There was this nagging feeling inside his head that wouldn't settle until he found out what had happened at Aulder and Bartie. He felt guilty every time he remembered the news report, thinking of the people that could've been trapped inside the store. He had to know for certain what Morgan had done.

He slipped into the parallel as he approached the Alhambra, and stepped cautiously into the foyer. Lola the werewolf was sitting on a sagging red velvet chair, painting her nails a glossy black. Cameron felt himself tense. They hadn't exactly parted on the best of terms.

"Go on up if you want to." Lola gave him a careless glance. "I'm not gonna stop you. He's in his room."

Cameron glared. "Why are you being nice all of a sudden?"

"Does a girl need a reason?" she said innocently.

"You do."

"Look, I've spent twenty minutes doing *these*. I'm not going to ruin them chasing you." She held her taloned hands up in front of her face.

He edged past, watching her carefully, then pelted up the stairs.

"Give my love to Morgy," she called after him.

He'd never figure girls out as long as he lived, Cameron thought. Last time she wanted to kill him, now she was more worried about chipping her nail polish.

An angry thud of heavy metal came from the projectionist's room where Morgan had his den. Cameron thumped on the door. The music stopped abruptly, and the door was flung open.

"What?" Morgan's face looked swollen, and his long hair had been cropped savagely close to his skull. A studded collar that might have suited a fierce pit bull was cinched around his neck. "Oh, it's you. Thought I told you to stay clear?"

"Well, I didn't. Surprise!" Cameron waggled his fingers like a magician that had just pulled off a particularly brilliant trick, but Morgan didn't smile. Feeling a little awkward now, he said, "Are you ok? What happened?"

"Felt like a change, didn't I?" Morgan rubbed at the skin beneath his collar, which had turned an angry red. "Come in then, if you've gotta."

The chaos of clothes and CDs Cameron remembered from last time had nearly all vanished; even the hammock had been folded away. A bulging grey rucksack stood on the floor.

"Going somewhere?"

Morgan shrugged. "Maybe. Need to get my head sorted. See if I can get my control back, before I next go wolf."

"You weren't going to tell me?"

"Don't need to, do I?" He balled up a T-shirt, and stuffed it in the bag.

"I thought we were... mates," said Cameron, a little helplessly.

"Yeah, cos I steal your stuff, then you lock me up in your granny's basement. That makes us great mates, doesn't it?" Morgan laughed, a harsh and angry sound. "Look, you *know* what I am. I'm dangerous. You don't know what I might do..."

"Like start a fire in a shop?"

Morgan's eyes flashed at Cameron, and he instantly regretted what he'd said.

The werewolf paused momentarily in his bundling. "Something like that, yeah."

"What made you do it, Morgan? There were loads of people in there, people who have nothing to do with the parallel—"

"Couldn't help it." Morgan's face had taken on a haunted look. "There was this voice in my head – old and frosty. Said I was special, one of winter's wolves. I couldn't *not* do it. You wouldn't understand."

Cameron remembered the way the giant had spoken to him. "You're wrong. I *do* get it. I heard it too. Listen—"

"Not interested. Don't care." The werewolf yanked the drawstrings of his backpack. "Run away, Shorty, before you regret it."

Cameron's face fell. "Fine. I'll go. After tomorrow I might not be hanging round much more anyway. Things'll be different." He moved towards the door. "By the way, mate? Hate to break it to you, but that collar looks stupid. Punk's dead."

"Yeah? Well, so would you be if I hadn't set that fire," Morgan growled. "So don't come to me all goody-goody now."

"Boys, boys, must we bicker?"

The door had opened while they argued, and a woman stood framed in it, a satisfied smile on her face. Cameron recognised her at once; she'd been with Morgan in Aulder and Bartie, casually detonating door probes with a flick of her hand. There was something different about her now, though. She seemed older. She'd smartened up her look too. An elegant red dress flowed down to her knees, and her black hair hung in dark waves around her shoulders.

Cameron felt Morgan's breath at his ear. "Forget what I said. Forget everything, and get away now. You don't want to be near this one. She stinks of death and cobwebs..."

The woman snaked across the room, and cuffed him smartly round the head. "Bad doggie! No!"

Morgan's eyes flared green, and his mouth contorted into a snarl, but he made no attempt to duck or fight back.

"What makes you think you can go around hitting people?" Morgan had been acting strange and aggressive all day, but Cameron still felt a huge debt of gratitude to the werewolf. He pulled himself up to his full height. "Just who are you anyway?"

The woman raised a sculpted eyebrow. "Aren't you going to introduce me to your friend?"

"Mrs Ferguson, this is Cameron," said Morgan sullenly. "Cameron, this is Mrs Ferguson."

Cameron did a double take, and looked again at the young woman. "Nah, it's not. I've met Mrs Ferguson; she's a curtain with attitude." He shook his head. "Trust me, this isn't her."

"Oh, but I am, delicious boy." The woman looked rather pleased with herself. "You met only my old avatar before, that disgusting, worn-out relic. I've finished with it entirely. Don't you like my new body better?"

"It's alright," he said warily. "You'll have a hard job pulling off the sweet old-lady act now, won't you?"

"I have other, more interesting games to play." The woman laughed, and twirled on the spot. "I'm so pleased you appreciate my new look! But then, you always did like Eve, didn't you? I think her body suits me very well indeed!"

22. New Eve

Cameron's jaw dropped. "You can't be her. You can't be," he whispered. "Eve's just a kid."

"Humans are so weak," said the woman dismissively. "The shock of taking her over completely aged her body a good seven years at least. Now, every step I take, every breath I draw only adds to the decay."

"I don't believe it..." Cameron backed away, but even as he spoke he knew it was the truth. Growing up had stretched Eve's face out, creating angles where her features had once been round, but the woman in front of him still had Eve's mocking smile and her upturned nose – she'd even had her hair in pigtails the last time he'd seen her, back in Aulder and Bartie.

"You can't do this!" he shouted. "Give her back! Get out of her body!"

"Careful, mate," warned Morgan. "You don't want to make her angry."

"Leave my vessel? Oh, I don't think so," the woman smirked. "Even if I wanted to, I don't know if she's still in there. My presence can be a little *overwhelming*, shall we say?"

Cameron's mind raced back to Mrs Ferguson's creepy flat. The hidden letter Eve had shown him suggested she was not the first; there had always been a child servant working there. Now he understood what had happened to all those mysterious sad faces in the pictures cluttered round the living room.

"Grandma Ives told me you made your avatars, but she never said how..." He stared at the woman in horror. "You make them from the bodies of the children that work for you, don't you? And when they're old and used up, you just move on into the next."

"Waste not, want not. Where else would I get the raw materials?" The woman laughed, a surprisingly girlish giggle. "Once I take the time funnel from your grandmother, the process shall be fully under my control. There will be no need for me to carefully ration every moment. My avatars will last as long as I choose! I shall be able to wander freely in the Humanian world at last. Who knows what I'll get up to?"

"You're sick," Cameron spat. "You're a monster—"

"No, dear. Just a daemon." She flashed him a glittering smile.

Rage flooded through Cameron. He wanted to hurl himself at this awful creature, to grab her and shake her till she stopped her smirking and taunting, and went back to being the sad little girl he'd once befriended...

His hands fell helplessly to his sides.

He turned to Morgan. "C'mon. Let's get out of here. We don't have to talk to her."

Morgan did not move. Cameron shot him a worried glance. The werewolf had been still and quiet throughout the whole exchange. What was up with him?

"All packed up I see." The woman-who'd-been-Eve cast her eyes over Morgan's newly tidied room. "Were you planning to run out on me, our contract half done? I don't appreciate that at all. Just as well I took measures to bring you to heel."

"What does she mean, Morgan?" said Cameron urgently. "What's going on?"

"I told you before, back at the store. Me and her had a deal."

"You didn't tell me who she was, though! How could you work for her?"

Morgan stared down at his boots. "I've been trying to get out of it."

"Unfortunately for you, that will not be possible." Eve-Ferguson (as Cameron was starting to think of her) rolled back the sleeve of her dress, revealing a coil of wool wrapped around her wrist like a bracelet. She stuck a finger between the strands, and twisted until a loop formed around her fingertip. "Let's have some obedience."

Morgan's face reddened, and his hands leapt to the spiky collar buckled round his neck. Cameron guessed at once that a ring of Mrs Ferguson's wool lay beneath, in much the same way the girl Eve had been controlled. If that was true, there was nothing he could do – only Mrs Ferguson could safely remove it.

He eyed the open door nervously, tensing himself to make a break for it if he had to.

"Don't get any foolish ideas about running." The daemon-woman seemed to have read his mind. "I have only to turn my finger..."

Morgan gave an agonised choking cry.

"...and the dog will do exactly as I say. Can you really outpace a werewolf?"

"No. No, I can't," said Cameron grimly. "But I don't have to. You'll never get the time funnel now; I'll make sure of it. I don't care what it means for me, or for dad, or anyone else. You can't just run around in someone's body, like a new set of clothes! People are worth more than that. *Eve* was worth more than that."

"You don't understand. You are my insurance. Until Ives brings me the funnel, you shall be staying with your Auntie Ferguson." The woman turned to Morgan and issued a command. "Tether your little human friend."

"I'm sorry, mate. I've gotta do this," Morgan spoke in a hoarse whisper. He pulled a belt from his rucksack and bound it roughly round Cameron's wrists. "Just try to hold on, ok?"

Cameron didn't even reply. He felt angry and sad all at once. He wasn't even sure who he should be most furious at, or most frightened for. Was Eve lost forever now that Mrs Ferguson had taken her over completely? Could he rely on Morgan at all? And what was going to happen to him? He couldn't even begin to think what all this might mean for the resurrection spell...

He stumbled down the stairs of the cinema, following in the wake of Eve-Ferguson's billowing red dress. He barely even noticed when the woman paused in the foyer to drop a handful of coins into Lola's lap.

"I did right to summon you, then?" said the girl eagerly.

"You did splendidly," Eve-Ferguson said, and swept out into the street.

Mrs Ferguson's flat seemed to be in the process of redecoration. Most of the little china nick-nacks and ornaments had vanished, and an exploratory corner of the wallpaper had been peeled back, revealing a pattern of roses and thorns beneath.

"I've been hidden away in this little corner so long! I've become as dull and tired as those bodies I used to inhabit. They became old and cautious so quickly. It's time I reached out again." The heavy curtains were drawn across the window, but Eve-Ferguson showed no desire to materialise in daemon form. Her new avatar stalked impatiently round the room, her high-heeled shoes clicking on the wooden boards. "And you, little human... so silent! Perhaps you'd like a drink, a hot chocolate while we wait for your grandmother?"

"Oh, do me a favour." Cameron raised an eyebrow. His hands were still tied and his wrists were starting to itch. "You honestly think I'm going to fall for that?"

"Modern children are so suspicious. It's a wonder I get anything done." She threw herself on the sofa and sprawled pathetically, like a pampered cat denied a bowl of cream. "So what are we to do to pass the time? I do so hate to be bored."

"There's only one thing I want to talk about," Cameron muttered.

"Oh yes?"

"Tell me how long he's been working for you." Cameron jerked his head in the direction of Morgan, who was lurking by the door. The wolf boy stared back at him, his green eyes unreadable in the gloom.

The woman laughed. "Whatever does that matter?"

"It's about trust. You wouldn't understand."

"Very well." Eve-Ferguson gave an elegant shrug. "When your grandmother offered to seek the time funnel in exchange for my conductor, I decided to keep an eye on things. Why pay out if I didn't have to? I simply hired the best tracker I could to go where I could not. If you were successful, his instructions were to intercept and bring the object of power directly to me."

"So you're a cheat as well as a monster," retorted Cameron. "That figures."

The woman's face twisted in anger. She rose swiftly from the sofa, strode across the room and took Cameron's jaw in a vice-like grip.

"You have a silver tongue," she snarled. "Take care I don't have cause to pluck it out and keep it as a souvenir."

He tried to twist free from her cold fingers, but he couldn't push her away.

"*I am a daemon of my word!* If Lady Ives brought the funnel to the barter table and I failed to pay up, then I would be dishonoured. But if I were to seize the object before the exchange could be made, then more fool her. My honour remains intact. Do you understand?"

Cameron made a garbled sound through his pinched mouth, which was the closest he could get to saying yes.

"Good." She released her grip, and returned to the sofa. Cameron waggled his jaw painfully, checking everything still worked.

"Shall we continue?" she said, her composure apparently restored. "The werewolf failed me. First of all he bungled the lift, taking only part of the funnel. Then he had the audacity to return the missing part to you. That's when I decided to teach him a lesson."

Cameron looked at Morgan, at the tight collar, the roughly cropped hair and the bruises on his face. The boy looked away, unwilling to meet his gaze.

"Like I said. You're a monster," Cameron said quietly.

Eve-Ferguson tossed her hair. "He's lucky I didn't muzzle him as well."

From down the passageway, the doorbell chimed.

"I believe that may be your insufferable grandmother." Eve-Ferguson rose and turned to Morgan. "Take the boy to the kitchen and keep him quiet! If you don't it'll be worse for you both."

The L-shaped kitchen was stacked with dirty dishes, their surfaces streaked with red and brown stains. There was no Eve to clear it all away. The alcove where she had kept her few possessions was empty, the tiny camp bed folded up. *She probably wouldn't fit it now anyway*, Cameron thought, and he shuddered. What would it be like to wake up one day and discover you were ten years older? That you'd missed your teenage years, and done all your growing up while you were asleep?

Morgan untied the belt from Cameron's hands, and slung himself into a chair. He picked up a discarded knife, and began to idly pick chunks of mud from the treads of his boots.

Cameron rubbed his wrists and glowered. "Is that it, then?"

"Won't be long now," Morgan muttered, his attention apparently focussed on his task. "Then we can get out of this hell hole. My contract's void once old Ferguson gets her hands on the funnel."

"What did she offer you? It must have been something pretty good."

"Money. Human spending money."

"That's all?"

"*That's all?*" Morgan mimicked. "You try crashing in a mouldy cinema, scavenging clothes and scraps, and nicking CDs from shops. See how you like it. I wanted to live a bit, that's all. That's not wrong, is it?"

"It doesn't matter." Cameron shook his head, now feeling a little guilty. "It's just I thought we were mates, and all the time you were working for her—"

"No, that's not fair!" Morgan thumped the table with the hilt of the knife. "Maybe at the start that's all it was. But you had to go and help me, didn't you? Hid me away when I lost control. You didn't have to do that. I *owed* you because of that. I gave you back the claw, tried to tell *her* I'd never got it in the first place. But she got all snoopy. Moved into her new young body, and started going places. Started following me about, checking up on me. The only way out was to run."

"And that's when I showed up, asking questions," Cameron said. Morgan's strange behaviour the past two days suddenly made sense. "All the time you were trying to tell me to stay away, to get me to go. I didn't listen."

"Yeah. Kind of annoying that." Morgan threw a hardened pellet of mud into the sink, where it clinked into the stack of dirty dishes. "Did you know you could be annoying?"

"Me? I'm perfect." Cameron grinned despite himself.

"Yeah, yeah. Whatever." Morgan finished cleaning his boots and hurled the knife after the mud pellet, a little too hard. A plate shattered nosily, and the werewolf sighed. "Aw, she's gonna have my hide for that."

"Shut up for a bit, will you?" Cameron moved across to the door. From the corridor he could hear the muffled sound of conversation. Eve-Ferguson's amused tones duelled with Grandma Ives' brittle voice.

He could still shout out, call the whole deal off. They couldn't stop him. But what would happen to him and Grandma Ives? Ferguson might force Morgan to go wolf. She might even call up her daemon form in the curtains. He remembered her sharp teeth from the time he'd fed her. He'd never discovered what her full powers really were...

He felt Morgan's hand tight upon his shoulder. "C'mon, Shorty. You and your nan were always gonna give Ferguson what she wanted in the end."

"Maybe." Cameron wriggled, uncertain if Morgan meant to be reassuring, or if this was his warning to keep quiet. "I never knew Eve'd end up as Ferguson's avatar..."

"So we both agreed to things we regretted later, yeah?" said the wolf boy softly.

"Do you reckon Eve's still in there? Can she be brought back?"

"I dunno. Let's worry about us first, eh? Try and get out of here alive."

Cameron turned round and looked at Morgan. His face was pale and serious. "Ok. Good plan."

There was thump from down the hall: the sound of the front door closing. Eve-Ferguson's voice rang out, summoning them back to the living room.

The time funnel stood on a side table, its sand sparkling. Eve-Ferguson examined it with delight. "It's mine at last. Just think of the places I can go, the flesh I can consume, the new prey I can draw into my web. All of Edinburgh Humanian shall be my hunting ground. Nothing can stop me!"

She turned to face Cameron. He shrank away, appalled by the raw hunger in her eyes. She didn't look like Eve at all.

"Now, delicious boy... whatever am I going to do with you?"

23. Out of the Mouths of Daemons...

"So you've got the funnel. Well done. Thanks for sharing." Morgan stepped forward. "That means our deal is over."

He unbuckled the spiked collar from his neck, and threw it to the ground. Beneath it, as Cameron had guessed, ran a loop of Ferguson's wool. Morgan's hands tore at it and it crumbled apart, falling to the ground in a fine dust, its power gone.

"I'm free now." He grinned broadly, exposing his teeth. "Anything you want to do to him, you gotta come through me."

"How touching! The werewolf has found a pet human." Eve-Ferguson's tone was mocking as usual, but she looked a little uncertain. "All these guard-dog heroics are unnecessary. The boy is in no danger from me."

"So I just imagined you threatening to pull my tongue out?" said Cameron sourly. "Nice joke."

"A rouse. I was provoked," she snapped. "Until the conductor is returned to me, I'm bound by my contract with Lady Ives. You are strictly off the menu."

"You mean I could've got away at any time?" Cameron didn't know whether to feel angry or relieved. "And you couldn't stop me?"

"Perhaps," said Eve-Ferguson, her mouth twisted into a mischievous smile. "But you didn't know that, did you?"

A rumbling growl ran through Morgan, and his hands flexed convulsively. Cameron shot him a worried glance. He was starting to behave like he did back at the cinema, when he'd felt the moon's call.

"Get a grip, Morgan. You can't do anything! That's an avatar. If you hurt her, you're really hurting Eve." He gestured to Morgan to follow him, and turned to go.

"Of course," purred the woman, "the delicious irony is you are safer here with me than you will be with Lady Ives..."

Cameron stopped. "And how do you work that one out?"

"Have you never wondered what she wants the conductor for?"

"C'mon. You know she twists everything..." warned Morgan.

Cameron ignored him. "I know fine what it's for! She's going to bring back Dad. You'll have to do better than that."

"Oh no, that's not her plan at all." Eve-Ferguson's smile grew wider. "She doesn't have the skill. It's very, very difficult to return a soul that has left this world. It's much less difficult to extend a life that already exists..."

"Whose life?" said Cameron. "You're not even making sense—"

"How old do you believe your precious grandmother is?"

"Seventy. Eighty maybe. I dunno. I've never asked..."

Eve-Ferguson shook her head. "Much, much older. And yet, for all her cunning, all her dark knowledge, she can't last forever. She needs a fresh dose of human life energy, channelled through the conductor—"

"You're talking nonsense now," said Cameron stubbornly. "The conductor's for Dad."

"That milksop? He was a disappointment to her through and through! Why would she waste time on him?"

Eve-Ferguson laughed, and for the first time Cameron felt the tiniest twinge of uncertainty. All the time he'd been with Grandma Ives, she'd never once said a good word about his dad.

"She might not have liked him," he said quickly. "But she can still do it. She's going to do it for me—"

"Such an innocent! You matter no more to her than your father did," said the daemon-woman maliciously. "It's *your* precious life she wants, dear boy; and she will have it, in order to prolong her own."

The daemon's words stung Cameron as if she'd slapped him hard across the cheek. "No, she wouldn't do that. She couldn't..."

"Ferguson's lying, Cameron," interjected Morgan. "Like she did before. You're so close to getting what you want. She's messing with your head—"

"I know that! I'm not stupid!" Cameron shouted. His heart was beating fast. "All the things Gran's done for me... she couldn't use me like that..."

"Ives may care for you, in her way. But that won't stop her sacrificing you to save herself. Such acts are not without precedent." The avatar paused, as though dredging ancient knowledge from the depths of her daemonic mind. "There was once a mountain tribe with the most amusing little custom. All their chiefs ruled for one year exactly. They were given every courtesy, every luxury. Their merest wish was granted. Their people truly did love them – but at the end of that year, they still slit their ruler's throat." She shrugged elegantly. "The same will happen to you, little King Cameron. Your time in the sun is nearly over."

"I don't know why I'm even listening to this!" Cameron's voice had become an angry whine. Why hadn't he left already? "I don't believe you, I don't!"

"Well, that's your privilege, however wrong you may be." Eve-Ferguson moved over to the table that held the time funnel, and for a moment seemed mesmerised by the fall of the sand. She looked up. "Still here? You may go. I have no claim on either of you – for now."

"That news is full of win," rumbled Morgan. "We're out of here. Now."

Cameron still lingered. He couldn't help himself. He had to know where the daemon's extraordinary story had come from. "How can you *hate* her so much, to say things like that?"

Eve-Ferguson's eyes narrowed. "Ives and I were sisters once, of a sort. And when sisters fight, they fight with tooth and claw. You understand?"

"No. I never had a brother or sister," he muttered. "It was just me and Dad most of the time."

"Then that's one pain you've been spared. But believe this, human. However much I detest Ives, however much it delights me to thwart her plans, I still speak the truth. By the Hill and the Fort and the Shattered Rock, I swear: return to Lady Ives, and she will take your life—"

"This is so *over*," Morgan lunged forward. He shook his head furiously, and the spiky fuzz of his clippered hair wriggled like a nest of worms, lengthening even as Cameron watched. His teeth glinted at the corners of his mouth, and his voice was guttural and savage. "Stop now, or I'll make you stop, whatever that means for the human whose skin you hide under."

Eve-Ferguson's jaw dropped open, almost comically wide. For a moment, it looked as if the woman was utterly astonished by Morgan's threat. She staggered back, and collapsed on the couch, the colour draining from her face.

"Not so tough now, are ya?" jeered Morgan.

Eve-Ferguson didn't reply. Her eyes rolled back eerily in their sockets, and suddenly Cameron was on his guard. "Watch out, Morgan, I've seen this before. Ferguson's not in there any more!"

"Sharp as ever, dear boy," hissed a voice from the curtain. The heavy velvet crumpled and contorted, revealing the daemon's fire-red eyes and drooling mouth. Its face pushed and wriggled its way forward. Eight wiry legs began to rise up and take form.

"You dare to threaten me in my own domain? I see another lesson is in order." Ferguson's mouth opened, and she spat thread from her throat. The dark and sticky strands shot across the room, and wrapped themselves around Morgan's leg, pulling him off balance. The

246

werewolf fell to the ground with a yelp. At once Ferguson began to swallow the thread, each huge gulp jerking the boy closer towards her slavering jaws.

Morgan's fingers scrabbled desperately for purchase.

Cameron ran to him, grabbed his hands and held on. "I've got you!"

"Keep back, human," threatened the daemon, managing to speak despite the slimy strand projecting from her throat. "You may be untouchable for now, but dog-meat I shall have!"

The gloopy strands grew taught, as Morgan kicked and struggled. His feet were in the air now, as he was drawn towards the mouth in the curtains, a living rope in a human versus daemon tug-of-war. Still Cameron held on. Morgan's hands were sweaty, and he could feel them starting to slither from his grasp. He searched around wildly for something he could use. He let go, and Morgan thumped to the floor. The daemon cackled in delight, and with great noisy gulps, began to reel in its prey.

"Mate, don't leave me!" Morgan yelled.

Cameron seized a poker from the hearth.

"Have a bit of faith!" he shouted. He struck down with the poker on the sticky thread, spearing it again and again. "Nice – try – but – dinner's – cancelled!"

The thread splintered, breaking into smaller strands, then at last giving way. The daemon roared in frustration.

Morgan leapt to his feet, and he and Cameron pelted for the door.

"Mark my words, boy," howled the daemon. "Return to Ives and you will die!"

They didn't stop to listen. They ran and ran, leaving far behind them the neatly ordered streets of colonies houses and the hunger of the curtain-daemon.

24. Going Home

Morgan gobbled his chips ravenously. "These are *so* good. There's nothing like nearly getting eaten to give you an appetite..."

They were walking down the Cowgate, a street that snaked through the belly of the city. Tall old buildings rose up on either side, joined together by huge stone bridges that had been turned into streets so long ago that the people who strolled along them rarely noticed they were crossing a valley.

Down in the parallel version of this alley, a bustling market had gathered. Brightly coloured lanterns shone over barrows selling food, and the air was filled with the smells of cooking. A surly, antlered daemon put their chips into a bag, and offered them a choice of oddly coloured sauces and dressings. To Cameron's relief, Morgan plumped for regular vinegar. He wondered vaguely if the stallholder had been part of Hairtman's gang at Aulder and Bartie, but he didn't dare ask.

Morgan pushed the greasy poke towards Cameron, but the boy didn't want any more. "What's up? Not hungry?"

"Nah, not really," said Cameron gloomily. "I'm still trying to figure out if Gran wants to kill me." Saying it aloud made it sound ridiculous, but he couldn't entirely shake Mrs Ferguson's words from his mind.

"Oh, that," said Morgan between mouthfuls. "Think about it. Ferguson had given your nan the conductor, her deal with me was over – she doesn't like being out of the game. She just wants to throw some chaos into the mix, yeah? Ferguson lies, we both know that."

"That's just it," Cameron said. "I'm not sure she does. She plays games, and only tells you what she wants, but I don't think she often lies. Honour and rules are too important to her, in a weird kind of way." An idea struck him. "Can't you tell, with your super-wolfy senses?"

"Sometimes. But not with that avatar. It doesn't move like a proper human, you know? It's a dead thing pretending to be alive." Morgan rubbed a greasy finger across his nose. "Ferguson never warned me I'd end up collared if I disobeyed her..."

"But she didn't say she *wouldn't* do that, either, did she?"

"Um, no," said Morgan, looking doubtful. Logic games weren't really his strong point. "My head hurts. You can't trust her though. That's what I mean."

"It's not just Ferguson," muttered Cameron. "Remember when I told you why I wanted the funnel? You didn't reckon Gran could bring Dad back either."

"Doesn't figure she's gonna kill you instead, does it?" scoffed Morgan. "Talk a tiny wee bit of sense."

Cameron's cheeks coloured. It didn't make him feel good to ask questions like this. It wasn't that he didn't trust his gran. Not exactly. There'd been so many times she hadn't told him everything: about Mrs Ferguson, the Temperatori, Montmorency... But when it came to the really important stuff, he knew she'd been there for him. She'd taken him in when he'd had nobody else left in the world. Why would he take the word of Mrs Ferguson over that?

He thought for a moment. "Werewolves have been around Edinburgh a long time, right?"

"As long as Mother Moon has shone her fat face down," grinned Morgan. "So pack-talk says."

"So what's the word about Grandma Ives? You *must* know she's alright, really. How long do you think she's been about for?"

"The pack knows she trades between worlds, so they're a bit wary of her. They don't like anything that might set humans poking about, finding out about us and the parallel. I reckon she's been around for one or two wolf-lives at least."

"How long's that?"

"I dunno. Plenty of moon-cycles. A while. We're not like your sort, always writing things down, scribbling away." Morgan scrunched up the paper bag, and slung it across the street. "We prefer to *SING!*"

He threw back his head and howled, long and loud, straight from the wolf within. His voice reverberated, echoing along the tunnel-like shape of the Cowgate, and causing several stallholders to drop their ladles or splutter in surprise.

"You mad eejit! What's up with you?" hissed Cameron.

"I'm alive! Alive and fr-ee!" Morgan laughed and whooped, sprinting round the stalls and barrows that littered the street. "That's gotta be worth celebrating!"

His rush of energy was infectious, and Cameron soon raised his own voice in a yell of delight.

"Noisy, noisy wolf-kin!" chided a whiskery old daemon in a tweed coat. Beneath her cowl, her face was pointed like a seal's. "Not the 22nd yet, hmm? So take your noisome howling away!"

"Lighten up, Grandma. Go catch a fish!"

"Nice bit of dog-fish I'll have, skewered with my spiker," said the creature darkly. "You watch out."

"Oooh, scary!" taunted Morgan, and danced away.

"What happens on the 22nd?" said Cameron, trying not to laugh.

"It's world-split night, isn't it? Old fishwife selkie there'll need to be back in Cramond harbour if she doesn't want to get stuck in the wrong skin. Can't you just see it, a seal stranded in the centre of Edinburgh..."

"...barking at the tourists, begging for fish!" sniggered Cameron.

"I'll be a wolf," Morgan added, sounding a little proud. "Not a moon-mad thing, but a full werewolf. You see, everything daemon becomes properly daemon again. Humans become more like themselves too, I s'pose. It's not like the crazy mash-up of the parallel, where you get chips 'n' monsters all at once."

"*For on that night, all things turn to their true nature*," said Cameron, remembering Grandma Ives' words.

"That's right. You got it," said Morgan.

Cameron stopped laughing. In the excitement of their escape from Mrs Ferguson, he'd forgotten how little time they had left. Tomorrow night was December 22 and the deadline for the spell. All the parts had to be collected by then – and he was meant to be building the icon.

Morgan was still full of energy. "Hey, do you wanna risk Kitty's Tavern? They've got some wild drinks there. Or there's a cavern I know that's for the win. Tunes you wouldn't believe—"

"I can't."

"Aww... Why not?"

"I've got somewhere to go, and I'm not looking forward to it."

"Are there gonna be monsters? I'm in the mood for a scrap," said Morgan, swinging round a lamppost.

"Not the Edinburgh Parallel sort," said Cameron. "I've got to go back home, you see. Back to Cauldlockheart."

They shifted back to Edinburgh Humanian, and caught the train from Waverley. Enclosed in the plasticky warmth of the carriage, Cameron watched the darkened outlines of trees and fields slide past. A bored-sounding voice read out a roll call of stations, and the static crackle of the speakers reminded him of something...

The fortune-telling globe... What had it said? *Old hearts shall seek to capture young, to add to their stock of days.* At first he'd reckoned it was a warning about the Temperatori. Then he thought it could be about Eve: the ancient Ferguson-daemon had taken her body and stolen all her childhood. If Ferguson's slippery words were true, it could even be about Grandma Ives, and her plan to take his life—

No. He shook his head hard to clear it. It did him no good to start thinking like this. He *knew* those globe-things were useless.

I'm going to get myself together, find the things for the icon – and get on with the spell. I'm not going to get caught up in one of Mrs Ferguson's twisted games.

He glanced across the table. In the fluorescent lights of the carriage, Morgan looked pasty and a little sick. He flinched when someone bumped into him as the train went round a bend.

"What's up? Too many chips?"

"Nah, they were awesome. It's just the further I get from the city, the harder it is to shift back. I kind of lose the scent of the parallel."

"You didn't have to come." Cameron picked at a dried-out lump of chewing gum welded to the underside of the table. He wanted to leave it alone, but his fingers kept creeping back.

"Course I had to. You got me away from Ferguson. I owe you. Again."

Cameron's face twisted. "You need to stop that 'I owe you' rubbish. If you don't want to help, don't. Get off at the next stop."

"Hey, no need to get touchy," grumbled Morgan. "I want to, alright? It's just I'm not used to being so far away from the parallel, and Daemonic."

"You've never told me what it's like? Daemonic, I mean. I've never been that far."

"Best not. Humans who go there come back dead or mad. Both, sometimes."

"How can you be dead *and* mad?"

"You don't want to find out." Morgan pushed back his hair irritably. It had sprouted during his bout of wolfish anger, and although nowhere near its old length, it now half-covered his eyes. "It's not a good place for people who don't belong there."

Cameron looked away, out into the night. The train was clacking over a bridge, and far below him he could see the lights of ships moving about on the water. "Yeah, I know what that's like."

"Cauldlockheart's not your real home?"

"It's where I grew up. Dad told me we stayed in Edinburgh when I was small, but I don't remember that much. Then we moved, a few years before Mum went. I never really fitted in at school there. That's why I first took up with Amy. She's not from round there either."

"She your girl, then? Amy?"

"Amy's nobody's girl but her own," said Cameron smartly. The chewing-gum pellet came loose from the table with a crack. He peered at it. "Gross. This is so old, it's nearly a rock. A dinosaur must've stuck it there. A gum-chewing tyrannosaurus."

"What's a dinosaur?" said Morgan blankly.

"Seriously? You don't know?"

"No."

Cameron looked at him in surprise. Morgan *seemed* to be human, a boy not much older than he was – but every now and then he was forced to remember Morgan was something completely different. "It's a great big lizard. They lived millions of years ago."

"But you get them on trains sometimes?" Morgan glanced over his shoulder, as if he expected to see one walking down the aisle, pushing a trolley.

"Not often."

"Oh."

Cameron felt the corners of his mouth twitch in response to Morgan's puzzled expression. Despite all that had happened, it felt good to be able to smile a little. "Never mind. We're nearly there."

A stream of commuters stepped from the train, heading for taxis and cars parked by the little station, getting ready to go home.

"C'mon, we'll get the bus." Cameron headed down the station steps. His foot slithered a little as it touched the pavement. It got colder here than it did in the centre of the city. He'd kind of forgotten that.

A line of people had gathered already, their breath puffing out clouds in the night air. At the back of the queue, a burly boy in trackie bottoms and a sweatshirt was stabbing at his mobile and scowling.

Wayne Sneddon. Last time he'd seen him, Sneddon had chucked a footie boot in his direction because Cameron had been daydreaming about music and let some stupid goal in...

"What's up?" said Morgan.

"Nothing. Let's go a different way—"

But Wayne had already seen them. A slow grin spread over his features. "Hey, it's Loony-Tunes Duffy, the boy with the voices in his head. Thought you'd run away."

"Well, I came back, didn't I?"

Wayne glared at Morgan. "Got yourself a boyfriend?"

"No," said Cameron. "He's not even really a boy."

"Huh?" Wayne's eyes narrowed. He noticed Cameron's leather jacket. "Cool top. How's about givin' it me?"

"No, I don't think so."

"You *so* didn't want to say that—"

"Do you want me to take care of this monkey?" Morgan spoke amiably, but the set of his jaw told a different story.

"Guess I'll have to make you hand it over..." Wayne drew back his fist.

Sneddon was a lot *squatter* than he had remembered, like a sort of squashed-up bulldog... Pretty daft-looking when he was angry, really. Cameron felt his confidence growing. "You're not that tough. I've faced worse things than you."

"Yeah, like what?"

"Oh, I dunno. Winter Gods and werewolves. Time-eating bats and talking curtains. Why would you scare me?"

"You've lost it. You've finally gone totally psycho," jeered Wayne, but his voice sounded a little uncertain.

"Try me." Cameron stared him straight in the face. "Do I look like I'm bluffing?"

There was a moment when time seemed to stand still. *That's it*, thought Cameron, *I'm definitely for it now*. Then, miraculously, Sneddon's left eyelid started to twitch.

"You're different," he said suspiciously.

"He's not on his own either," said Morgan. "So think carefully about what you're going to do."

"I've gotta go meet my crew anyway." Sneddon waved his mobile in Cameron's face. "You see you're not about when I get back."

He spat on the ground, then turned and walked away, heading in the direction of the town centre.

"He's scared all the time, him," said Morgan.

"You're kidding." Cameron was still amazed he'd managed to avoid getting thumped.

"I'm not. He stinks of it real bad. Either that or he doesn't wash." Morgan glanced about at the nearby houses and the shivering queue of people. "Why did your dad want to come here anyway?"

"Gran told me once he ran away from the parallel. He wanted out." Cameron sighed, remembering way, way back to the first time he'd ever met his gran, and how his dad refused to let him have the music box. "I don't know if that's exactly true. Maybe he just wanted to take me away from it all. Keep me safe."

"Guess you can't ask him now." Morgan spoke sympathetically, noticing how Cameron's face had turned pinched and haunted-looking.

"No, I can't. Not right now. But maybe tomorrow night I can."

Cameron turned his key in the lock, and pushed the handle. He frowned and tried again, this time pressing a shoulder to the door. With a protesting groan it opened, scattering a slew of letters and copies of the local paper across the floor.

Morgan lifted his nose, scenting the air. "There's been no one here in ages."

"You don't need super-senses to work that one out." Cameron pressed the light switch, but nothing happened.

There was the soft *whuppp* of a lighter being struck, and Morgan held up a flame. "Better?"

"Candles," said Cameron, "under the sink, for power cuts and posh dinners. Not that we had lots of those. Posh dinners, I mean."

After a few minutes rummaging, they had a flotilla of candles standing on various old saucers and plates. Morgan's features seemed angular and wolfish in the flickering light, his green eyes shining like lanterns.

Cameron explained about the icon. "I'll need to do that bit; find some things that were really connected to Dad. But I also thought..."

"Yeah?"

"I can't believe Dad would've sent me to live with Gran if she really was bad." Cameron paused. "But there's loads of things about how he... went... that never made any sense. I just need to make sure he never left me a message or some kind of clue. Maybe you could help look."

They set to work, their candles creating little pools of light as they moved about the gloomy house.

Two hours later, Cameron had a collection. He examined the bits and pieces scattered across the bedspread: Dad's baseball cap, ragged round the seams; a photograph, his face startled but happy, snapped as he got out of the van; a battered orange storybook that he used to read aloud when Cameron was little; a favourite mug in rich dark red, the inside stained from a million cups of tea; the checked shirt he wore when he was slobbing about the house; a few old films he'd loved to watch when he and Cameron were having a lads' night in.

It had been hard to know what to pick. Dad was just Dad. Cameron hoped he'd made the right choices.

He rooted under the bed, searching for a suitcase or bag to put them in. It felt so odd, moving around Dad's old bedroom like a thief. His hand touched the shoulder strap of a rucksack – that'd do. Carefully, one by one, he began to put the objects into the carrier.

A thump, followed by a stifled yelp, broke his concentration.

Morgan appeared at the doorway, rubbing his elbow. "I nearly got squashed by a wardrobe; I took one step towards it, and it half fell over. Knocked me flat."

"Yeah, it does that," said Cameron absently.

"Cheers for the sympathy." Morgan scowled. "What've you got there?"

"*Puss in Boots.*" Cameron closed the little orange book. "Dad used to read it to me all the time. He did daft voices for all the characters. I never knew he'd kept it."

Morgan looked unimpressed. "What do cats need boots for, anyway?"

"It's not important." Cameron shrugged. "I've got the stuff for the icon. That's what matters."

"Did you dig up anything else?"

"Not really. Angry letters. I knew Dad and Gran didn't get on. It doesn't tell me anything I didn't know. What about you?"

"I might've nosed out something. You'd better come see."

Cameron shouldered the rucksack, and followed Morgan to the spare room. It had always been filled with leftover furniture. He used to play in there when he was small, dodging his way round the stacks like he was exploring a jungle.

"In here, really? It's just old junk."

"Yeah, and killer wardrobes."

They were standing on a circle of bare floorboards, an island of free space amongst the clutter. He frowned as his eyes adjusted to the light. "It's tidier than I remember. He must have been clearing up..."

"Maybe that's when he found this." Morgan shone his candle over a shoebox. The inside was stuffed with yellowing newspapers and, nestling in the centre, was a fortune-teller globe.

"Not another one," Cameron moaned. "They're no use at all."

"Proves he went to the parallel once though, doesn't it? Maybe that's why he kept it. Bit of a trophy..."

Cameron examined the prognosticator. The glass was grey and dull, and the wires frayed. "It looks broken."

"The magic field round here is pretty low, but you can sometimes get a 'last message' replay." Morgan fiddled with the wires and there was a rush of static.

"*By the Hill and the Fort and the Shattered Rock, I pronounce: fleet of foot like a fox, your death rushes to embrace you across the sand, until you can run no more, no more, no more...*" The prognosticator's voice faded to a whisper.

"That's it," said Morgan. "There's no more power."

Cameron sat down heavily on a paint-spattered chair, and put his head in his hands. In his mind's eye, he saw Dad moving about the packed room, perhaps more cheerful than usual because he'd finally decided to clear it all out for good. Then he'd found the prognosticator. He probably didn't even remember he owned it, but when he'd touched the glass – maybe even by accident – out it came with that awful message. If Dad had already been scared of the parallel, that must have *terrified* him...

"Gran said he was running from something. She said he was always running. Is this what scared him away?"

Morgan moved over, and hunkered down by the chair. "So what do we do now? It's your call, Shorty."

Cameron rubbed his knuckles in the corner of his eyes. "I'm still never going to know for sure – I'm never going to understand unless I bring him back."

He sighed. "I'm not going back to Gran's tonight. We'll go see Amy. Her mum'll give us a couch to crash on or something. I just need a break from all this."

"Don't you want to stay here? In your own place?" said Morgan gently.

Cameron looked about the room, at the towers of junk and the lopsided wardrobes. An old pair of his dad's work boots still stood by the door, waiting for him to scoop them up and pitch them into the back of his van.

"No, let's go. It's not really home any more, is it?"

25. Samson and Delilah

"Cameron! How nice to see you!" Rachele Giovanni bent and kissed him on the cheek. "You've brought a friend. From your new school in the city?"

"Something like that," said Cameron. He didn't really want to lie to Amy's mum. She'd always been pretty good to him. "This is Morgan."

"Hi," mumbled Morgan.

Amy's mum kissed Morgan's cheek too. "Now we're all friends. Come in, come in."

She waved them through to the front room. Strands of tinsel were looped around the walls, and in the corner by the TV, a Christmas tree winked between red, green and yellow like a set of over-excited traffic lights.

A pang of envy ran through Cameron's chest. It was all so normal.

"Three days off from the hospital they've given me. That's all. Time to wrap presents, unwrap them, cook food, do dishes, then back! What kind of holiday's that?" Rachele filled the kettle. "But you don't want to talk to me, do you? You want my useless daughter."

"A–M–Y!" she bellowed at the ceiling, causing Morgan to blink in surprise.

There was the sound of footsteps on the stairs, and the lounge door opened. "I'm *busy*, Mum. I can't just quit everything because you forgot how to work Sky Plus—"

"Hello, Amy," said Cameron. "Happy Christmas."

Amy's mouth opened and closed a couple of times, then her features rearranged themselves into a slightly forced smile. "Hey, what's up? Thought you were never coming."

The posters in Amy's bedroom had nearly all changed. Over her desk, where there used to be a patchwork of magazine scraps, a vast corkboard now hung, covered in Manga-style cartoons. Powerful warrior women fought elfin boys wielding swords. Lizard creatures roared and skyscrapers fell. In one corner, a huge clockwork robot stomped into a building that looked like their high school, whilst the teachers and pupils screamed and fled. Amy had always been into drawing, but she'd usually kept her scribbles hidden inside folders Cameron was forbidden to browse.

"These are good." Cameron scrabbled around, searching for a free spot to put down three scalding hot cups of coffee. Amy's mum had insisted on giving them snacks. "Really good. Did you do them all?"

"No, it was the magic drawing pixie. Who do you think?" The corners of Amy's mouth relaxed slightly, and Cameron could tell she was secretly pleased. She flipped her laptop open, and with a few expert swipes of her thumb, sent some music thundering through the external speakers. It was one of those girl singers who hammered her piano and hit notes pretty randomly, as far as Cameron could tell, but he recognised Amy's strategy: the music was insulation for her mum's prying ears...

So he wasn't in the clear yet.

She gestured for him and Morgan to perch on the edge of the bed, whilst she commanded the only chair. "So. Still not dead then?" She glared at him from beneath her fringe.

"Um, no. Why would I be?"

"The fire! At Aulder and Bartie, remember?" she hissed. "TV said the manager couldn't be found. No one's sure if he did a runner, if it was all an insurance scam. But I didn't know, did I? You never told me you were safe."

"Sorry." Cameron stared at the knees of his jeans, remembering the angry way they'd parted. "I wasn't sure you wanted to talk to me any more. After what you said."

"If I was really going to stop talking to you cos you acted weird, I'd have stopped a long time ago, wouldn't I?" she said. "Idiot."

"I guess."

"I was just... you know... concerned."

"So we're good, then?" ventured Cameron.

"For now, yeah."

They both grinned at each other, and for a moment it was like things had gone back to how they used to be, before Cameron moved away.

Morgan crunched a crisp.

"So what's the story with him?" She nodded her head in the direction of Morgan. "Chatty, isn't he?"

"He," said Morgan, "is Cameron's mate. What's the story with her?"

"She," retorted Amy, "was Cam's mate since before even that ratty coat of yours was new."

Cameron had the uncomfortable feeling his two friends were not going to like each other. "Guys, guys, just chill – ok? It's been a difficult day." He rubbed his head. He'd come here for a bit of peace and normality, but he wasn't sure he was going to get it.

"Looks like it has. 'You've been hauled backwards through a hedge', as Mum says. Could do with a tidy up." A look of pleasure spread across Amy's face. "Hey, tell you what... new victims!"

She rummaged in the clutter on her desk, and produced a pair of scissors. Blades open, she advanced on Morgan. The boy lurched backwards, spilling his crisps.

"Easy tiger!" she said.

"Relax," said Cameron. "She's not about to stab you. At least I don't think so..."

Amy examined Morgan under the bedside light.

"Well, what do you know? The boy's got cheekbones." She clacked her scissors together briskly. "So, how's about it – you Samson, me Delilah?"

"What's she on about?" said Morgan suspiciously.

"Sheesh, you know nothing! Delilah was a chick in olden times that cut off her warrior boyfriend's hair. All his power was in his locks, so he woke up feeble, like a teeny tiny kitten." She grabbed a hunk of Morgan's tangled hair. "Your strength's not in that 'do', is it?"

"Um, no. That'd be daft."

"Well, you've got nothing to fret about, have you?" She smiled.

Amy set about her work in a blizzard of confident snips. Her haircutting was like her drawings, thought Cameron, all angry fuzzy lines, but they came together and somehow worked.

"Are you back, then? For a visit or properly?" Amy had noticed his rucksack.

"No. Maybe. I dunno," said Cameron awkwardly. Amy had always been the one he'd talked to, but just as before, he was struggling to think of a way to explain his problems.

"What would you do," he said eventually, "if there was something you wanted badly, really badly, and you'd nearly got it. But you had to trust someone, someone who you'd never really entirely figured out, someone who seemed like they were there for you most times, and others... well, they dropped you right in it."

"You're way too cryptic for me, sunshine." Amy gave Cameron an odd look, the meaning of which he couldn't figure out. "I reckon if I wanted this thing so bad, I'd go for it. If you don't ever try, you don't get. I know that."

"Am I done yet?" said Morgan in a bored tone.

"Art takes time, ok? Patience." She fired off another couple of snips. "There, all finished!"

"It's not bad." Morgan scrutinised his reflection in the mirror. She'd crafted his recently sprouted hair into a lopsided cut, high and choppy on one side, long and straggly on the other. "Thanks, um, Delilah."

"No problem. You're a bit less nineties grunge and more you." She sniggered. "Just a wee bit emo."

Later that night, they watched a movie on Amy's laptop, some dumb comedy about a lost car.

Cameron yawned. "I've had it. I really have to get some sleep."

"You can use Rob's old room. I've cleared it with Mum." Amy paused the DVD. "Scruffster gets the couch downstairs."

"Hey, can't we finish the film? I need to know what happens—"

Amy shot a look at Morgan. "Maybe. If you're good. And you don't eat *all* the crisps."

To Cameron's relief, his friends seemed to be getting along a bit better now; they'd been laughing at the same bits in the movie, and sharing a bowl of chips and dips. He gave them a weary smile. "Night guys. Play nice."

Amy's brother had left home a year ago, but her mum still kept his room on. Cameron moved a pile of shirts from the bed, and settled down. The muffled sounds of the movie next door reassured him Amy and Morgan hadn't murdered each other yet. He closed his eyes, and let his attention drift...

His mind kept returning to Mrs Ferguson's warning. He couldn't let himself believe there was any truth to it, but like a swarm of un-swatable flies, her words kept buzzing round his head.

He sighed angrily, and turned over. He tried imagining instead a set of scales, to balance out all the possibilities. On one side, he set the good things he knew about Grandma Ives: the fact she'd taken him in; her pride at his world-shifting talents; the way she'd let him have his first guitar, and encouraged him to help out in her music store... Above and beyond this, there was her promise to bring Dad back, made right at the moment when he was hurting so badly he could scarcely think. It had been a strange and scary offer – but it was also the one thing in the world he knew could stop that pain...

One side of the scales clunked down. Win for Grandma Ives!

What did he have to weigh against all that? In comparison, Mrs Ferguson's story was a flimsy spiderweb of lies. She'd do anything to spoil Grandma Ives' plans; she'd admitted as much to his face. And as for her claiming Gran was older than he'd ever guessed...

A memory flashed into his head – *an old photograph of a family sitting stiffly in formal clothes* – from the mouldy suitcase he'd found squirrelled away in the basement of Scott and Forceworthy. He recalled the face of the girl who'd reminded him of Grandma Ives. Could it really be his gran after all? She'd never wanted to talk about her childhood, always kept her past hidden...

For all her cunning, all her dark knowledge, she can't last forever. It's your precious life she wants, dear boy; and she will have it, to prolong her own: Eve-Ferguson's voice came back again to haunt him. He could see her mocking expression, the cruel set of her mouth...

He tried to lose the image, but he wasn't in Rob's bedroom any longer. He was on the beach now, the shore at Wemyss he'd dreamt about before. He saw his dad's van, its bonnet propped open. A sandy-haired figure whistled tunelessly as he poked about inside.

"This is all because of you. All of it," said Cameron sadly.

The man did not speak. A slight smile played around his lips, as though he'd just puzzled out a problem.

"I don't know what really happened to you. I might never know," said Cameron.

His father looked up. For a moment, his eyes seemed to meet Cameron's.

"Dad? Can you hear me?" Cameron's heart leapt, driven by impossible hope.

His dad's mouth opened, but no words came out. A look of horror ran across his face. Cameron realised his father was actually looking over Cameron's shoulder, into the distance. Cameron whipped round.

He saw a figure in a cloak. The same one he'd seen the first time. It was moving across the sands towards them, darting from shadow to shadow.

Cameron's dad turned and ran towards the sea.

Fleet of foot like a fox, your death rushes to embrace you across the sand... The prognosticator's voice echoed in the night air.

This is it, Cameron thought. The moment the globe's prediction had come true for his dad. Filled with a surge of anger, he confronted the hooded creature that was fast approaching. "Keep back. I won't let you have him!"

He looked around for something to hurl, some weapon to defend himself. Meanwhile, his dad ran on, on into the waves, the water sloshing round his knees as he took great crazy strides.

"Dad, wait!" he shouted. "Don't go that way! There's no way back!"

A sudden spasm of pain – the creature grabbed him by the shoulders, and shook him hard. He fought and fought to get free, his flailing hand clutching at its robes. It gave a shriek of displeasure, and the heavy hood fell back.

Paper-thin white skin was stretched over a distorted skull that seemed part human, part animal. The jaw and nose were grossly extended into a snout, the teeth sharp and savage. All around the head, a halo of fine silver hair stood out crazily. The eyes weren't eyes at all – they were two pitch-black tunnels that seemed to go on forever, leading down into the darkest of all possible pits...

Cameron screamed.

"Hey, hey! Are you ok?"

"Wha—?"

"Wake up, Cameron! Are you alright?"

Morgan was shaking him.

He looked at the werewolf boy in fuzzy confusion. "Bad – bad dream. Was I shouting?"

"Only loud enough to wake the dead." Amy's face was a picture of concern.

He sat up, still shaking slightly from the shock. "Don't say that. It's not funny."

"Oh, Cameron. I'm sorry..."

"Never mind. I'll be fine," Cameron mumbled. "I just need a moment..."

In the white-tiled bathroom he splashed his face, trying to wash away the salt and horror of the beach. *It was only a dream*, he told himself. There was no way he could know if that terrible contorted monster had really driven his dad to run into the sea... No way at all – *unless I bring him back.*

He let the water out of the sink.

On his way back down the corridor, he heard his name. His friends were talking about him. Unable to help himself, he lingered by the door.

Amy was speaking: "Did I say the right thing earlier, when I told him to go for it? He won't talk about it, but I kinda get the feeling you know exactly what's going on..."

A pause, then Morgan's low tones, "Mostly. But it's complicated."

"Are you gonna tell me?"

Another pause. "No."

"Why?" Amy's voice was raised now.

"You can't help."

"You arrogant—" She broke off. Cameron smiled, despite himself. Morgan had a close escape there.

She continued: "Then *you* are gonna have to watch out for him, Morgan. Ok? Whatever this big thing is, if I can't help, then you'd better."

"I would, but..." Morgan sounded awkward. "Tomorrow night's gonna be difficult."

Amy's voice raised again: "*You've got plans?* Something more important? I thought he was your mate."

"It's a family thing. Sort of a tradition, an anniversary. Makes things difficult."

"Like how difficult?"

"Pretty difficult. I don't get a choice."

World-split night will affect Morgan too... He'd be a proper full werewolf. Cameron felt his heart sink. There was no point asking Morgan to come with him; to watch his back and be his wingman that night. He would have to face Grandma Ives and the resurrection spell alone.

He pulled the door open. Amy and Morgan looked startled, but he acted as if he hadn't heard a thing.

"It's ok, guys. You can go back to your movie." He yawned, vastly and deliberately.

"Sure," said Amy, a little uncertainly. "You know where we are, right?"

"Yeah, I know. Have sweet dreams, guys. I'm going to try to."

The next morning, he left a Post-it note stuck to Amy's door:

To M&A,
I've got to go back.
Wish me luck.
Cameron

26. World-split Night

"Cameron, you're safe! I'm so relieved." Grandma Ives rose and held her arms open to embrace him.

He lingered by the door. "Are you?"

"But of course!" She tilted her head, peering at him curiously. "You do know how important you are to me, don't you?"

Important for what? He looked away, unable to meet her gaze. "I suppose."

"Where on earth have you been?"

"Cauldlockheart. By the time I'd got the stuff for the icon, it was too late for the train. I stayed at Amy's." He opened his rucksack and laid on the table the things he'd found. "Do you think these'll work?"

He studied her reaction. She seemed frozen for a moment, then her hand reached forward and touched the baseball cap, and stroked the soft material of his dad's checked shirt.

She cleared her throat. "I wish you'd let me know where you were, but yes, these will do." She went to a drawer and returned with a reel of fine brass wire and a set of clippers. "We have to bind them all together, do you see? We must provide a route for the power to run along."

She looped the wire through the buttonholes of the shirt, then briskly round and round the band of the cap, knitting the objects together into a sort of lumpy mound. "Do you think you might continue? There's something I need to find."

He nodded, taking the tools from her. She returned carrying a silver locket on a chain he'd sometimes seen her wear. She pried at the edges, and the oval container sprang open.

"A finishing touch," she said, her voice breaking slightly. She lifted out a lock of sandy hair. "Your father's, from when he was little. I could never quite part with it..." She placed it on top of the pile.

"Why did you keep that?" Cameron was astonished. "You don't even like him! You've never said a good word about him—"

"I liked him well enough when he was a boy," she said sharply. "What came later... well, there were reasons. Maybe second time round, things will be better." She turned, and walked towards the door.

"Hold on," he cried. "I need to ask you—"

"Yes?"

Are you really very old?

Do you really want Dad back?

Did you really take me in... just to use me?

The words fell apart in his head. He couldn't say them to her. Not now. He *must* believe the resurrection spell would work.

"Nothing," he said.

"I have things to prepare, books to re-read, the artefacts to check. Everything must be perfect if I – if *we* – are to succeed. Finish the icon, Cameron. Finish the icon. It'll all be over soon."

She hurried from the room.

"This has always been a place of power," said Grandma Ives.

They were standing by a tumbledown ruin that rested on an outcrop some distance up Arthur's Seat. On midwinter's night, three days before Christmas, the parkland beneath them was almost empty. Only a couple of dog owners trudged across the frosty grass, cursing every time their pets chose to sniff and linger, rather than walk on.

Grandma Ives wore her Aulder and Bartie hiking boots, along with a grey wool coat and knitted hat. She'd insisted Cameron wrap up too, producing for his benefit a padded jacket, thick sweater and gloves. He'd eyed the new kit dubiously, but he was already glad of its warmth. He rubbed his hands together, and shoved them in his pockets.

"Do you see down there?" Grandma Ives raised her spiked walking stick. "That's the remains of Holyrood Abbey, founded by King David after a mystical encounter with a ferocious stag – or at least that's what he believed it to be."

Cameron saw the hexagon lattice of a great church window, lit up by white floodlights against the night sky. The building behind it had collapsed, leaving the ornate window eerie and empty, like a honeycomb abandoned by the bees.

"Let me guess," he said. "The stag he saw was a daemon, really, a Cervidae."

"One of Hairtman's ancestors? Perhaps. King David and his monks were not the only ones drawn here." The tip of Grandma Ives' stick swung left, covering an elegant mansion nestling beside the abbey. "Holyroodhouse, a seat of royalty ever since James IV decided Edinburgh Castle was too high flown and draughty. And there –" her stick twitched on, pointing to a construction shaped like a row of upturned rowboats, "– the Scottish parliament, where the politicians squawk and flutter like a brood of fox-scared hens. They were going to put it on Calton Hill, but that same old power brought them here eventually."

She puffed her cheeks, and turned on the spot, her climbing stick now gesturing shakily to the hill they were still to climb. "Up, up, above us, by Samson's Ribs and on Dunsapie Crag, the Iron-Age people built their forts. They sensed the energy that lurked here, and knew that height offered safety: an advance warning of enemies on the march. The daemons held a parliament here too once. Those that lost in debate were flung onto the crags for the crows to pick their guts. They had a novel approach to democracy."

"Mitchell and Astredo came here too, didn't they?"

"They did. They found their pressure point here, a locus where the boundary between the worlds was weak. But even their great magic could not fully separate the realms of daemon and human, and in the gap they opened up..."

"...Edinburgh Parallel was formed."

She smiled at him proudly. "You've learnt so much these past months. You've become a most worthy successor."

He stole a glance at his grandmother. "Do you think they did right? Mitchell and Astredo, I mean. Did they make the world any better, splitting off all the magic and daemons?"

"Great people and great daemons can do terrible things. The reverse is also true: terrible people and daemons can do things that are great. Close up, its sometimes hard to tell which is which."

The admiration in her voice was clear, and a chill ran through him that was nothing to do with the wind. "But if people end up getting hurt, that's always bad, isn't it?"

The old woman dug her stick into the rocky soil, and upturned a flat grey stone. They watched a beetle scurry for cover, its shell black and shiny as liquorice. "If you had to kill an insect to save yourself from a deadly bite, would that be wrong?"

"Well, no... maybe not. If it was you or it."

"If a hundred people had to die to save millions more, would that be wrong?"

"I'm – I'm not sure," stuttered Cameron.

"What about one person, just one person being lost, to save another you cared for dearly?"

Her eyes flickered with amusement. "Shall we proceed? We have a fair bit of climbing to do, and I'm not getting any younger."

She turned, pulled her collar high around her neck, and continued the ascent. Cameron followed, listening to the *tap, tap* of her walking stick, searching for grip in the frozen ground.

Whoo-ooooooo-eeee-ooooo!

A strange whistling whine echoed across the hillside. Cameron paused, searching for its source. To his right, the ground dropped off steeply in a slope that ran all the way to the meadow below. To his left, a curtain of craggy rocks marked the distance they had to travel to the next plateau. A flash of white some way down the path caught his eye, but when he glanced again it was gone.

Whoo-oooooooo-eeeeee?

The sound came again, oddly plaintive this time. It sent a shudder down his spine.

"Come along, Cameron. What's the matter?" Grandma Ives had noticed he was lagging behind.

"I thought I heard something. A weird sort of noise..."

"An owl, perhaps, or a fox."

He shook his head. "I'm not sure it was..."

"Whatever it is, it's likely more scared of us than we are of it," she said dismissively. "Daemons may be real, but that doesn't mean we should invent imaginary ones to hinder us. Keep your eyes on the path! This next bit is treacherous."

She set off again, and Cameron reluctantly followed. He had the strangest sensation they were being watched...

They climbed for another twenty minutes until they came to a point within sight of the summit where the ground levelled out. A small loch huddled beneath a lumpy crag, its waters black and frozen. They had travelled so far by the light of the stars, but now Grandma Ives drew a torch from her knapsack and clicked it on. She cast its yellow beam from side to side, muttering and trying to get her bearings.

Cameron picked up a stone, and skimmed it across the surface of the loch. It bounced once, and hit the ice with a crack. A group of birds scattered, rising into the air with a barrage of angry cries.

Whoo-oo-oo-oo-oo-ooo!

Again he heard the strange sound, but this time it seemed almost to be laughing. He whirled round.

"If you've quite finished playing pitch and toss?" snapped Grandma Ives.

"Sorry."

"We need to go round the back of the loch, behind that overhanging rock."

She led the way, leaving the main path and tramping through some thick undergrowth, coming to rest by a v-shaped crevice in the rock. An overgrown holly bush had almost entirely concealed an opening, but even if Grandma Ives had not chosen to stop, Cameron would have known that this was the place.

"This is it, isn't it?" The music he heard whenever he shifted into Edinburgh Parallel had risen unbidden in his head.

"It is. It all began here." She held back the prickly holly with her stick, and they inched their way past, into a small cave. The air was musty, stinking of earth and long-dead campfires. Cameron's boots crunched on a discarded beer can.

"We're not the only people to come here."

"Maybe not. But the first in a while to know its significance." Grandma Ives handed Cameron a bundle of thick candles and a box of matches. "Set these round about and light them, would you?"

He did as he was told, searching for nooks in the walls or flat stones to put them on. As each candle was lit, the inside of the cave revealed itself. The rock walls were a reddish-brown, and the ground mostly even. Its roof was arched like a church, but it was the rear wall that really caught Cameron's attention. A series of large cracks zigzagged out from a single blackened point, about the size of his fist. It was as if the rock had been struck by a colossal hammer, and then frozen at the moment it was about to shatter.

Not knowing quite why, he took off his glove and ran his hand along one of the zigzags. As his fingers traced the jagged course of the rock, the Edinburgh Parallel music sounded again in his mind, a note ringing out for every lump and bump.

"There's a fault line for each member of Mitchell's coven, created when they focussed their magic on the pressure point," said Grandma Ives, watching him.

"By the Hill and the Fort and the Shattered Rock..." He lifted his hand from the fragmented surface.

"What's that?"

"It's what those globes-things say. It just came to me somehow." *Old hearts shall seek to capture young, to add to their stock of days:* that's what it had predicted, in its deep and crackly voice.

"I told you not to listen to them," said Grandma Ives. "No good can come of it."

Ferguson used that phrase as well, when she swore Grandma Ives was going to kill me...

He shivered. "Daemons say it too, sometimes."

"They don't say it lightly, and neither should you."

"Why not? Does it mean something?"

The old woman smiled and shook her head. "You never know who might be listening." She delved into her bag, and took out the magical battery, along with a long, thin shape wrapped in sacking. She picked at a knot, her lips pursed. "Here, Cameron. Be useful. Your hands are more nimble."

The knot finally gave way, and Cameron unrolled the material to reveal something like an iron spear, a little longer than his arm. It was tipped with a sharp arrowhead and at the other end with a flat disc. The entire rod was stained a dark orangey-red, although whether this was due to rust or exposure to some bloody liquid, he couldn't tell.

"This has to be the conductor..." Prickles ran through his fingertips as he lifted it from the cloth.

"Give it to me." Grandma Ives took it eagerly and placed it next to the battery, close to the rock wall.

"The icon next?"

"Yes, yes. The icon. Set it between them."

He opened his rucksack and carefully removed the bundle of objects. A stray gust of wind blew into the cave, catching inside the sleeve of his dad's shirt and making it flap about. For an instant, Cameron imagined he could see his dad's arm, flailing wildly above the waves, searching for someone to grab on to, someone who never came...

He yelped and dropped the icon.

"What's the matter?" hissed Grandma Ives. "Do hurry up!"

He knelt to examine the bundle. His dad's favourite mug had cracked on impact. Beneath the tea stains, he could see dazzlingly white china.

"It's broken. The mug's broken..."

"We've no time to worry about that now."

"Yeah, but will the icon still work?"

"It will have to. Put it in place!"

Numbly, Cameron obeyed. He found a small stone to weigh the shirt down, and placed the icon on the ground.

"We are doing right, aren't we? Bringing him back?" he said in a small voice.

Grandma Ives snorted. "It's too late for indecision, my boy. Far too late."

She plucked the bonnet from her head, and shook out her hair, which fell in a silver curtain to her shoulders. She took off her heavy coat, and dropped it to the floor. Beneath it she wore a long dress in brilliant red, rather different from the blacks, greys and greens Cameron had seen her in before.

"No harm in dressing for the occasion, is there?" she said, noticing his surprise. "Shall we begin?"

Without waiting for a reply, she took the conductor in one hand and the battery in the other, and brought her outstretched arms together. As the conductor and battery neared each other, a deep sonorous hum filled the cave, like the engine of an aircraft slowly gaining pace.

"Even after all this time, they still function together." She gave a smile of satisfaction. "How very ingenious those Makaris were—"

"Never mind joining their fan club," Cameron said. "Just get on with it! Make the spell. Bring him back."

She turned to face the rock wall and began to chant, her voice rising in pitch and speed:

"On this eve,
When old times are close,
And the soul of one world,
Cries out to another,
Let the chasm be open,
Let magic flow freely,
Let daemon and human,
Once more be brother,
Mitchell and Astredo,
Grant the boon that we yearn,
On this moment of moments,
When things to their true nature turn!"

A clap of thunder echoed through the cave, forcing Cameron to cover his ears. Tiny bits of earth and pebbles shook loose from the cave roof, as the ground itself seemed to rumble and vibrate. The rock face in the rear wall began to ripple. At the centre of the fault lines, the dark fist-shaped point started to rotate and open. It swirled round and round like a whirlpool, and began to grow.

Grandma Ives flung her arms wide, and threw her head back in triumph.

27. The True Nature of Things

"I can't look – it hurts." Cameron backed away, and raised his hand to his brow. His eyes throbbed not from light at the centre of the void, but the very lack of it. It had a special sort of blackness, like staring into the opposite of the sun.

"Try to hold on. It's stabilising," cried Grandma Ives. "Not long now!"

The tremble in the ground was subsiding, and the hail of dust and soil from above slowed to a patter.

"The route of magic is open to us at last." She turned to face Cameron. "I have one last lesson for you, if you care to learn it?"

Some instinct made Cameron check behind him, making sure his route to the cave mouth was safe. There was nothing to stop him running...

He licked his dry lips, willing himself to have courage. "Go on, then. Show me."

Grandma Ives brandished the conductor. "As you know, Mrs Ferguson adapted this to use upon her avatar. It opened a two-way channel, so she could place her intellect and life energy inside another's body whenever she chose. But that is not the only way the conductor works. By reuniting it with the battery, we can force it to reset, to return to its original function..."

"Why are you telling me this?" He stared at her. "Tell me how this brings back Dad!"

"Watch." She levelled the conductor's spear tip at the top of the battery, and pushed. A slot clicked open, allowing the battery to slip over the arrowhead and slide down the conductor's shaft to the middle, where it locked in place with a clunk. There was a sudden wild crackle of power, and the humming sound increased.

Grandma Ives swapped her hold, gripping the conductor by the battery at its centre now, like an athlete wielding a javelin. "With the battery located *so*, the flow of life energy is restricted to a single direction. Now it is vitality alone, *pure life-force*, which the conductor transfers to its owner from the... desired... target."

She lowered the conductor so its spearhead pointed directly at him.

It looked even more like a weapon now – aimed right at his chest.

"The icon," he insisted. "What about the icon?"

"What about it, indeed?"

"Don't play games," he shouted. "Show me how it works!"

She shook her head slowly. "What possible use do you think it is?"

He glanced at the icon, that odd little collection of objects. Just a shirt, an old book, a photograph, a watch, a lock of hair... a pile of bits and pieces that had once belonged to someone he loved.

"Don't say that." Cameron's voice caught in his throat. "It's got to work..."

"It *did* work. It kept you believing, for just long enough." Her eyes were grey and cold. "Long enough to bring you here."

Cameron felt as if the ground was falling away from him. He knew for certain where all this was heading now. He wanted to close his eyes, and stuff his fingers in his ears – but that wouldn't stop a thing. "I don't believe it – I won't," he muttered. "Mrs Ferguson *can't* be right. She warned me about you—"

"So you knew." A look of admiration played across Grandma Ives' haughty features. "You knew what this was really all about."

"I didn't want to believe her! I believed in the spell. I believed in you..."

"You knew," she repeated, "but still you came. That was brave. I said you'd have to be brave, back at the start."

"This is crazy," Cameron protested. He couldn't – *he wouldn't* – accept that this was really happening. "Even if all the stuff about Dad coming back – even if everything you told me was just some twisted joke – you still don't need me! The battery is full of life energy from the customers at Aulder and Bartie. You can use that!"

"Don't be foolish," she said calmly. "I'm not a Makaris daemon. I'm human. If I am to live on, I need a transfusion from a single donor. A compatible life, one my body will not reject. Why do you think I chose you?"

Shock slammed through Cameron. His voice became an anguished howl. "Is that all I am – something *compatible*?"

"You are the best donor there could be. And your world-shifting skills are excellent, far superior to your father's. I shall retain those after my transfusion."

So even his training, her delight in showing him another world, had been a lie. Everything he'd enjoyed – everything he thought he'd shared with his gran these past months – she'd always had another motive.

He still could have turned and run, but anger made him stubborn.

"I thought when you took me in it meant something!" he shouted. The truth hit home. "You don't care about me at all! You never did!"

"Not at first," she said. "But the more I got to know you, the harder it became."

He searched her face for some hint of understanding.

"You can't go through with it." He willed her to change her mind. *Say it, Gran. Say it! Pull us back from this moment.*

She smiled sadly. "I would say this is going to hurt me more than it will hurt you—"

In a lightening quick movement she thrust the conductor forward, aiming just below his ribs. The arrowhead speared through his jacket, and cut into his flesh. A shaft of pain shot through him.

He looked down, staring dumbly at the sticky red patch that was spreading across his jacket. "Don't do this. Please don't."

She paid no attention. She jabbed her palm against the flat disc of the conductor. There was a sizzle as it made contact, and she gasped. "We're locked together now. There's no way out until the spell is done."

A multicoloured stream of light began to snake along the conductor, running from him to Grandma Ives. He tried with all his might to pull out the arrowhead, but it was stuck fast inside him, as if it had grown there. There was an awful tugging sensation inside his chest, as though a fist had closed around his heart, and now it was beginning to squeeze and pull...

Like a DVD playing in reverse, images flashed into his mind: *Sneddon glaring at him from the bus stop; Ferguson spitting thread; Lola pruning her nails, pretending not to be interested. Then the Winter God's old and frosty voice, "The only ivy I know creeps and creeps until it kills. Do not trust it."*

Another warning! Just like he'd had from the prognosticator, from Mrs Ferguson... He hadn't paid them any attention. He'd been so focussed on Dad, on bringing him back... Why hadn't he listened?

"You can't do this!" he cried out. "You're my gran. You're family. Families don't try to kill each other!"

"What do you know about families?" she snarled. "Dying is what they do best! Don't you know what it was like before your cosy little twenty-first century life began?"

New images forced their way into Cameron's mind. Faces from the photographs he had found in the suitcase, but these pictures moved and spoke...

Grandma Ives' mother, Euphemia. She would play the piano for hours like a woman possessed...

A brood of sisters and a brother, with whom Grandma Ives loved to squabble and fight...

Grandma Ives as a little girl, walking with her father. "Look at the funny man, Papa! Perched on the branch of the tree, with wings upon his back. The strangest melody came into my head..."

"Not a man, dearest, but a daemon! You have your father's skills, at last." He lifted her into the air, twirling her in his arms...

"We were prosperous, happy and blithe." The light from the conductor was running up her arm, travelling over her entire body, bathing it in colour. "Five years was all it took for disease to claim them all. I had to fight *so hard* to stay alive, to keep going all on my own. Everything I've made for myself in this life I've had to grab by tooth and claw. Why should I give it all up now?"

"But – but how can you?" It was getting hard to force the words from his lips.

"Don't you see?" She spoke pleadingly. "I tried to play the doting grandmother, to bring you gifts, but Malcolm would have none of it. The only thing which kept him from severing the link entirely was the promise you would inherit – my money, my house, my shop – the things I never gave him."

"He – had – to struggle," Cameron gasped. "He – had – to – scrabble and scrape... You made him."

A look of distaste ran across her face. "He was such a disappointment. How could something so lily-livered, so weak ever have sprung from me?"

"You always told me he ran away – away from the parallel." Now Cameron understood the awful truth. "But really, he ran away from you—"

"It was necessary. To bring you to me, I had to be rid of him—"

"No!"

Another jolt ran through Cameron, worse than the pain he felt as the conductor drained his life.

He remembered the creature beneath the cowl in his dreams, with its wild silver hair and terrible features.

"It was you – you on the beach the night he died..."

Her eyes narrowed suspiciously. "How could you have known?"

"But – your *face*," he moaned. "You were a monster! What did you do to your face?"

"What are you talking about? It wasn't my face he ran from." She rubbed her hand over her features. Her skin was thicker now, fresher and pinker than Cameron had ever seen it. "It was the blade in my hand. Can you imagine? A feeble old woman, and he fled into the sea rather than confront me."

More images flashed into Cameron's mind...

A young Grandma Ives was dancing around a great hall lit by elegant candelabra. The man in her arms had blue skin, patterned with crescents and stars. Everyone was envious, for she was the prettiest, the cleverest, the best of them all...

She beamed ecstatically. "Oh, what it shall be to recapture my lost youth! This time there shall be no mistakes, no wasted opportunities."

Cameron swayed giddily on his feet. He was getting weaker by the second, and if it weren't for the conductor tip buried in his midriff he would've fallen.

Grandma Ives looked radiant and youthful, all her wrinkles smoothed away. The colour was returning to her hair, a dark rich brown replacing the grey.

In Cameron's head, his memories raced, faster and faster, further and further back: before he came to Edinburgh, before his dad died, before he'd ever met

Amy... *How many more memories do I have?* Back to when Mum was still about, back before he'd even started school...

Whooo-oooo-eee!

By the mouth of the cave, Cameron saw a sudden flash. The holly bush shook wildly...

A huge white wolf tore in, his green eyes flaring brightly, a growl echoing round the confined space.

"Morgan..." croaked Cameron. Was this another vision, something plucked from his mind as his grandmother stole his life? "Help me!"

The wolf leapt forward, throwing himself at Grandma Ives. Instantly, he bounced back with a whimper and hit the ground, as if he had struck an invisible wall.

Grandma Ives laughed. "Foolish dog – the tools of the Makaris protect their operator! While the magic works, I am invincible!"

Morgan threw back his head, and howled. He surged forward again, and once more was flung back, his furred body slamming hard into the rock walls.

"Everything you have is mine now, Cameron," Grandma Ives gloated. "All of it, all of it is mine! I shall live on!"

Everything. Everything. EVERYTHING!

Her cry of triumph sparked a desperate idea. With almost his last breath of life: a solution. *Everything* he had was being taken and given to her...

What will happen to her if I'm bitten by a werewolf?

Would the bite pass straight on to her?

What would happen to him?

He had no time to think—

"No, Morgan, not her! Bite me, *bite me!*" he gasped.

For just a second, the wolf hesitated. Then, darting past the cackling figure of Grandma Ives, he leapt. His paws thudded onto Cameron's chest, and his teeth sank deep into the boy's shoulder. Cameron barely even felt them break the skin...

Then...

New life flooded into his body. His limbs zinged with potential, like a wound-up spring; if he could run, he would run forever...

New information charged into his brain: the smell of the grass, the stories of the wind and the call of the moon...

The world he had known all his life was just a pale shadow of the *real* world, which danced and leapt and sang in the scent-realm of the wolf.

Cameron felt *marvellous...* and *hungry...*

His eyes met Morgan's, and Cameron knew he understood.

In front of him, Morgan's wolf-shape was rippling and shifting. The paws pressed firm to Cameron's chest were now more like thick white-furred arms, tipped with strong, clawed hands.

A new strand of brilliant white light entered the stream travelling along the conductor. Grandma Ives shouted out in rage, and tried to pull her palm from the disc, but it was stuck fast.

"No! What have you done?"

"No way out, Gran, remember?" Cameron's voice sounded deeper and more powerful than he'd ever heard it before. "No way out!"

Morgan's jaws snapped open, releasing their grip on Cameron's shoulder. His dog-like muzzle was struggling to form words. "I'll – get – her. Tear – her – apart!"

Cameron's eyes shot to his grandmother. The white wolf-light had run the length of the conductor and was snaking all over her body, dancing about like lightning.

"You could've saved Dad," he snarled. "Instead you did this! You made it happen!"

"Stupid boy – have you still not realised?" Grandma Ives gave a terrible coughing laugh. "Mortal death is a door. Once it closes behind someone, there's no way back. No matter how you strike, no matter how you beg..."

Her free hand clawed at her chest. Just as Morgan had become less wolfish, now she was becoming more so. Her features distorted with a snapping, popping sound, her face stretching into a new and terrible shape. Her jaw elongated, just as her nose cracked and surged forward, twisting together into a crude version of a snout. Her hair bleached to silver and zigzagged crazily around her skull. Long yellow teeth shot out from her upper lip, and her ears crawled up the side of her head, growing into points.

She screamed, and the sound was more animal than human.

"*Good* – for – things – to – *die*," Morgan growled, the fur on his head furrowed into deep ridges. "*Bad* things. Like Ferguson. Like *her*." He shook himself furiously, and became entirely wolf again. His heavy paws left Cameron's chest, and he leapt away to prowl round and round the cave, his eyes blazing green and angry.

The deep humming sound of the conductor was slowing, and the tugging sensation in Cameron's chest felt at last like it was letting go. He stared at the monstrous old wolf woman, still locked to him by magic. The life-force she had stolen had been entirely overwhelmed by the werewolf's bite.

On the cave wall, the dark vortex started to swirl and close... Then, with a final crackle, the conductor shut off and clattered to the ground.

Cameron gasped and pawed at his front, but the wound had sealed over instantly, forming a huge and angry welt. With the wolf power transferred on to Grandma Ives, his own remaining energy was fading fast, and he felt pitifully weak.

"If – I – am – wolf," snarled a guttural voice. "Then – as – wolf – I – will – devour!"

The creature that had been Grandma Ives hurled towards him. With no time to draw breath, he shot backwards as fast as he was still able, blindly thumping his head *hard* on the rocky cave wall. Red light flared across his vision, and he slid in a daze to the ground.

In the same instant, Morgan leapt forward. The two colossal beasts – one white wolf, the other a hideous mix of human and animal together – met each other in mid-bound.

Cameron's eyelids flickered closed...

He forced them open, but his head reeled and ached and he was losing the battle to stay conscious. Images of Morgan and Grandma's fight flashed before him:

Morgan on the ground, swiped hard by Grandma Ives' long white talons...

Grandma Ives pouncing, her yellow teeth above Morgan's neck...

Morgan twisting, and rolling out from under her. His huge wolf head lowered, as he charged forward...

Grandma Ives falling, tumbling backwards into the pitch-black vortex. Morgan's muzzle wide in a triumphant leer...

Claws grabbing Morgan's fur, pulling him backwards too. His rear paws scrabbling valiantly on the ground of the cave, digging in the dirt, trying to find purchase. The ever-shrinking vortex dragging him in as well—

"No! *Morgan!*"

With a last, desperate burst of consciousness, Cameron half-lurched, half-fell forward. His hands seized on the white brush of Morgan's tail. Morgan yowled, a cry of pain and terror, but Cameron held on – like he was never, ever going to let go.

His eyes started to close once more. The last thing he saw was the creature that had been his gran tumbling helplessly into the void, spinning round and round like a rag hurled into a washing machine, and the rock wall swirling shut.

Then the darkness finally took him.

28. Curtain Call

Morning came, bathing Arthur's Seat in a reddish glow. The light snuck around the leaves of the holly bush, and played upon the face of a boy sleeping on the cave floor.

Cameron's eyes blinked open. He took in the fuzzy outline of a figure, standing by the cave mouth. It seemed to be wearing his dad's checked shirt and cap...

He sat up too quickly, and groaned. A dull pain nagged him from his shoulder, the back of his head throbbed like mad, and his entire body felt as if it had been hit with a hundred tiny hammers.

The figure turned to him. "You're awake, then."

"Morgan..."

"Who else?" The werewolf had returned to human form with the dawn. "My proper gear's stashed in a tree trunk. It's crazy cold though, so I borrowed these. D'you mind?"

Cameron hesitated, just for a second. "No, it's alright. It's not like he needs them any more."

"Cheers." Morgan looked awkward. "Hey. Sorry about your dad, Shorty."

"It's ok. Really." Cameron paused. "I lost him ages ago. I just didn't want to admit it." His words took him by surprise, but he realised they were true. All this time he'd spent running around, rather than just dealing with it...

"I still miss him though. I'm definitely always going to miss him."

Morgan moved over, and sat beside him, his back propped on the damp cave wall.

"There's something the pack says: 'You howl for the things you need, and you howl for the things you can't have.'"

Cameron shot a glance at Morgan. "Is that what I've been doing, then? Howling?"

"Maybe. Thing is, sometimes you can't tell what sort of howl it's gonna be. Not till you've let it out." Morgan scratched his head. His hair had snaked back to its old length; all Amy's careful snips and cuts were gone.

"What happened to Gran?" Cameron started to say. "Oh yeah, I remember..."

"It's what she deserved," Morgan said darkly. In the pale morning light, Cameron could see the wolf boy was bruised all over from his epic fight.

He thought of the slavering beast his gran had become. The elegant old lady he'd thought he'd known was entirely gone.

"In the end she was just like – like the monster in my dream." He stared at the dark, fist-shaped point at the rear of the cave, and the fault lines that zigzagged out of it. "How is that even possible?"

"You've got the Edinburgh Parallel inheritance running through you, Shorty – that whole mad mixed-up gap between Humanian and Daemonic. All sorts of things fall into it – some of 'em drift out as well. Maybe it was a warning..."

"Yeah, well. Next time, I want a text. Something helpful and easy to understand." He shook his head. "What am I saying? Like there's going to *be* a next time... Dad, Mum – Gran even – they're all gone now. There's no one left but me."

A hand biffed him, gently but firmly on the shoulder.

"Ow! What d'you do that for?"

"If you're so alone – who did that?"

"Very funny." Cameron grimaced as his shoulder throbbed again. The bite from the werewolf's jaws was still very fresh...

"Do you think I'm going to end up going like... *her*?" he asked in a small voice.

"Take off your coat. Lemme see."

Gingerly, Cameron removed the jacket. "What do you reckon?"

"Tricky." Morgan sniffed. "The wolf is in the blood. You're born a wolf, or you bite someone and, if they live, the blood takes hold. That's how it goes, usually. But you passed it straight on, no blood involved. I don't think anyone's ever done that before."

"Do you reckon it's all gone?"

"Probably," said Morgan, after a moment's thought.

"Are you lying to me?"

"Would I?" Morgan grinned. "Truth is, I don't know."

Cameron felt a strange mixture of fear and excitement. For the few brief moments the werewolf had been part of him, he'd felt *great* – but he also remembered what Grandma Ives had turned into. "Bitten humans don't turn out right. You said they never learn to control it."

"What do I know? Maybe they never had the right teacher," said Morgan. "I'm going to have to re-learn my control for moon changes too. Maybe we can learn together."

"How long till the next moon?"

Morgan whistled. "Good while yet. Over three weeks."

Nearly a month to wait till I find out what I'll be...

"We'll deal with it when it happens – if it happens." Morgan spoke reassuringly. "The important thing is how do you feel? Right here and now?"

"Every bit of me hurts, but more than that..." Cameron's stomach rumbled. "I'm absolutely starving."

Morgan laughed. "Yeah, me too. Let's go eat."

"Hold on a bit..."

"What? C'mon..."

"You do know you've totally got no trousers on, right?"

They gathered their stuff together and made their way down the hill, heading for the hollow tree where Morgan had left his proper clothes. The werewolf had Grandma Ives' long wool coat slung around his shoulders. His bare feet and legs looked odd sticking out the bottom, but Morgan didn't seem to care about the stony ground beneath his soles.

"So what are you gonna do now?"

"I don't know." Cameron stared at the city spread out beneath them. Some street lamps were still glowing, lighting up the winter morning, and there was the distant thrum of traffic as people hurried about their business. "Go back to Gran's place or her shop, I guess. It's going to take a lot of sorting out, but I reckon they must be mine now."

Morgan paused mid-stride. "Seriously?"

"Seriously. If Dad and Gran are both gone, who else is there?"

"You've still got the battery and the conductor." Morgan tapped his rucksack. They'd found both parts lying separately on the floor. "The only ones left in the worlds, I reckon. There's plenty daemons would pay big time for those." He stopped when he saw the look on Cameron's face. "Ok, maybe not. We can bury them in the basement, or throw them in a loch. As long as that old *bizzum* Ferguson doesn't get them, I don't really care."

"Maybe she should, though," said Cameron quietly.

"You what?" Morgan nudged him hard. "I'm not helping that crazy Weaver again as long as I live—"

"Easy! Still recovering here, you know?" Cameron moved out of Morgan's reach. "It's Eve I'm thinking about. Ferguson's still living in her body, and the time funnel means she can stay there as long as she wants. I think we should do something."

Morgan's face was grim. "Ferguson hollowed out Eve's head, and took up squatters' rights. You've gotta face it, mate. Eve's gone."

"No, no, I don't think so." Cameron shook his head. An idea was beginning to stir... "The first time I met her, Ferguson took over Eve, just for a moment; to try and trick me. When she was done, Eve was Eve again."

He'd seen the conductor work. More than that, he knew about its power firsthand: the victim was helpless to remove it, while the recipient of the energy was protected. If only he could make that knowledge work for him...

"I'm going back to Mrs Ferguson's, even if you won't."

"Don't you want to keep your head down for a bit, not go sticking it where it's gonna get bitten off?" Morgan looked uneasy.

"I can't – because I'm not going to run away," said Cameron fiercely. "I'm not going to ignore other people hurting. That'd make me like Gran – and I'm not going to be like that. All these weeks I spent risking everything to find the funnel and then the battery. Something good's got to come out of it."

"Ok, ok. I reckon you're mad, but I'll go with you," grumbled Morgan. He held up a warning hand. "But we'd *so* better get breakfast first."

If Eve-Ferguson was surprised to see Cameron, she didn't let it show. She opened the door of her little flat, and spoke smoothly. "Do come in. And where is your little doggy friend today?"

"He's busy."

"Such a pity," said Eve-Ferguson with a flicker of amusement. "Give him my regards, won't you? Tell him I haven't forgotten him."

They walked through to the living room. Cameron's heart was thumping. It was insanely daftly dangerous to face up to Ferguson in her den, but he knew he had to try. He'd spent all day thinking over everything he'd ever learnt about Ferguson and all her strange quirks; the way she liked to act out roles, play games and make deals. He'd put it all together, and made a plan.

He was going to have to play this very carefully...

"Now, what can I do for you?" Eve-Ferguson arranged herself on the sofa. "As you can see, the time funnel is working splendidly. I've been using this body continuously, and it hasn't aged a second. Not a wrinkle, not the slightest white hair. Don't I look divine?"

"Yeah, you look great," said Cameron, as earnestly as he could. "Brilliant, in fact. Why would you ever want to go back to your gross old daemon form now?"

Eve-Ferguson paused. "Naturally, here in Edinburgh Humanian, this shape is the most convenient. And how is your grandmother this fine day?"

"Dead," said Cameron bluntly. "Or vanished. I don't care which."

"Really," purred Eve-Ferguson, "this is most gratifying! My advice was useful, then?"

"Very useful," he said, fighting to keep the bitterness out of his voice. "I'm grateful you helped me see Gran for what she really was." He delved in his coat, and drew out the conductor. Eve-Ferguson's eyes flashed greedily.

"So I'm returning this to you, as agreed. I'll give it back, then you and me are finished. You stay away from me, and I stay away from you, ok?"

"As you like. My, things really are going my way!" She pressed a button on a remote control, and some strident operatic tones boomed out of a concealed speaker. She stood up and started to sway gracefully to the music. "I have the conductor, I have the funnel, I have my smart new avatar... Would you care for a dance?"

"Do you know, I think you're turning human?" mused Cameron. "You think you're so powerful, and so clever.

But you're just the same as us. You've hidden out so long, you've forgotten what you really are."

"I assure you, I have not," the avatar said icily.

"Prove it."

"Excuse me?"

"Show me your true face." He swallowed hard. *This part is so important. I have to get it right...* "Or don't you remember how?"

"I'm not sure you cared for it much when you saw it last."

"That's an excuse," he goaded. "I'm guessing that means you can't. You've lost the knack."

"Now you're being vexing." Eve-Ferguson glared. "Body transference is not a parlour game. I'm perfectly comfortable as I am."

"Oh well." Cameron stood up and tucked the conductor back into his jacket. "Then I'll just take this home with me—"

"That wouldn't be wise," said Eve-Ferguson quickly. "In fact, I believe I would be forced to do something very unpleasant..."

Cameron thought quickly. *I have to say just the right thing to nudge her in the right direction.* "You tried to trick me like that before. You can't harm me though, can you? Gran saw to that with her contract."

"Faulty logic," she hissed. "With the death of your tiresome grandmother, the contract is null and void."

"Ah," said Cameron triumphantly, "if the contract is broken, then, I don't owe you a thing. I don't *have* to return the conductor. I can keep it myself." He turned and headed for the door. "Two can play that game."

Eve-Ferguson leapt to her feet. "GIVE ME THAT!"

"Why do you need it, anyway?" Cameron tossed the conductor from hand to hand, taunting the enraged avatar. "I reckon you're settled in that body for life."

"It's a daemon's right to change her mind," insisted Eve-Ferguson. "I'll grow tired of Eve eventually, and then I'll take someone else—" She lunged forward, trying to snatch at the conductor, but Cameron danced away.

"Ha ha! Too slow!"

The avatar tried again, but Cameron dodged round the back of sofa. Every time she grabbed for the iron bar, he darted the opposite way.

"Not pulling the strings of your puppet fast enough, are you?" he crowed. "I can keep this up all day..."

"This is a needless waste of energy." Eve-Ferguson stopped and smoothed her hair with an irritable flick of her hand. "If I materialise, you swear you'll give me the conductor?"

"I promise I will let you have it," he said, choosing his words very carefully.

"Then we have a deal. Much good that it will do you! I think I shall shortly be very hungry..." She sat down on the sofa, crossed her arms in a pointed fashion, and allowed her eyes to roll back.

Over by the curtain, the material began to contort, and the face of the daemon started to form. "This is what you wanted, is it, boy?"

"Just what I wanted." He mentally crossed his fingers. *The plan has to work!*

"You will give me the conductor now?" the daemon rasped eagerly.

"Oh yes," he said. Then he shouted, "Now, Morgan, now!"

There was a terrific crash of cracking glass. Ferguson's crooked features barely had time to register surprise as the window behind her shattered into a thousand pieces. Morgan barrelled through, his long army coat wrapped protectively round his face. Ferguson's curtain ripped from its rails as he charged in, and fell to the ground in a heap.

"How dare you!" Ferguson screamed. "I shall take such vengeance..."

All round her head-body, legs began to sprout as her spidery shape struggled to pull itself free from the material.

"Grab it, Morgan, quickly! Bring it over here!"

Morgan snatched and bundled the curtain, and dragged it over to the sofa.

"What are you doing?" Four of Ferguson's legs were free now, waving and wriggling in the air. Cameron ducked as she spat thread from her throat. It shot over his shoulder, and coated a light fitting in sticky streamers.

"Not so fast!" He could only guess at where the bizarre creature's vital organs were... Gritting his teeth, he stabbed down with the conductor, piercing into the underbelly of its head-body. Ferguson shrieked furiously. In the same instant, Morgan seized Eve's palm and pressed it to the other end of the conductor. He held it in place as her body flopped lifelessly from the sofa. Multicoloured light began to race along the rod.

"What are you doing? You just wait!"

Morgan eyed the daemon fearfully.

"Don't worry, she's stuck in place till the magic is over," gasped Cameron. "Come on – come on – come on! Work! Transfer her out! Bring back Eve!"

On the floor, Eve's body began to tremble and shake like she was having a fit. Her eyes rolled in their sockets, and froth formed at her mouth.

"Get ready," prompted Cameron.

Morgan nodded. "I am."

Eve gave one last ferocious jerk, and the light stream began to slow.

"So, take my avatar from me, would you? Confine me to this one body. I'll show you what I can do..." roared the daemon.

"Now!"

In one smooth movement, Morgan pulled his lighter from a pocket, flicked it to conjure a flame, and held it to the corner of the curtain. The thick material caught easily, and the fire swiftly spread.

Ferguson howled. "No, you can't! Have pity!"

"Like you had for all those kids whose lives you stole?" said Cameron.

"They were just toys."

"No. They were real people."

The flames licked over Ferguson's spidery body. Her legs kicked and flailed, then slowly fell limp. With a last gurgle, the face collapsed back into the burning material, and vanished.

"I'm sorry. But someone had to stop you." Disgusted, Cameron turned away.

Morgan swept a blanket from a nearby armchair, shook it open and dropped it over the flaming curtain. He started to beat out the fire with great heavy stomps, a grim half-smile playing round his angular features.

Cameron knelt down by Eve. Her face was as pale and empty as if she was a fine china doll. There wasn't even a whisper of breath from her lips.

"Come on, can't one good thing happen? Come back to us!"

"Cameron, mate, she's too far gone," said Morgan gently. "Ferguson didn't leave anything of her."

Cameron studied the girl for any tiny hint of life. He felt so helpless and stupid; he had no idea what to do. *Idiot boy*... That's what Eve had called him, back when they'd first met...

The thread...

"No, wait – I *am* an idiot!" Cameron shouted, causing Morgan to jump.

He frantically lifted aside her collar. The thread was still there, looped around her neck, but horribly blackened. It must still be linked to Ferguson somehow. Dare he remove it? She still wasn't breathing – he had no choice. He snatched at it, and it dissolved into powdery strands. As the last fragment fell from her, Eve gave a long rattling gasp. Her eyes opened blearily, and she looked up at Cameron.

"Idiot boy," she murmured. "What are you doing here? Why do I feel so strange?" Eve sat up, and eyed her rescuers groggily. She pulled herself to her feet, and stumbled as she tried to move towards them.

"These aren't my legs!" She looked down and wailed. "They're miles too long. What's going on?"

Cameron steered her away from the mirror over the fireplace. "I'm not sure you want to look in there just yet. You're in for a bit of a shock... You've grown up really fast."

"No, I want to see!" Eve protested. Then she noticed the gap where Ferguson's curtain had hung. "What's happened? Is she gone?"

"Yes. She's gone," said Cameron.

Eve stared out into the street at a clear and frosty afternoon. "All the time I've been here, I've never seen out of that window..." She held out a shaky hand, and laughed. "Look, it's snowing a bit. Can we build a snowman?"

"Are you ok, love?" A smart-looking woman had appeared in the garden, and was staring at the broken window with an expression of alarm. "I'm from next door. Is old Mrs Ferguson alright?"

"She's gone away," said Morgan firmly. "She ain't coming back."

The woman gave them a hard look, taking in the dazed young woman in the red dress, the two teenage boys, the broken glass and the charred remains of a fire. "Right. What's going on?"

"Home improvements," said Cameron. "That curtain had to go."

"Oh, really? We'll see about that..." The woman hurried away.

"She's off to call the police," noted Morgan. "We should get out of here, slip away to the parallel."

"Hold on." Cameron had spotted an old-fashioned rotary-dial phone nestling on the sideboard. "I still don't have a new mobile, and there's a limit to how many times Amy is gonna forgive me."

Morgan nodded. "Make it quick." Eve was still watching the snowflakes, and he put a steadying hand on her arm. The girl gave him a confused glance, but didn't push him away. "This one's going to need some help," he said quietly to Cameron.

Cameron dialled the number. "Amy? No, I'm still not dead. Pretty alive really. Great, in fact." He listened for a bit. "Yeah, Morgan helped."

"Tell old Delilah to hurry it up!" said Morgan.

"Listen, I can't really talk, but I'll come see you soon. Promise. What am I doing for Christmas? Nah, I'm not with family..."

He glanced over at Morgan and Eve: the werewolf and the girl who grew up in her sleep. They were an odd pair, he reckoned, but then, he wasn't exactly ordinary either...

"I guess I'm going to be spending it with friends," he said, and smiled.

PARALLEL
POINTS

The Daemon Parallel is a complex and
dangerous world, in which many players
have a stake, and everyone has their own
agenda. Use these Parallel Points to work
out who might have the upper hand...
GOOD LUCK on your journey
through the Parallel!

CAMERON DUFFY

A new face on the Parallel, Cameron is known to be an adept world-shifter, and skilled at wriggling out of tight scrapes. Enemies take note: will throw caution to the wind in his quest to bring back his dad...

STRENGTH	5
SPEED	5
AGILITY	8
INTELLIGENCE	8
SPECIAL POWERS	6
COURAGE	9
DANGER RATING	4
FEAR FACTOR	2

MRS FERGUSON

Be wary of this daemon's avatar! Mrs Ferguson's skills include possession. mesmerism and a handy way with thread. A strict observance of rules and rituals may help you, but keep an eye on the curtains...

STRENGTH	6
SPEED	6
AGILITY	6
INTELLIGENCE	8
SPECIAL POWERS	9
COURAGE	2
DANGER RATING	10
FEAR FACTOR	10

GRANDMA IVES

Premier trader between the worlds, what she lacks in physical prowess this player makes up for in knowledge. Seek her out at Scott & Forceworthy's, but beware: she doesn't like ditherers...

STRENGTH	3
SPEED	2
AGILITY	2
INTELLIGENCE	10
SPECIAL POWERS	6
COURAGE	3
DANGER RATING	6
FEAR FACTOR	5

MORGAN

Said to be 'the best tracker in town'. A fast runner and light-fingered, this free agent may be persuaded to nose out secrets. Find him at the Alhambra Cinema, but time your visit carefully...

STRENGTH	7
SPEED	8
AGILITY	8
INTELLIGENCE	5
SPECIAL POWERS	8
COURAGE	9
DANGER RATING	7
FEAR FACTOR	8

TEMPERATORI

The only source of the sought-after Time Funnel. If you wish to summon the bat-like Temperatori, you must dare to crack open its egg.
Likes: poetry, running water, eating days...

STRENGTH	8
SPEED	9
AGILITY	7
INTELLIGENCE	4
SPECIAL POWERS	9
COURAGE	2
DANGER RATING	8
FEAR FACTOR	8

MR HAIRTMAN
(CERVIDAE DAEMON)

Proud manager of Aulder and Bartie, Mr Hairtman will take great pleasure in directing you to the correct department for your purchase. But watch out for traps along the way.

STRENGTH	5
SPEED	7
AGILITY	5
INTELLIGENCE	3
SPECIAL POWERS	7
COURAGE	3
DANGER RATING	5
FEAR FACTOR	5

WINTER GOD

A seasonal spirit, never seen at the same time as his sunnier brother. Special powers include time travel (winters only) and telepathy. Doesn't take kindly to being kept in one place...

STRENGTH	10
SPEED	4
AGILITY	2
INTELLIGENCE	9
SPECIAL POWERS	10
COURAGE	5
DANGER RATING	4
FEAR FACTOR	6

AMY

This player is thought to be human, and without world-shift powers. Despite this terrible inconvenience, she is determined, fiercely loyal, and skilled with a pen or paintbrush. Secret weapon: sarcasm...

STRENGTH	4
SPEED	5
AGILITY	5
INTELLIGENCE	7
SPECIAL POWERS	1
COURAGE	6
DANGER RATING	3
FEAR FACTOR	4

Have you discovered the Discover Kelpies website?

Adventure
Animals
Environment
Friendship
History
Laughs
Legends
Magic
Monsters
Secrets
Spooky
Thrills

Discover Kelpies is *the* website to visit if you love books!

- Read all about your favourite Kelpies books and authors
- Check what is happening on our blog
- Read exclusive extracts of new books
- Enter competitions
- Discover new books in your favourite subjects whether you love adventure, animals or magic!

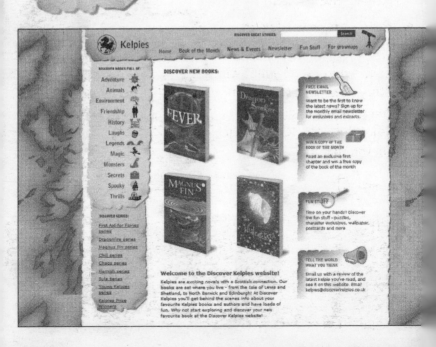

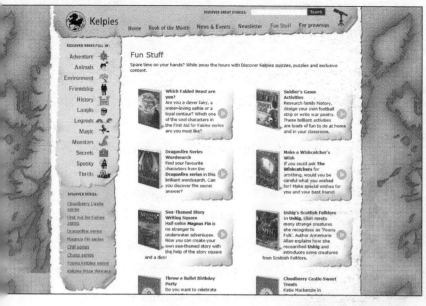

How can *you* get involved?

- Sign up to our Discover Kelpies eNewsletter

- Send us reviews of your favourite Kelpies books

- Take a quiz, write your own story or make a wish with our Fun Stuff page (new fun things are being added all the time!)

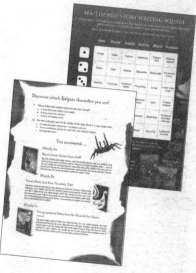

Scan me!

Log on now at
discoverkelpies.co.uk

ALETTE J. WILLIS

The new boy at school tells 12-year-old Edda he can help her stop being afraid by building a golem – a mud monster. A spooky story, both quirky and funny, about facing your fears.

Winner of the Kelpies Prize 2011

JANIS MACKAY

Join half-selkie hero Magnus Fin on three exciting underwater adventures as he struggles to save the sea, his selkie family and Neptune's treasures.

Magnus Fin and the Ocean Quest *Magnus Fin and the Moonlight Mission*

Magnus Fin and the Selkie Secret

 The Magnus Fin books are also available as eBooks

LARI DON

Helen and her fabled beast friends face treacherous tasks and dangerous monsters in three thrilling adventures.

 The First Aid for Fairies books are also available as eBooks.

First Aid for Fairies and Other Fabled Beasts

Wolf Notes and Other Musical Mishaps

Storm Singing and Other Tangled Tasks